NOT GOOD ENOUGH

NOT GOOD ENOUGH

James Robert Moore

MUSWELL
PRESS

First published by Muswell Press in 2025
Copyright © James Robert Moore 2025

Typeset in Bembo by M Rules
Printed by CPI Group (UK) Ltd, Croydon CR0 4YY

A CIP record for this book
is available from the British Library

ISBN: 9781068389306
eISBN: 9781068389313

Our authorised representative in the EU for product safety is
Easy Access System Europe, Mustamäe tee 50, 10621 Tallinn, Estonia
gpsr.requests@easproject.com

Muswell Press, London N6 5HQ
www.muswell-press.co.uk

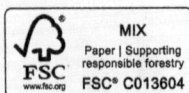

CHAPTER ONE

G eorge Crawford is the most perfect man on the planet. He's insanely attractive, but not in a way that makes anyone feel inadequate about their own looks. He has a wonderful relationship with his mum and dad. He works hard and has goals and dreams that he actually achieves. He writes his daily pages and gives to charity and volunteers his own time to teach young people from low economic backgrounds about how to get into business. His jawline is solid, his hairline thick and strong, he's a good mover and knows all the words to 'Rapper's Delight'. His storytelling is charismatic, his jokes never too wordy and they always have a killer punchline. He knows how to do first aid and he once saved a colleague from choking on a piece of roast chicken. On weekends you'll find him in the gym, where the sweat he produces makes him glisten rather than redden – he can play tennis and chess, and always knows that one niche answer in a pub quiz. He's unflappable in the kitchen, where he bakes and creates delicious, hearty dishes that lie on beds of *jus* or that come with a parmesan *tuile*. He's earnest and doesn't show off about his salary, which is above average for someone his age working in an office in the City of London. He loves animals and the environment and once nursed a baby bird back to health after it flew into the patio doors. Mothers love him. Straight men are in awe but unthreatened by him. Women wish he was interested in them, or at the very least that he had some bisexual tendencies – but sadly for them he doesn't, because George Crawford is my boyfriend – and I fucking hate him.

★ ★ ★

The doorbell chimes. I push George off of me – a little more forcefully than I intend. He doesn't stir. Downstairs is a mess. Empty seven-quid bottles of Prosecco decorate every surface. My mouth tastes fuzzy. The doorbell peels again. Niamh, my best friend, housemate and unpaid therapist sticks her head out of her bedroom doorway, last night's heavy mascara forcing her eyelids to remain firmly closed.

"If that's Ocado or something I'll kill you. It's my half term. Choose the afternoon slot." She recedes back into her pit with a loud grunt. As if I could afford Ocado.

I can make out the silhouette behind the glass.

It's Mum.

My-working-class, bull-in-a-china-shop mum.

I specifically said Farewell to her last week. At the small Costa in the station. We had one latte each, shared a slice of almond Bakewell and she was back on the next train twenty minutes later. We do this once every three months. Twice if there's a birthday or a bank holiday. But of course she's decided to turn up at the house, in person, on the day my life is completely over.

"Where is he then?!"

"Mum, what are you doing?"

"Well I couldn't let you go without saying goodbye to Gorgeous George – your better half – could I?"

She barges past me, uninvited, revealing Leanne in the

doorway. Hair down to her calves, like she's been styled by Cousin It.

"Hi Fuck-Face!"

Leanne holds up a very obviously homemade sign that says 'GoOdbYe gorGoeus gEorGe'. Usually I'd take delight in pointing out that she's put the E and the O the wrong way round in the word 'gorgeous' but I just can't muster the energy.

"Jesus, Leanne, did a five-year-old make that?"

"Fuck off."

"Why isn't my name on there?"

"It is."

She points to a small amendment in the bottom right-hand corner which says, 'and bye Fuck-Face'.

My nineteen-year-old half-sister is baffling to me. I don't understand how we came from the same womb. In fact I've often wondered if I was adopted – prayed for it even.

"Mum, is that Granny in the car?"

"Oh yes, there's no point in letting her come in, she'll only settle," Mum says as she frumps down on the living room chair.

"So, what, you're just going to leave her there?"

"Calm down, I left a window open."

I wave to my eighty-five-year-old granny. She doesn't wave back. Leanne is trying to stick the sign up on the wall with tape.

"Don't do that, it'll mark the walls. Mum, can you tell her?"

She tears a large piece with an obnoxious ripping sound. Mum coos at her, then catches my expression of horror.

"Oh, don't give me that look. We're here because I thought you might want some help packing."

Post-sixteen, Mum has never helped me with anything; I took myself on the train to college open days, booked my own driving lessons, moved myself into halls. I Had to Fend for Myself at Sixteen, she'd repeatedly say, And It Never Did

3

Me Any Harm. Her response to any of my protests was that she'd spent enough money on me over the years, and on top of this my dad hadn't paid her any maintenance all through my childhood. I assumed this was primarily because she had no idea who my dad actually was, therefore it was quite hard to send him a letter demanding money for my upkeep.

"I've done all the packing already, obviously, because ... well ... it is today that we're supposed to be leaving."

"What do you mean 'supposed'? What's happened? What have you done?"

My stomach does a single somersault.

"I haven't done anything, Mum," I try to say as casually as possible, collecting bottles and half-destroyed pots of hummus which at some point over the evening became ashtrays.

"OK well, you won't have packed properly, there's a technique to folding clothes, let me see."

I block Mum's advances towards the staircase. I can't face seeing George yet. I wouldn't know what to say to him. About Mum being here. About what happened last night.

"Don't go up there. He's still asleep."

Leanne abandons the make-shift sign, her interest suddenly piqued.

"Oh let me go and wake him up, he'll want to give his future sister-in-law a goodbye kiss."

Leanne's sexual perversion towards my boyfriend has never gone unnoticed by me. I caught her with a pair of his dirty boxer shorts when we stayed at Nan's two Christmases ago. She said she was checking to see if they needed washing, but she'd never been anywhere near any cleaning products in her life. This from the girl who once tried to heat up a lasagne in a tumble-dryer.

"Can you both just go ... I've got things to do. You can't be here now."

The cistern of the toilet flushes and there's a shuffling of feet down the stairs. My heart drops quickly into the vicinity of my arsehole.

"Well fuck a duck, who's this then?" Leanne licks her lips, her eyes wild.

Axel smiles. His hair is perfectly wavy. He's only just woken up, yet he could be about to step onto the catwalk.

"Yo, I'm Axel, I live here now."

I only met Axel for the first time a mere twelve hours ago. He's the ridiculously attractive American who is taking over the lease on our bedroom, because George and I are flying to New York City tonight. George has got a promotion at work which means we're being relocated for the next year – potentially two. Our new home is a twenty-third floor apartment in Downtown Manhattan. It has a gym, a concierge and a swimming pool in the basement. It didn't take me too long to quit my job at the coffee shop next to the tube station and decide to go with him. That's the best part of being with George – he likes exploring and has an extremely well-paid job, and I'm his other half so he has to take me along for the ride. The polyester hot dog costume I was wearing last night at our American-themed fancy dress leaving party stares at me from a crumpled heap by the television. It makes me heave a little. I hate fancy dress at the best of times. I hate it even more now. Leanne jabs me in the ribs.

"You've picked the wrong time to move out, big bro."

I can't help but look at Axel's crotch. I think everyone in the room is staring at Axel's crotch. He pulls one side of his extremely tight white briefs away from his bum cheek. I'm conscious that my face is red. I try to rub my embarrassment away, but a fleck of mustard-coloured face-paint falls to the floor. Mum stands, spreading her arms wide.

"Hello Axel, I'm Charlie's mum, and this is my daughter Leanne. We're just here to wish the best thing that ever happened to Charlie a fond farewell and make George promise not to get bored of him whilst they're out there in big old New York! I mean, really I just want to thank George for finally giving Charlie something to do with his life!"

Axel throws his head back and laughs.

"Dude, this lady is roasting you hard this morning!"

I imagine Axel being run over by an articulated lorry.

"Mum, would you and Leanne both mind just sort of . . . well pissing off really, I'd be ever so grateful."

Mum's bottom lip protrudes, and in a baby voice she says she'll miss George so much, but it's muffled by the strain of me pushing her through the front door. Leanne takes out her phone and snaps a picture of Axel who is now splayed – legs akimbo – over the sofa. His eyes are closed but he's definitely posing. Leanne stops in the doorway.

"When will we see you again?"

"I don't know."

"I didn't mean you," Leanne pouts, "I meant fitty over there."

"He's gay, and even if he wasn't he wouldn't go anywhere near anyone who shops online at Nasty Gal."

I slam the door firmly closed.

Leanne's fingers flick a V shape at me but the glass diamonds in the window are frosted so it could also be a peace sign. I lean my head against the door for a moment, glad for the silence.

"Yo, do you mind if I grab a shower before I start moving the rest of my stuff in?"

Axel sticks his hand directly inside his pants. Leaves it there. Perhaps something has fallen off after last night and he needs to check it's still attached.

I want to say something; say that when I mentioned What's Mine Is Yours before I went up to bed last night, I wasn't referring to my boyfriend of nine years. Instead I find myself making him a cup of coffee and chopping up a banana and explaining how the shower has to run for three minutes before the hot water comes out and how to open the back door because the lock is sticky and what the password is for next door's Wi-Fi because ours goes down frequently. He thanks me by kissing me once, square on the lips.

"I had a really fun night, thanks for everything man. Good luck in the States, we'll miss ya."

And with that, the Scarlett Woman walks up the stairs. His bottom rising and falling like a perfectly set jelly. A jelly that you want to set on fire.

I stand alone in the lounge and stare at The Wall. I want it to explain itself. I've sat against that Wall and eaten noodles out of a carton whilst George massaged my feet. I danced against it when I turned twenty-three, twenty-six, twenty-nine, thirty. I've blue-tacked Happy Birthday banners and tinsel onto it. Leant advent calendars next to it. I painted it the colour of "Spiced Squash" with Niamh whilst Alexandra Burke won *The X Factor*. I've cleaned Halloween blood off of it, put a glass to it with George and listened to the neighbours arguing, hung a picture on it of all of us at our graduation ceremony and up until now completely and utterly taken it for granted. It's always just been there. Solid. Unmoving.

Now I look at it, and I don't recognise it at all. I want to punch it. Make a hole in The Wall with my fist and ask it what I ever did to deserve seeing my boyfriend pressed up against it with someone else. Someone naked, and beautiful, and American. But I know it can't answer me, because no response to that question would ever be good enough.

* * *

By the time I arrive at the coffee shop both my housemates, Niamh and Dylan, are there – Dylan already halfway through a Full English. How they slipped out of the house before I did, and without me seeing, I've no idea. Despite Dylan's constant inhaling of anything and everything deep-fried and never touching a vegetable, his cheekbones have never filled out and he's remained a neat thirty-inch waist throughout his twenties and well into his early thirties. The bastard. His beautiful black curly hair falls in little ringlets across his face, and his dark green eyes are always his most commented upon feature when he's on the pull. Niamh – who shares my metabolism – is poking at a single piece of grapefruit. I thought it was only people in Hollywood films who ate grapefruit for breakfast in front of billowing white curtains, but apparently British teachers do it too. Niamh is the coolest, snappiest dresser I know, with a seemingly endless stream of fashionable garments, matched always to her little heart-shaped beauty spot that she paints on her cheek every day. Her long, red hair is today tied up in a ponytail that makes her look both studious and a total rocker at the same time.

Niamh shakes her head disapprovingly at me as I take a seat at our favourite table by the window.

"I wasn't going to come, but after you woke me up with all that moaning at your mum, I thought, sod it, I'm up now."

"I didn't know she was coming."

"Honestly, you two need to communicate more."

"We communicate enough. The less communication with that woman the better."

Dylan, Niamh, George and I went to the same university, and have lived together ever since we graduated, because splitting bills four ways means I can afford a Pret for lunch once a week.

The last of our motley crew, Zachary – who is always notoriously late to everything – we picked up a few years ago at a party, but I don't really remember a time without them being in the picture. That's what happens in big cities. You end up with all these different friends; friends that you potentially made at a party, or at 4 am in McDonald's, or through a mate of a mate of a mate, but the story of how you met is eventually taken over by the story of what big life event you got each other through – meaning you're now inseparable, and forever linked.

Dylan clicks his fingers to silence us.

"Sorry I was so pissed last night Charlie boy, we had an emergency – big pile up on the motorway so it was all hands on deck in A&E. Pretty rough to be honest. So when I got to the pub I just wanted to forget it all, you know? I definitely overdid it on the shots."

"Don't be silly, you were fine . . . I hope everyone was OK."

"Well no, they weren't, obviously. It was a pile up."

"Oh right."

I'll order something small. Maybe just a tea. My head hurts. Dylan grabs my hand.

"Let's cut through all the small talk and get to the real point here."

A drip of ketchup flicks from his mouth and onto the Formica table. I stare at it for a bit too long, apprehensive of what he's about to say. Maybe he heard George and Axel too.

"And what's that?" I say.

"That my new housemate, Axel, is basically a fucking supermodel."

Dylan loads up a photo alarmingly fast on Instagram.

"He's put this up from last night already. The balls to come dressed as a slutty sailor when you don't really know anyone there, I mean, he can go down on my ship any time."

Niamh's eyes widen.

"Dylan, he's smoking."

"Isn't he!"

"No, I mean he's actually smoking. In the bar. Look."

Of course Axel thinks he can just light one up inside and get away with it. Because of her profession as an educator of the next generation, Niamh is a stickler for promoting a healthy lifestyle and uses her knowledge to berate us on every occasion. Last year she gave us a very unnecessary two-hour PowerPoint presentation on why we should cut out sugar. She used a pack of twelve donuts as a demonstrative tool and was furious when George, Dylan and I ate them the minute she started packing away the school projector.

"He'll be cutting his life expectancy short by at least two years."

Niamh hands the phone back to a physically salivating Dylan.

"Forget that, he's just fucking hot isn't he, and you were all over him last night Niamh, so don't play the Virgin Mary today," he says, shovelling baked beans into his mouth.

They go on talking about Axel's looks for the next eighteen minutes. I time them from the clock on the wall. A fly lands on Dylan's bacon and rubs its spindly legs together over the strip of white fat. He doesn't even notice.

Apparently Axel is a personal trainer and there's a photo of him smiling with someone from *Bake Off* and Tom Daley. Clients of his they presume. Sexual conquests of his they further speculate.

"But Tom's married," I muse, to nobody in particular.

Dylan once told me that All Gay Men Can't Keep It in Their Trousers, and I just thought he was being cynical and bitter because he'd not found anybody to share his life with yet. He's had numerous boyfriends since I've known him, but the relationships are short-lived, contained to pockets of six months or less, and he moves on from them alarmingly fast. Now Niamh and he are discussing how another couple we know have started sleeping with other people behind their backs. I feel a wave of nausea wash over me. Finally, Zachary struts in. Their moisturised, ageless hands are holding countless shopping bags. Zachary told us they were non-binary last year and would from then on be using the pronouns they/

them/their and I've never been more proud to learn so much about gender and sexuality from somebody so brilliant, patient and understanding.

"Sorry I'm late darlings; I came as soon as I could."

Dylan narrows his eyes. "Via the sales?"

"Don't be silly, this was all full price. George not joining us?"

"Erm, no he's comatose. Standard." I say quickly, even though George is usually the first one up and about before any of us.

"We were just discussing my fit *new* housemate," Dylan says through a mouthful of scrambled eggs.

"*Our* fit new housemate," Niamh corrects.

I try to beckon the waiter over, hoping it's not too early for a gin and tonic – or an absinthe.

"Oh darling I know. I've been up all night stalking his social medias. That's why I can't take these glasses off – there's more bags under here than you could find at Fendi."

Dylan thrusts his phone at Zachary.

"Did you see this one?"

"Of course, babes. I chatted to him loads last night, I brushed his bicep at one point and I've still got a semi."

It's another torso picture. If Axel walked in now fully clothed I don't think any of them would recognise him.

Zachary works in PR. They were always going to work in PR. I don't even know what PR really is but I always knew Zach was going to do it because they only ever wear black and talk into their phone exclusively on speaker so they look like they're a contestant on *The Apprentice*, and those people always work in PR.

I look around the cafe to distract myself and spot a man in the corner looking over at us. We catch eyes and he hurriedly bows his head back to his book. He must think that we're those enviable close friends who do nothing but brunch and laugh and brunch a bit more. Maybe he even wistfully wants to join us. Or perhaps he's more comfortable finding solace in someone else's story. I blink really slowly hoping to end up in someone else's story. It doesn't work.

"We need one final toast to celebrate your departure, Charlie. Oh garçon!"

Zachary flicks their hand. The waiter – who's been ignoring my desperate waves the entire time I've been here – saunters over. He's wearing a shirt covered in sad-looking cartoon foxes and has a large hole where a nose piercing should be. His expression gives a faint odour of low job satisfaction.

"We'll have a bottle of something sparkling, chilled," Zach says without looking at the plastic-covered menu.

"I can do you some Fanta" the waiter sighs.

"Fantastic!"

He slumps away to the fridge.

"Full of sugar is Fanta," Niamh tuts.

"What time are you going to the airport?" Zachary asks.

"I'm not going."

Over by the counter, the waiter drops a can and it bursts – shooting carbonated water all over the man with the book. I wish that he'd dropped it on me instead so I could excuse myself to the bathroom. My group look equally puzzled.

"What are you talking about?" Dylan wipes his chin with the back of his hand, "You've got your suitcase right there."

Before I left – and after I'd put all the empty bottles in the recycling and repotted the succulents that Niamh knocked over at one point – I went upstairs, took my ready-packed suitcase and decided to rip up my plane ticket. Except George had downloaded an app with the tickets on, so I had to go onto his phone, get the confirmation number, go to the website, download the paper tickets and then go to the internet cafe around the corner to print out both plane tickets. Then, and only then, could I tear up *my* ticket and sprinkle it all over the still-sleeping

12

George. It was worth the effort. As I dragged my case out of the door, Axel appeared – dripping wet in my towel – and hugged me goodbye and for some reason I let him, relaxing my whole body into his warm, lime-scented hairless skin.

"We know it's a big move for you, but New York is incredible, it's probably just nerves." Zachary nods their head in agreement with Niamh and adds, "I'm sensationally envious."

Dylan puts down his fork, "Anyway, if you'd suddenly panicked and were changing your mind – which would be ridiculous – then what would you even do?! You've quit your job and you haven't got anywhere to live anymore, and I'm sorry but you're not dangling someone as fit as Axel in front of me and then taking him away again."

I didn't think of that when I ripped up the ticket. Or maybe I did. I have got my suitcase after all. The waiter puts four cans of Lilt on the table. Zachary takes out a non-ironic monocle and inspects one, their eyes narrowing.

"What vintage is this?"

"Sort of 1999, circa the playground."

"Retro vibes hun, love it."

Zachary's phone beeps.

"Oh God, I totally forgot I had a meeting with Amanda Holden this morning about bringing back Rear of The Year, do you remember that? Anyway, she wants to bring it back but make it classier, and not so sexualised, you know?"

"It's called Rear of The Year. It's literally judging someone's arse, how do you make that not sexualised?" says Niamh.

"I don't know, but we're meeting at The Ivy and Amanda's paying so ... Niamh, Dylan – you still on for dinner at ours tonight? Steve's making boodle-nese."

"Oh God, is there a cure?" Dylan clutches his chest in mock horror.

"No, it's spaghetti Bolognese but the noodles are made of butternut squash instead of pasta. It's the only way I can get

13

you to eat a vegetable and stop the spread of scurvy that's desperate to infest your rotting insides. Right, bye darlings."

Zach puts on their coat, then gives me an awkward hug, telling me that New York is incredible, and says to keep in touch, and then they've gone, completely unaware that I'll be seeing them sooner than they think.

Dylan turns to me.

"What's really the matter Charlie?"

I want to tell them. I do, and especially to Dylan. I usually tell him everything. But the words can't form properly in my throat. My face feels wet and I realise that my eyes are leaking. Niamh whisks me into a hug and dries my cheeks with a rough paper napkin from the table.

"We know you're going to miss us, and of course we'll miss you," she's saying to me, as great big gushing sobs start to pulse from my gut, "but you've got George with you, plus you'll meet the American equivalent of me and Dylan, and they'll be much more fun than us boring English tossers who can't handle their alcohol."

"I hate Americans though," I say through a swig of Lilt.

"I know, we all do, but they love the English, darling, you'll make friends in no time. Just tell them your Nanny was Mary Poppins; they love that shit."

I have nine years' worth of memories tied up in this friendship group and now everything is about to change. Dylan says I need to focus on the glass of complimentary fizz I'll get on the plane but that's especially irrelevant because it was only George that was in Business, I was in Economy, and the only complimentary thing you get in Economy is shame and regret, and maybe a packet of peanuts.

The man with the book looks over and we lock eyes once more, mine now red and swollen. He's glad to be dining on his own today. There's enough drama written amongst his slightly sodden pages. He doesn't need any more.

14

Before I know it, I've been jostled between Niamh and Dylan and I'm standing outside in the street with all my worldly possessions.

Dylan wipes under my eyes with his thumb and says that he'll always be at the end of the phone whenever I need him, but he's in front of me right now and I say nothing.

They wave me off as I walk down the road towards the bus stop that takes me towards home. Except I can't go there because what is home now?

My pocket vibrates. I don't even need to look to see who it is. I gallantly wave back at the pair, mustering all the energy I have. I watch them turn around and go back inside to have another flat white before they continue their day. In relative normality.

I keep walking forwards.

I have absolutely no idea where I'm going.

CHAPTER TWO

You see, it all went wrong once we left Vauxhall last night.

★ ★ ★

I'm staring at George now from across the dimly lit bar. He's got this energy that makes everybody want to be his friend. Even earlier on, when he walked in – twenty minutes late as usual – you felt the entirety of the room take an in-breath. He's gorgeous. I'm very lucky to have him, and everybody tells me so.

When I first introduced him to my mum eleven years ago she went pale. A little droplet of sweat appeared on her furrowed brow. You're His Boyfriend? she stuttered, curtseying like he was a member of royalty. George just laughed whilst wrapping her in a firm hug. I think Mum knew everything was going to be alright when George was around. He made her feel safe. He makes me feel safe. She stopped asking me what I was going to do with my life after I finished university. It didn't matter. With George I was going to be unequivocally happy.

The wordless music in the bar is loud. I'll have a sore throat tomorrow from trying to make myself heard over the bass-heavy thrum. Niamh is asking me what I want to drink, but George's cowlick has been blown about in the wind and I want to go over and sort it out for him. I know he'll hate the pictures afterwards if I don't.

"Too late. I've got you a Sambuca."

Niamh knows how incredibly frustrating I find this, because we all understand the unwritten rule when buying rounds is that a shot doesn't constitute a proper drink. And if you're going to buy them, then you also have to follow this up immediately with a longer-lasting beverage, but her temper can be biting so I accept the clear liquorice in silent defeat. Niamh is currently dressed up as the 47th President of the United States. The security guard nearly refused to let her in she's that convincing. The orange powder she's used on her face has been stripped away in a little oval above and below her mouth where she's been slinging back everything she could get her hands on since she finished school at 4 pm. It makes her look like a circus clown.

"What did you use to get that colour? The texture looks weird."

"Wotsits. I crushed them up in the staff room. It was my Deputy-Head's idea." Niamh downs her shot in one and shudders.

"What are you going to do whilst George's working in the Big City every day then?" she rasps, her tongue hanging momentarily loose.

"Become a lady of leisure, the role I've always been destined to play."

"Oh fuck off, Charlie."

"No seriously. I'm going to be a proper trophy husband; make dinner, and go to yoga, finally join a book group, and—"

Niamh rolls her eyes and moves back to our assembled friends. I pour the Sambuca shot onto the floor. It's already sticky so nobody will notice. Dylan lurches over.

17

"Are you going to stare at George all night, or do I actually get to spend time with you before you leave me?"

"Sorry, I'm just so happy to see him having a good time."

I step in the Sambuca puddle. It looks like I've wet myself.

"Charlie, he's had six beers and a Jägerbomb, of course he's having a good time."

The fake breasts inside Dylan's Hooter's top jiggle as he leans across the bar to order more beers. I want to ask him where he got them from, but the inevitable anecdotal story will take up most of the night.

"The house will be very quiet with the two of you gone."

"Oh come off it, Dylan, I'm surprised you're even aware of our presence. The conveyor belt of South London's eligible bachelors moaning their heads off in your bedroom often made me think you'd forgotten you didn't live alone."

He's blushing now. Dylan loves that we know how much attention he gets. One time a conquest of his accidentally walked straight into our room in the middle of the night – drunk and completely naked – and tried to spoon me. George was away on a conference and in a sleepy stupor I just assumed he'd arrived home early. I got quite the fright when this Gentleman Caller started whispering How Hard Do You Want It Baby – George would never be so crude. Although I was flattered to be asked with such intense consideration for my needs.

I admire Dylan for being able to Do Life Alone. He takes himself on solo holidays all the time, and despite usually having some sort of man hanging around in his back pocket, he's never struck me as the settling down type. Whenever I try and picture a romantic future for Dylan, I'm not sure who I see standing by his side.

Dylan raises one of his neatly trimmed eyebrows at me and makes his way back across to our reserved area, flashing a bit more bum cheek with every swish of his tiny skirt. He slides

18

in next to Niamh, just as George is clambering onto a stool and shouting for everyone to listen.

"Everybody, thank you so much for coming tonight. I'm so fucking excited to get away from London and into the Big Apple, but I'll miss you all so much."

God he's just so wonderful. Even the way he says the word Fucking sends a jolt of goosebumps up and down my body. Shit, I didn't slick his cowlick down. I gesture with my fingers for him to flatten it. He doesn't see.

"I'm very fortunate to have so many wonderful pals here to say goodbye, but it's only goodbye *for now*. Don't forget us."

Dylan pipes up with his usual trope of Who Said We Were Going to Miss You, which is ironic because two Fridays ago I spent an hour and a half on our kitchen floor consoling his Prosecco-fuelled tears at the thought of me not living with him anymore.

George is thrusting his glass in the air and saying something about life being a journey, but I can't really understand him properly. He's definitely had too much. He can't stop grinning when he's the wrong side of sober. His dimples bloom. Niamh says I need to say something too, but I'm not comfortable when it comes to public speaking. My mouth goes dry and I end up saying something inappropriate or terribly unfunny, not like George. Nonetheless, I find myself suddenly standing on a chair, besides my partner, clearing my throat and wondering how I can put into words how lucky I am to be going on an adventure with the man I love.

"To my Gorgeous George, I can't believe I get to share this with you, and I'm beyond thrilled to be starting our new life together in one of the most incredible cities in the world."

I can see Dylan trying not to cry. He's pinching the skin between his thumb and finger. My voice wavers and I swallow down the happy but salty tears at the back of my throat. I turn towards George to steady myself and slide my hand into his.

19

"I love you so much, Georgey."

Raising our intertwined arms up – like we've just won first prize in the competition of life – I let my voice carry around the room, "To Gorgeous George!"

Everybody repeats and glasses clink appropriately. George lunges forward and clasps my hands. Those thickly skinned, healing hands. He leans his head on my shoulder. The smell of his aftershave is instantly calming. He's so perfect when he's being sentimental.

"I just want to say to you," he slurs, "that I ... need to be sick."

And with that, my lover runs to the bathroom to heave up six beers and a Jägerbomb. I hope everyone's clear of the firing line.

★ ★ ★

We're back at the flat in the Dodgy End of Wandsworth. George is vomiting furiously into the toilet. I've put a wet, cool flannel on the back of his neck to counteract the sweating. I'm confused as to what he's possibly got left in the tank. He slumps his forehead onto the porcelain.

"Ew, it tastes like avocado."

Zachary passes him a towel.

"You're a millennial hun, everything tastes like avocado."

I'd been wondering where Zachary was – they missed the speeches at the pub and most of the night – but I've come to realise that the less you ask the better. Zach's an enigma. A male Victoria Beckham but somehow with a smaller waist. I'm surprised they're sticking around – if one speck got on their designer blacks I've no doubt we'd get a dry-cleaning bill sent through on the WhatsApp group.

"That's it, up it comes," I say as I rub George's back, lick three fingers and finally slick that bit of hair down. He looks up at me, his eyes like saucers I could fall into.

"You're the best, you know that?"

George leans up and plants a sloppy kiss on my cheek, somehow managing to slip his tongue into the corner of my mouth. He's right. It does taste of avocado. But there's something slightly attractive about his helplessness.

"I think I've wet myself a bit."

Or, maybe there isn't. George gets up and gazes around the bathroom, his pupils not quite turning at the same speed as his head.

"Where's Axel?"

He stumbles into the shower curtain and one of the rings snaps off. There goes the deposit.

"He's so hot, I've flooded my basement twice tonight," Niamh growls.

"Fuck off, he's mine. Anyway I thought you were into girls at the moment," Dylan barks back.

"I'm into whoever I want to be into."

"Alright, Peter Pan-Sexual, stop being greedy."

"You sound like my fucking dad."

They begin to square up to each other – like a comedy duo playing for laughs. I intervene. I'm not in the mood for a pantomime.

"Neither of you are allowed to shag the very nice chap who is subletting our room, it's incestuous."

I know they're only joking, but on occasion I do feel this little burn of something in my stomach when Dylan talks about who he wants to hook up with. I feel this protective barrier start to rise. I wouldn't want him to get hurt. To be frank, his and Niamh's constant battle to sleep with the most people is something they really should have left back in our university halls. Niamh sits on the edge of the bath, sucking on her vape.

"You won't be here Charlie, so what do you care? Plus I've never had an American."

Zachary twirls around from the mirror.

"I have darling, it's very performative. It's easier to masturbate."

The door bangs open announcing the arrival of Axel into the now very crowded bathroom. Axel says nothing and instead greets us all by swiftly removing his stripy cotton sailor's top and swirling it around his head. I assume he's spilt something on it downstairs, but then he says, "I heard some-one needed their deck scrubbing and rigging climbed," so my initial assessment that he's a Bit of a Prick is correct.

Niamh and Dylan appear to love it. Dylan's practically dry humping him and Niamh's somehow managed to get herself on Axel's back. She's finally taken her Trump toupee off and her sticky auburn hair is matted to her forehead. Ideally this wouldn't be happening whilst my boyfriend is being sick all over the linoleum. Zachary offers me a menthol cigarette.

"How did you manage to get those? Aren't they illegal now?" I ask them, not smoking it, but wafting it around to mask the smell of vomit.

"Oh, I know people," Zachary says nonchalantly.

As Niamh, Dylan and Axel collapse on the floor in fits of laughter, and Zachary sticks their head out of the small window above the sink, puffing circles of smoke into the freezing night-air, I watch George hiccup – and somehow, even in this state, he makes my heart swell.

I let everyone have their fun. Everything I need is right here.

★ ★ ★

At around 3 am Niamh pushes the front door shut with purpose.

"That's the last of them gone. Night poofs."

She sways across the living room towards her bedroom, lurching like a salmon trying to swim upstream. Two feet before her door, she walks straight into the small side-table, taking two succulents and a signed picture of Alan Rickman from the table with her. There's a crash from inside her room.

"Is she dead?" George asks vaguely.

A loud guttural snore tells us she isn't.

Dylan and Axel are slow dancing in the middle of the lounge except there isn't any music. Nobody appreciated the Spotify adverts playing after every third song so the party descended into silence a few hours ago and the inane drunken circular conversations began. Most of Axel's sailor costume has been disbanded – shipwrecked somewhere in the house – and Dylan has lost both the silicon tits from his t-shirt. Bits of mud and feathers and glitter lay trodden into the mangey white rug that's followed Niamh from her childhood bedroom. Most of that isn't even from tonight.

I try to pick up George, but he's too broad for me. All that last-minute exercise he's been doing has clearly worked. He's practically bursting out of his Oxford shirt. He was worried that he wouldn't be taken seriously enough in an American office if he wasn't in good shape. In comparison, I'll be attending all social mixers in a large black bin bag.

"Dylan, can you get Axel a duvet for the sofa please?" I say.

"I'm busy, Charlie, can't you see?"

Dylan loses his balance and steps back, catching himself on the bannisters. Axel spins around and clatters over to the mirror where he begins an unusual mating habit with his own reflection – winking, blowing kisses, flexing his muscles and rather alarmingly whispering, You're Hot. Dylan gives me a side eye.

"Yeah, I'm not normally fussy about cock, but even I can't handle this. Goodnight."

He doesn't like it when he's not the centre of attention. The mood has changed. The prey is weakened and the game isn't as fun anymore.

"No Dylan, wait, help me."

23

"He's your boyfriend, and I've only just met that one. I've got plenty of time to get to know him better, especially when he's all moved into the room next to me."

Dylan reaches the top of the stairs and disappears. His bedroom door slams. Although he hasn't helped in any way, I do feel relieved that we don't have to listen to the thud thud thud of Dylan's bed against our bedroom wall tonight, especially when we need some decent sleep.

I turn to my boyfriend, who having seemingly discovered an unhelpful second wind is unbuttoning his shirt.

"George, you need to sober up or you'll feel so rough on the plane tomorrow evening."

"Yes, Sir!"

Axel tumbles onto the floor besides him. His muscular back arranging itself immediately across George's legs.

"Axel, how often do you go to the gym?" George mumbles.

"Like, twice a day."

See: Prick.

"Twice a day! You don't even know where the gym is do you, Charles?"

I offer him a glass of water. He wafts it away.

"He thinks lifting a chicken bake from Greggs is a workout."

Axel and George laugh. I fail to see what's funny about pastry.

"You need to come to bed now please."

"Pfft, Charlie, shut up, let's have a nightcap."

"We don't have anything left, George."

He clambers up, sending Axel into a slump onto the rug, and heads to the kitchen. I follow closely behind, uncertain of where this is going. George begins to rifle through the cleaning cupboard.

"Ohh, this looks exotic."

"George that's Toilet Duck."

I snatch it off him. When he's like this, I wouldn't put it past him to try and use anything as the basis of a Blue Hawaiian.

"Boring!"

"Well, you say boring, I say, safety conscious."

We go back into the lounge and I plump the spare duvet and tuck it into one side of the sofa.

"Say goodnight to Axel and then come upstairs and sleep."

I emphasise Sleep like a discerning Victorian Nanny. George looks at me. His eyes narrow. He hates being told what to do. He murmurs something I can't make out. I turn to Axel who, like a quick-change artist, is now wearing only the smallest pair of briefs I've ever seen, despite having not moved an inch from the spot on the floor where we left him. I look only for a second but manage to count a minimum of eight fully formed abs.

"Help yourself to whatever you want, Axel. This is pretty much your place now, so what's mine is yours."

Axel rolls onto his tummy and farts. Maybe that means Thank You where he's from in America.

I head upstairs as he and George both cackle uncontrollably. Give it five minutes and George will be up here. I know when he's had enough and needs to sleep it off. He can be a bit minty with me sometimes, but he'll apologise profusely in the morning. He'll do that thing with his mouth where he pouts and looks like he's going to cry, and he won't even need to say anything because he knows I'll forgive him for anything. Then we'll have our last breakfast in bed in this house – this faithful house of eight years where we've laughed until we've cried. We'll say goodbye to our friends, hold hands as we make our way through departures, and then chime our champagne glasses in the apartment after we've touched down in our new life. In my head I begin to pick out which films I'm going to watch on the plane but before I can make a definitive list my eyes become heavy and I feel myself dribble, satisfied, onto the pillow.

★ ★ ★

I look at my phone. It's 3.45 am. I've drunk so much water that I can feel it pushing against my bladder. I roll over. The other side of the bed is untouched.

I pad across the landing. I can hear voices. As I step downstairs the voices become more monotoned. The further I descend the less I can hear any actual words, just a sort of hum.

The hum becomes a moan.

The moan turns into gasps.

I peer around the corner into the living room and there is Gorgeous George with his back against the wall and his legs wrapped around Axel's waist and Axel's perfectly round bottom is thrusting backwards and forwards backwards and forwards over and over and over again and George's mouth has made this little round O shape and his eyes have rolled into the back of his head and his cheeks are flushed this deep pink colour that I've never seen on him before and there's a silvery sheen of sweat gliding down Axel's thick strong back and George is saying something; George is saying Harder and Axel is saying I'm Going to Come and George is pleading Come Inside Me Please and as Axel's arm muscles tense and hoist George further into the wall and George makes this almighty groan of sheer pleasure I find my legs have carried me silently back upstairs and I'm lying in bed and I realise I've been holding my breath for the past two minutes.

Shouldn't I be dead by now? I think I want to be dead.

★ ★ ★

To my surprise, I am still breathing. I'm staring up at the ceiling, having counted exactly how many little semi-circles there are in the plaster. A bit like when you'd finish your exam early so you'd try and see how many bricks were in the wall of the sports hall. The door opens and George falls into bed. I

26

don't know how much time has passed since I went downstairs and saw them. He swings his arm over me and immediately begins breathing heavily. Air whistles out between his neat white teeth. It smells sweet. His body exudes heat and lust from every pore. I wonder how long it took him to finish after Axel had. I try and scramble the thought from my head. There are two hundred and one circles on the ceiling – not quite so perfect.

* * *

It's been five hours since I left Niamh and Dylan outside the coffee shop. It was a surprise to me when I looked at the time. I'd been staring at the small, black-beamed hut in the centre of Soho Square – the only place I could think of to go – since what felt like the beginning of time itself. My phone alight with so many missed calls that the battery was showing a paltry 12%.

We spent an afternoon here last year, for London Pride, all of us together. Niamh had bought a load of glitter and poster paint from her classroom and we'd enjoyed a giddy morning of colouring each other in – marred only by Dylan's accidental use of PVA glue to stick two yellow pipe-cleaners along the line of his eyebrows that he then couldn't get off. Looking around at us all, sprawled on the desolate wasteland of the square in the July heat, an overwhelming feeling of joy sloshed around my body. Of course the five gin-in-a-tins coupled with a small oncoming dose of sunstroke were contributing to this, but the consistent laughing and dancing and hand-holding made my heart nearly burst from my chest. How lucky was I to know these people? My people. George had undone his shirt all the way to his naval, and his trim torso was almost blinding it was so perfect. Boys kept coming up to him and chatting, offering him a can or slipping their hands around his Rainbow underwear waistband, but each time he'd politely smile, point me out, wish them a Happy Pride and carry on being the life and soul of the party.

How could I have got him so wrong?

The grass has all but disappeared now, replaced by hard, brown mud. Exhausted from the relentless stomping of picnickers in the summer and the bitter frost of the winter, it'll soon come out of hibernation, ready to go another round.

I didn't know where else to go, but I knew I couldn't just stay in the park all night, and so I found my legs carrying me to Pimlico on the bus to Steven and Zachary's.

Their flat is luxury personified. They have a spice rack, an umbrella stand and a kettle that whistles, which means they are actual grown-ups. Steven cooks exotic meals that he's learnt on his travels around Cambodia or somewhere else that I couldn't point out on a map, and says things like, Nobody Even Touches Prosecco Anymore, It's All About Crémant, and, I Find One Can Never Own Too Many Items From Le Creuset, and, Everything Should Be Served With a Sprinkling of Cilantro – which turns out to be the American word for coriander. Why he can't just call it coriander like everyone else I'll never know. He's not even from America. He's from Bromley.

Ever since Zachary and Steven met – in a gay bar – he's become a firm fixture in our group of friends. Personally I was very happy with it being George, Niamh, Dylan and I in the house, with Zachary only a short bus ride away. The five of us were a motley crew. Five is a nice number. It means nobody has to sit on their own when you go on Inferno at Thorpe Park – because Dylan won't go on rollercoasters so it makes us an even foursome for sharing a carriage. Steven makes Zachary happy, I can see that, but I find him slightly intolerable. Dylan says that makes me a Bad Friend, but if that were true then I would have told Zachary my honest opinion of Steven, and although I've done that a couple

28

of times it was under the influence of Pinot Grigio so that doesn't count.

I hover my finger over the doorbell. I've been doing that for the last three minutes. I just can't bring myself to push it. Through fatigue I accidentally tap it and as Steven's voice crackles over the intercom I consider for a moment putting on a French accent and saying I've got the wrong number, but then I remember their flat is so well-equipped that they have a camera alongside the buzzer.

"Charlie? You know this isn't the airport don't you?!"

I can't think of a suitable response, so I find myself laughing and saying something about needing a wee. I don't. I haven't drunk a sip of water all day. My body is screaming with thirst. I should have taken the can of Lilt that Zachary never touched.

The door unlocks and after an excruciating lift ride where I consider pushing the alarm bell several times I find myself hugging Steven and feeling weirdly comforted. Steven's older than us all – he's nearly forty and that means he knows the secret to life itself.

I can smell garlic and tomatoes. Steven is wearing a chef's apron that says, "May the Forks Be with You". George loves *Star Wars*. We've seen all of them together. Even though he has to explain to me who the characters are every five minutes.

"You're a bit early if you're here for dinner buddy, I'm not expecting anybody for a couple of hours. Zachary's still at work, and I thought your flight was tonight or have I got that wrong?"

I can't be bothered to make an excuse. I'm already regretting coming here first, but I couldn't think of anywhere else to go, and the wind was getting up in the park. My hand aches from carrying my suitcase around. Steven wipes his hand on a tea towel. I tell him the flight has been delayed. He asks for how long and I stop myself saying it's been grounded indefinitely and instead politely ask whether he has any whisky.

29

I've never drunk it before, but in all good TV dramas when a character has had A Bit of a Shock another character always seems to pour them a whisky. They swill it round, then gulp it down in one go and seem to feel better. I throw the glass back and consequently choke. It burns my throat. Steven gets a cloth and I dribble slightly out of the left corner of my mouth.

"Where's George? Is he joining us for dinner too?"

The thing about being in a partnership is that everybody assumes you can't go anywhere by yourself. You're automatically gifted plus-ones even though the bride and groom have only met your other half once and could barely pick him out in a line up. When you do turn up solo, people immediately begin to ask you what's wrong, as if the sight of you on your own means you've had enough of your partner and fed their butchered remains to a couple of local foxes. I try to remember the last time I went out in public without George, but I can't recall. I've always been able to split the Uber, halve the cost of the birthday present and use him as an excuse for wanting to leave a boring party early. You can't do that when you're alone can you? Sorry I'm Leaving to Go Back Home, Alone, You Understand Don't You?

"He's not joining us, no."

My phone begins vibrating again. I push it down the side of the sofa.

"Well can I get you something else? I didn't realise you were a whisky drinker, and that was the last of the bottle. It's a shame most of it ended up in your lap. It was a good vintage that one."

I ask for some wine, any wine, and try to work out what I'm going to say when the others arrive. George will have called one of them by now, probably Niamh, and asked if she's seen me, but she hasn't contacted me, so maybe he's feeling too guilty. Maybe he doesn't even care and he's on his way to the airport already, having kissed Axel goodbye and said for him to come and visit. Fuck, I don't even know where Axel is from in America. What if it's New York? They'll be holidaying in The Hamptons at Christmas and I'll be drinking sherry through a straw, alone, because I'm too heartbroken and weak to lift the glass to my mouth.

Steven hands me a stemless glass of something so surprisingly clear in colour that I have to sniff it to make sure it's alcohol. The wine I buy is always yellow. As he says "Cheers," a flash of gold catches my eye. Steven is wearing a ring. On his left hand. It wasn't there when I saw him last week. And the week before that he'd been away to Paris with Zachary. Paris. A ring. I want to ignore it but I hear myself spit, "Oh God, you're not engaged are you?"

Steven freezes on his route back to the kitchen, turns slowly and asks me bewilderingly how I knew. I point at the smiling band of diamonds and slurp my drink like a petulant child. Steven bursts out into a wild Cheshire Cat grin and explains that he proposed to Zachary at the top of the Eiffel Tower – which is so incredibly heterosexual I can hear Kylie Minogue and Madonna clutch each other in terror. He begs me not to tell anybody if I'm still here when they arrive, as he and Zachary want to find the right moment together and I point out that he should probably take off the ring or wear the oven gloves until that time arises. He's mistaking my bitterness for tenderness and pulls me in for another hug. I don't feel as comforted this time. I'd never even considered how I would react to being cheated on but I am quickly discovering that it is in the category of Woman Scorned.

The next couple of hours pass rather hazily, as Steven tells me all about the latest case he's working on, (he's a high-powered solicitor, hence the spice rack, umbrella stand and kettle that whistles) and tries to engage me in several political debates. I spot a bag of unopened sweet chilli crisps and it sparks a rumble in my stomach, which untwists the knots it's been wringing for most of the day and I realise that I'm starving. I offer to help Steven with the cooking, which serves as both a rouse to get him to stop talking about politics and an opportunity to siphon away the majority of the cheddar he's asked me to grate. I've lost count of the amount of wine I've sunk but I'm verging on the level of not fit for flying. Good.

In a blur Zachary is home and asking me what I'm playing at, and I let Steven tell them my flight is delayed, but I think I'm mumbling something about it being cancelled, and Zachary asks me without any hint of irony whether I'm having a nervous breakdown and I laugh. I laugh hysterically at this and suddenly Dylan is there and Niamh, and with all the subtlety of a freight train I hear the word Engaged come from somewhere guttural within my throat, and through the momentary cheers of celebration and a look of scorn from Zachary, I see a large black hole spreading across the ceiling, and it's closing in on me and the voices of my friends disappear and I try to take one last gulp of wine but I'm falling into the darkness and a part of me hopes it's never going to end.

★ ★ ★

On my sixth date with George he asked me what I would do if I won a million pounds. Back then a million pounds was a very big deal whereas now it just wouldn't do at all. I looked away from *500 Days of Summer* playing on his university dorm television and considered my answer for a few short seconds.

"I'd use it to buy a lovely house for me and my boyfriend."

"Am I your boyfriend?" he mused.

I brushed a stray kernel of popcorn from his pyjama top and shrugged my shoulders.

"I don't know, are you?"

Turning to me, he took my face gently with both of his hands.

"Yeah. I think I am."

He kissed my forehead, pointed at the screen and said he hoped we would be partners just like Tom and Summer, who in the scene were running around IKEA and playing house with each other. I hope not, I thought quietly to myself – we were only twenty minutes into the film and I knew how it ended.

★ ★ ★

I'm lying on the floor face up and dripping wet. Niamh is shouting expletives at Steven who is holding an empty glass. He appears to be the reason I'm slightly damp. Dylan, his beautiful face very close to mine, has a hold of my wrist and is asking me in his best bedside manner if I can hear him. I can. I can hear all of them but for a moment I don't want to explain anything. Why I'm here. Why I've ruined everything. Why I passed out.

"He's opening his eyes properly now, look," Steven says over his shoulder, "Oh hang on, I need to check the boodles aren't burning."

Slowly I sit up and think about the countless times I've been helped off the floor by these three sets of hands – in clubs at 5 am; on the tiled floor of that apartment in Fuerteventura; at my grandad's funeral – and I know they'll lift me up every single time.

"You've got a lot of explaining to do," Niamh sternly reprimands me. I feel like one of her students.

Dylan wants me to sit on the sofa so he can make sure I haven't hit my head. There's not much up there to knock about anyway.

My mouth is dry. I look at my three friends, their faces fixed with concern. I remember spoiling Zachary and Steven's news so I stutter an awkward apology and study my hands. My suitcase is sitting expectantly in the corner of the room.

"George and I broke up."

They shift uncomfortably. With spectacular timing the sound of a cork pops in the kitchen and Steven says, "Shit, sorry."

Niamh straightens her skirt and asks me if I'm sure.

I want to laugh at this, but then think, am I sure? We haven't broken up. I've just got on a bus to Zachary's with my suitcase after ripping up my plane ticket. That's not a break up – it's a small journey using Transport for London.

Dylan takes his phone out of his pocket and starts tapping at the screen, saying he's going to call George but before I can stop him he's in the doorway chatting into the receiver, and I want to go over to him and beg him to hang up but I feel glued to the sofa. Niamh is stroking my hair. Zachary's bought me some water and they're both rebutting Steven's second offer of Crémant.

"George is on his way over here from the airport, he said he's been trying to get hold of you all day. He didn't know what to do so he went to Heathrow hoping to find you already there."

Niamh says I need to tell them what's going on but the words feel sticky and hot with betrayal in my mouth. All I can think about is Axel's bottom thrusting and George's eyes rolling back in ecstasy. I recall the only conversation George and I ever had about him being the Bottom for a change, and he said he had zero interest in doing that with me because he only wanted to pleasure me. I thought that was romantic.

They're all asking me what feels like a million questions, but I feel as though I can't say what I saw last night because what if they don't believe me? All they see in George is pure devotion and love. He was taking me all the way to fucking New York and I wasn't paying a single penny. But then on the other hand Zachary and Steven have been together for what feels like five minutes and they already live in their own place and get engaged at the top of Parisian landmarks. Why hadn't George proposed to me by now? It's been nine years. I mean, I know I don't have a job, and I don't have a direction in life. George was my direction, and maybe he's known all along that I wasn't marriage material and was just waiting for somebody more exciting to come along and I just didn't see it because I was coasting, not making any real effort with him, and now it's too late.

"What happened, Charlie?" Niamh says.

"It was George ... I woke up in the middle of the night and ..."

The buzzer sounds off, making me unnecessarily jump. Steven answers it and I hear George's voice through the speaker. That buttery, smooth voice that could talk me into walking off a bridge without hesitation.

I sway unsteadily to my feet. Everyone rushes to help but this time I can do it myself. I'm not sure if I had a coat this morning, but I've got my suitcase in my hand and I'm heading back down the corridor towards the lift and the doors chime open and there is George. George surrounded by three suit-cases. He looks at me, his blue eyes piercing through every part of me. My heart. Ouch, my heart. I want to fall into his arms and kiss his face a thousand times over and tell him I forgive him and I'll never do something as reckless as this again. What am I doing? I love him and we're going to New York together. We can still make the plane, I can look past what happened, I can, I know I can. He'll apologise and say it was a blip, a lapse in judgement, one last fling before the non-existent ring. How can I expect him to have been with me and only me for the past nine years? How outrageous of me. I annoy myself at the best of times, and he's stuck it out with me for nearly a decade! It's the least I can do to let him be ferociously shagged against The Wall by the very hot American he's only known for two seconds. I rush towards him and when I'm an inch from touching that flawless face, his eyebrows narrow and he draws back, the expression on his face turning, like he's smelled something souring.

"What the fuck are you playing at, Charlie? You haven't answered your phone all day. The fucking ticket ripped up all over the bed? I know you had reservations about going but you couldn't even have a conversation with me about it? You just disappear with your suitcase and don't even tell me you're not coming? This is my job, Charlie. This is a huge deal to me and you're acting like a child. Slumping off to Zachary's because, what? You've got cold feet? I've said to you plenty of times that if the move was too much then you didn't have to come with me, but oh no, typical dramatic Charlie, waiting until the day to suddenly change his mind. You're unbelievable."

The floor feels like it's dropping away beneath me. I can see Niamh, Charlie and Zachary gathered in the doorway, front row seats to the horror show.

"Stay here. Don't come with me. I'm sure the sandwich shop will take you back. Jesus. There's a time to start growing up, Charlie. More fool me for thinking that moment could be now."

And with that, George presses the lift button and the doors close and as they do, I look at him and see that there isn't an inch of what I saw in the early hours of this morning going through his mind. It's burned into my retinas but he's already forgotten it. He's found the narrative he's been waiting for – that I'm a fuck-up. A mess. A directionless liability. He's found his way out.

Dylan calls after me, but I take the stairs, two at a time, my suitcase flailing behind me, and throw myself out into the evening air.

I definitely did have a coat when I left this morning. It's fucking freezing. But I feel nothing.

CHAPTER THREE

At primary school I was the only child in my class who didn't have a dad. When I asked Mum who my father was she said there were three possibilities. Basically, I'm Sophie in *Mamma Mia!* except I can't sing and my grandmother is sadly nothing like Cher and doesn't own a helicopter either. I wanted to try and investigate – compare noses, eye colour, senses of humour with every man we passed on the street – but Mum told me not to bother as two of the people it could be were in prison and she thought the third option was dead.

At the Christmas Nativity every year we were always given two tickets for our parents, but I only ever used one for my granny. Mum always seemed to be working and Grandad didn't come as he didn't believe in God. Although in 1995 – under a new bohemian headteacher – we did an ill-advised production of *Fame* and that has nothing to do with the Bible and he still didn't come.

I came to enjoy being different. I was seen as a bit of a wild child with no father figure to keep me in check. I could walk into the playground on a Monday morning in December with wet hair and a hole in my left plimsole and other mums would smile sympathetically at me and something in that made me feel good. Hannah Fountain's mum used to pack an extra easy peeler in my BFF Hannah's lunchbox for me. I had a bit of purpose, some attention, being the odd-one-out. Hannah's parents slept in separate rooms and at her eighth birthday party we heard her mum call her dad a Sad Little Man in the kitchen and then they started shouting at each other whilst a magician twisted balloons into crowns in the lounge to try and distract us. When Mum picked me up, Hannah's mum said to her something like, *It's Better to Be with Someone and Be Unhappy Than Be Alone and Unhappy. Right?* And my mum hissed something about being late to pick up my sister from nursery and then ate both packets of Haribo from my party bag before we got home.

★ ★ ★

Jacob doesn't want any Fats or Femmes. I've never had to download Grindr before. The first time I knew about it was when Dylan had a guy over on the first night we moved into the house, and he tried to tell me that it was a friend of his, but I knew all of his mates, and a six-foot-five rugby player named Pietro was not one of them.

I'm holding my suitcase, shivering from the cold. I don't know how far I've walked from Zachary and Steven's place but my feet feel tired and my eyes are heavy with sleep. I think I've solicited Jacob. He hasn't asked me for any sort of payment, but that's essentially what this is. Really I would just like a sofa, or failing that a floor with a blanket, or even better the comfort of George's embrace.

"Are you moving in or something?"

Jacob is standing in his doorway, one hand seductively on his hip and the other propped up against the frame. He has the air of a 1940s matron chiding her son for being out past curfew, except he's only wearing a pair of grey boxers. They cling to his dark-haired skin in all the right places.

I struggle with my case into the hallway.

"Don't leave it out here, put it in my room. I don't trust that it would still be here when we're finished."

I've left half an Easter Egg, twelve pounds in cash and my Blue Peter badge on the living room table before and despite my concerns, Dylan and Niamh didn't go anywhere near them. What kind of people live here that would take a battered old suitcase? A sobering thought flashes through my mind: this man is a total stranger. My heart thumps and I can't fathom if I'm petrified or excited or both. I briefly try and recall my self-defence training in case I need it and then remember that I've never had any.

Jacob's room is very pink. Twinkling fairy lights shower the room with a warm glow. There's a framed Barbie doll on the wall and a sign that reads Gays Just Wanna Have Fun. I know I'm slightly under the influence but maybe I've got the wrong message with the No Femmes from his profile. Zachary has said to me that my irony levels are low. Coincidentally, so are my iron levels. I wonder if there's a correlation.

Jacob asks me what my name is again and for some reason I say that it's George, and a lump of regret claws at my throat. Maybe he isn't even called Jacob. Fuck, this is dangerous. I push my belongings – with difficulty – into the corner of the room and when I turn Jacob is standing so close to me I can smell his breath. Warm orange and a hint of peppermint. I make a mental note to ask what toothpaste he uses.

I don't know the protocol. The little sexuality I did have has been replaced with the charm of an over-excited Lush employee and suddenly I'm asking him questions more forcibly that I intend.

"What did you mean on your profile?"

"Huh?"

"It says no fats and no femmes. What does that mean?"

"I don't chat to fat people or guys that aren't straight-acting."

I immediately feel uncomfortable and yearn to point out

39

the problem with that, but before I can even formulate the argument he takes my arm and manoeuvres me onto the bed. As I tumble down onto the duvet, there's a loud high-pitched squeak, and it's not the mattress. Peering underneath me I've sat on what appears to be a Care Bear.

"Is this your sister's room or something?"

"I'm an art student," Jacob says by way of explanation.

My phone hasn't stopped buzzing since I left my friends wondering what's going on. I'm now thinking the same thing. My mouth feels fuzzy. The warmth from all the wine I drank is starting to wear off.

Before I know it my trousers are off. I can't even remember what underwear I put on this morning in my haste to leave. I look down. Oh, the ones with the hem hanging down my left leg. Perfect.

When Dylan entertains us with his sexual escapades it seems fun – PG-pornographic and cheeky. This feels a bit wrong. It all feels wrong.

Jacob is kissing my thigh and working his way towards the tatty hole in my boxers. I put my hands under his chin to stop him.

"Do you mind if we take a breather?"

He inhales sharply and sinks back onto his knees. His shaved head shines against the fairy lights. He must polish the top with something. A chamois leather, perhaps.

"I specifically said I didn't have long dude."

He might as well have been talking in Latin when we were messaging. I didn't understand anything he said. Poppers? Raw? BDSM? I'd gamely said yes to all three.

I'm not sure when I first discovered what sex between two men was but I do remember being very confused.

At school we only learnt about how a baby was conceived between a man and a woman. Sex was functional. Necessary to repopulate the planet, and useful for nothing else. We were given some horrific stimuli in the form of something called *The Body Book* which read, 'when a man and woman want to make a baby, the man's penis stops being floppy and hanging down. It stands to attention. Then he can put it gently inside the woman's baby-making hole'. I hid the book at the back of my wardrobe. I didn't know what a Baby-Making Hole was and I had no intention of ever seeking one out. Alice Jenkins in the year above me asked if I knew what a clitoris was and I said Yes, but when I went to Ask Jeeves later the results proved that my guessed answer of A Piece of Intimate Jewellery was sadly incorrect. I managed to just sign out of AOL – and close all the pop-ups of local woman who were apparently desperate to meet me – before Mum shouted upstairs that dinner was ready. We had salmon because Mum was seeing a guy who was the head chef at the local pub and she wanted to impress him, but sadly my internet investigations meant I couldn't stomach the pink watery flesh staring lifelessly up at me. I don't remember ever seeing that suitor again after that night and Mum told me suspiciously to never go into his pub. What she thought an awkward thirteen-year-old was going to do in the Dog and Duck I'll never know.

I got used to the continual revolving door that was her love life. Sometimes these men were around for a while – giving me lifts to school and browning smiley potato faces in our oven – other times I didn't even know their names. One face at breakfast would be replaced with another by the time I'd arrived back from homework club. I now realise that the noise I heard coming from her bedroom most nights was the sound of an orgasm, and not an exorcism as I'd previously assumed. Whenever I hinted about wanting to know more about sex, the conversation was shut down, swiftly, by her.

"I'm not telling you anything. You can't be getting anyone pregnant because we can't afford to look after a baby, Charlie. You eat me out of house and home as it is."

You could argue that not telling me about it increased the chances of me fucking it all up and suddenly becoming an unwitting teenage father, but luckily for Mum there was no chance of that happening.

When I got to university, I hid my virginity at the back of the wardrobe alongside *The Body Book* – which I still kept for tips in case I ever needed it – and buried my head into my studies. Boys and girls were snogging in the student union and at night I'd hear my neighbour screaming something about wanting to be eaten out and I'd listen with a glass to the wall and wonder whether I should call the campus security about the potential cannibal I was sharing halls with. I had absolutely no idea about sex of any kind. And certainly nothing about pleasure.

The first time George touched me I practically took his eye out I erupted so fast. It was like my body had been silently waiting for this moment without telling me. I had goosebumps on top of goosebumps for the next forty-five minutes. He laughed and smiled and said something about him not usually having that effect on guys, and although I was embarrassed I was incredibly excited that finally I had someone to teach me, and so my real sexual education began. He wasn't the first person I'd Done Bits with, but he was certainly the first person that made it feel good, made it feel right, made it feel like I wasn't dirty and disgusting.

We did it on all fours. And with me upside down. And whilst watching porn. And in the toilets half-way through a night out. And with my legs in the air. And once in my English Literature lecture hall on top of one of the desks and despite getting two splinters in the top of my thigh and losing one sock in the dark, it was the most whole I had ever felt.

I've only ever had sex with George. I fit with George. I don't know if I'll work with anybody else.

Jacob huffs loudly.

42

"I hate time wasters. Are you too pissed to get it up?"

I look down into my lap and see that there's nothing going on there. I've never had a problem before. In fact, it's usually the opposite. I've lost count of the amount of times I've been lounging at home with George and I've had to keep a cushion over my lap to avoid giving Niamh and Dylan a fright. George once told me I was insatiable. I'd assumed that meant I was enough for him.

Jacob is on his phone. Scrolling. Flashes of orange and blue brighten the room. I know he's an art student, that he likes pink, and he's internally homophobic and a fat-shamer but apart from that, this man in front of me could be anyone. He doesn't know the past twenty-four hours I've had. I suddenly feel very distant. There's nothing wrong with sex with a stranger. Dylan and Niamh, they've done it, and they brag about it. Peacocking the beautiful guys and girls they've shared the night with. Comparing notes and showing pictures. What They Taught You About Stranger Danger at School Was Wrong —People You've Never Met Before Always Give the Best Blowjobs, Dylan told me once, to which Zachary added, It's Even Better When You Don't See Their Face, Darling. I've always enjoyed their conversations, seen them as these fascinating enigmas – my window into the queer world because, quite simply, I don't know anything about being gay in London. About being gay in London in 2025. About being gay in London in 2025 and single. I actually don't know anything at all.

Jacob tells me he's got another guy willing to come over in ten minutes so if I'm not going to suck him off then I should leave. I squint and try to imagine George's face on Jacob, but the proportions are all wrong. I play with the corner of my t-shirt. I don't think he'd want to see me with my top off anyway. Jacob picks a piece of lint out of his belly button. He's looming over me with such confidence that I don't think I can even stand up to put my trousers on.

There's blood rushing to my head, so I ask Jacob if I can lay back for a couple of seconds; he flippantly says, "Whatever" and then I feel the heaviness fall away from my eyelids and before I know it I am asleep.

★ ★ ★

I wake up to the smell of incense. For a moment I think I can hear the faint sound of New York traffic in the distance. Then I see the pink fairy lights.

"You're a fucking heavy sleeper, man."

Jacob is sitting on the end of his bed. The bed which I am in.

"I'm so sorry, I just fell back and closed my eyes for a second and . . ."

"And now it's 8 am the next day. Yeah, I noticed."

He has a warm smile. He doesn't seem as harsh in the morning light.

"This is so embarrassing, I'd had a bit of a rough day and I guess I was still exhausted from the night before."

"It's fine, I've had stranger things happen on a hook-up, believe me."

I contemplate what could be weirder than a guy turning up with a suitcase, denying his host fellatio and then wrapping himself up in his duvet and refusing to wake until daybreak. Perhaps it's safer not to ask.

"Can I give you some money for letting me stay or something?"

"I'm not a sex worker."

"Well, I know that, but I could just give you a tenner?" I root through my pockets, "Well I don't have any cash, but I can send you a BACS when I get home – well I don't actually have a home but . . ."

"Sleeping rough?"

"No no no, God no, not that there's anything wrong with

44

that, you know, we never can tell why people end up on the streets and most of the time it's because they're escaping abusive relationships, but I'm not doing that, my home life is not abusive, genuinely, so I think what I'm trying to say is, well, I think I might stop talking and just leave?"

Jacob kisses his teeth.

"You're funny."

"Funny looking?"

"Nah, just funny."

He smirks. I feel bashful. My stomach protests loudly.

"Hungry?"

"Yeah, a bit, I haven't really eaten in a while. Just a bit of grated cheddar."

"Dude, are you sure you're not sleeping rough?"

"Really, I'm not. It's ... well, everything's a bit of a mess."

Jacob stands up and stretches his athletic arms above his head. His bones satisfyingly snap.

"There's a greasy spoon round the corner. I know the owner, and I could do with some free beans on toast."

★ ★ ★

By the time I've finished telling him about George and Axel, and fainting at Zachary's place, and what George said to me by the lift, Jacob is dumfounded.

"It's like an episode of *Eastenders*, man."

He mops the brown sauce from his plate with a piece of buttered bread and sloppily places it into his mouth.

"And you're both called George?"

I falter for a moment and then remember. Now should be the time to correct him but I don't. I've no idea why. I fleetingly feel like a spy.

"Yes?"

"So what, you're just gonna go from stranger to stranger on Grindr now?"

"Well no, that's not the plan. I mean, currently I don't have a plan."

"Look, we've all been cheated on, it's shit right, but people come into our lives for different reasons; maybe there's something you need to learn from this."

"To not let male models sublet your room?"

"Yeah, or to take a look at your own life for a second. It sounds like you've had a pretty comfortable ride with this guy."

I can feel my eyes filling. I rub them into placation.

"I suppose."

"Well comfortable is boring isn't it?"

"Your bed was comfortable last night and that wasn't boring."

Jacob slurps his coffee.

"London is like, the greatest city in the world to be single in."

I recall Dylan lamenting the lack of commitment gay men have in London, and Zachary walking into a restaurant one night to see the guy they were then currently seeing on a date with somebody else. It doesn't sound particularly charming to me.

"I'd rather just crawl inside this sausage sandwich and be left alone."

"Nothing worth having comes easy."

"Well you've clearly never been invited to move to New York for free."

Jacob wipes his lips with a paper napkin and a jolly woman collects his empty plate and calls him Darling.

"I ain't a psychologist, but I can tell you, running away is never the answer."

I picture Jacob and I as lovers. What a story that would be for the grandchildren. He's slightly grubby looking but I reckon I could see past the Rolling Stones t-shirt and the

46

battered Converse. He's very wise. I feel calm around him. That might be the three pain killers I took before we left the flat.

He scrapes his chair back.

"I've got to get going, got shit to do, and you've been staring at that sandwich since it got here."

"Oh OK."

"Safe travels, man. You got this."

I don't know whether to shake his hand or go for something less informal and hug. We are Good Friends now after all. I don't have a chance to decide because by the time I stand up he's already nearly out the door.

"I don't have your phone number!" I cry out.

He doesn't stop. The door closes and he turns the opposite way to where we came from and disappears. I presume this is because for the last half hour of our conversation his phone kept vibrating on the table with notifications from Grindr.

The jolly woman approaches again and asks if I want my food wrapped up to go, I say I would.

"It's a lovely day out isn't it?" she says brightly, "The sky does look extraordinarily clear for February."

The woman gives me a tied up brown paper bag and hands me a piece of paper with the bill on. I scratch my ears, nervously.

"Oh, I thought you knew Jacob, he said you were friends."

"Don't know him from Adam my love. He's in here with a different man most mornings for his breakfast though."

"Right, so, it's not on the house?"

"Nothing's for free these days my darling."

£18.50 for a fry up and a sausage sandwich. It seems the cafe isn't the only thing that's greasy.

★ ★ ★

Mum calls and asks me how New York is. I tell her that it costs £1.50 a second to call someone in America and she immediately hangs up. I'm back in Soho Square again, on a bench, with one leg up on my suitcase. I wonder what people passing by think my story is. Mum's phone call also drained the last of the juice out of my mobile. I've now gone completely AWOL.

There's a girl pushing a bike through the park. She nearly runs over a little Yorkshire terrier. Its owner calls her something obscene. George and I had spoken about getting a dog before he was offered the job in New York. I said yes, despite being heavily allergic.

I think back to what Jacob said, about not running away and pausing to look at your life for a second. I've been looking at mine from the moment I saw Axel's naked bottom. I don't have a life. George is my life. Was my life. So what do I do now?

CHAPTER FOUR

My local library used to do a reading competition every summer. You had to get through as many books as you could over the six weeks' holiday and were rewarded with a stamp for every one you finished. The first time I took part, at the age of seven, I had completely filled the entire card by the third day. The librarian looked down at me puzzled – as though I were a real-life *Matilda* – and said due to the cost of printing I couldn't have another card, but to save the six trips a day that I was currently making, she'd let me check out up to three books at a time. The thrill of this new bounty made me skip all the way home. I read Jacqueline Wilson and Enid Blyton and Roald Dahl and R. L. Stine – under a blanket and with a chair propped against my door – and every single *Horrible Histories* – the one about the Romans twice. These worlds were dangerous and adventurous and all mine. Now, twenty-ish years later, books are the one place where I can forget about what's going on outside, and time just seems to stop, and at the moment, I'd quite like to escape.

★ ★ ★

There's a smudge on the left lens of my glasses, but there's nothing to wipe it with so I take them off and quickly rub it against the bottom of my cable-knit jumper. The heating is blasting down the back of my neck and I can feel a slow trickle of sweat making its way along the hem, trying desperately to slip down my back. I called the sandwich shop and tried to take back my letter of resignation, but it was no use. The owner had filled the position as quickly as she could fill a panini. It's been a long time since I've been in an interviewer's chair, and my nerves are almost uncontrollable. I am David Blaine in a Perspex box above the Thames, except the box is made of asbestos, filled with snakes and on a plane directly towards the centre of the sun.

The interview is in the Waterstones on Trafalgar Square. The possibility that I could work in a bookshop is so overwhelming to me that I'm on the verge of hyperventilating. The first time I set foot in a Waterstones back at home I knew I wanted to work in there. I applied for a Christmas temp job four years in a row and never even got a response, which was problematic because I'd essentially only buy clothes ready for my stereotypical bookshop uniform – chunky knits, tweed trousers and glasses. Clothes which didn't give my eighteen-year-old self much street cred in the only nightclub in town on a Friday night.

The fact that I don't actually need glasses is an irrelevant detail. Ever since I got my first taste of the book world, I knew if I were to successfully infiltrate those quiet yet hallowed shelves then I needed to look the part. These are only the lowest prescription lenses, so I'm sure it'll be fine, and if I do fuck my eyes up then at least I did it for my art.

It has been exactly two weeks since The Break Up Which Wasn't Officially Named As A Break Up, and I've spent it sleeping at Zachary and Steven's house. Eventually, after wandering around Soho all morning with my uneaten sausage sandwich, I admitted defeat and got the bus to theirs. Niamh was there, with Zachary who was working from home. They were all sick with worry – Dylan had even called my mum, who assumed I was in New York. He'd told her I hadn't gone and she'd cried – not because I was missing, but because I hadn't gone with George. I didn't tell them about going to Jacob's – I knew they wouldn't understand, and to be honest I didn't understand why I'd gone there either. I'd told them that something had happened between George and I but I wasn't ready to talk about it yet, but it turns out I sort of didn't have to.

Once I'd plugged my phone in, got some charge and started to trawl though various messages, I realised that George had come clean about the whole thing to everyone. Well, almost. Nobody had mentioned anything about him having sex with Axel, but he did say he'd kissed him and I couldn't be bothered to correct his admission because it seemed irrelevant. George knew what he'd done and I felt as though that was punishment enough. He'd have to live forever with the knowledge that he had the capacity to cheat on somebody.

Niamh, Dylan and Zachary had all immediately scooped me up, and Dylan had even said he was excited at the prospect of being each other's wingmen on nights out. They all told me what a terrible person George was, and how disappointed they were in him, but he hadn't cheated on them, he'd cheated on me, so I knew that they would still care about him very deeply. It was my relationship with him that was over, not theirs.

George had rebooked his flight for two days later, telling his company that he'd had a family emergency which caused him to miss the first one. Granny always told me never to use that as an excuse because when she was twenty she'd tele-phoned her work and said she couldn't come in as her father was feeling under the weather and when she got home from an illicit picnic with my grandad that afternoon, her Dad had fallen down the stairs, hit his head on a shelving unit and died.

"You should be careful what you wish for," she often muttered whenever I complained that I didn't want to go to school. Little did she know that the thought of Mum taking a tumble down the stairs was actually enormously appealing.

The Waterstones manager calls me into a small, square office with framed pictures of Penguin Classics hanging on the wall and already I feel at home. She too has glasses and a crochet cardigan. I compliment her look, then immediately make a reference to my homosexual lifestyle so as to alleviate any fears that I'm coming on to her to get the job.

"I saw a lady wearing that very same jumper in The Royal Vauxhall Tavern the other night, and she just looked so gorgeous. It's a great cut and pattern."

She introduces herself as Noma, smiles appreciatively and tells me that she's hard of hearing, so if I don't mind speaking clearly so she can lip read she'd be extremely grateful. Noma asks me to talk to her about the last book I read. It was one I found on the shelf in the spare room at Zachary and Steven's. I'd last read it years ago at secondary school. It was super sleek – one of those classics with a reimagined cover. I sniffed the pages, thumbed through the first couple of chapters and immediately fell into its intrigue and mystery.

Being at the boys' place feels a bit like being in a spa – a spa with a constantly cheerful yet desperately sensible aunt and uncle – but for the first time since That Night I'm starting to feel a sense of potential serenity. There's always fresh bread from the oven every other morning and cocktails when I arrive home after a day of pounding the pavements with CVs. Plus, the real draw is that they aren't charging me a penny. Even I can put up with Steven's smugness for a rent-free couple of months.

"It was *To Kill a Mockingbird*. I'd read it at school, but my English teacher was terrible and I hated it, so I thought it would be a good idea to pick it up again – on my own

52

terms – and see what my opinion of it was now. I sometimes start a book and get bored within a few chapters, but when I come to it again at a different point in my life, I find myself devouring it in one sitting."

Noma scrapes a pencil across her pad, but it's only something short so I'm either giving her great answers or she's jotting down that she needs to buy oat milk on the way home.

"And that's what I love about books. The escape. The opportunity to experience things from the point of view of somebody else. I think the best way to sort through any difficulty you're going through in life is to pause for a second, see it from another angle and use that insight to make better-informed decisions. Reading does that for me. It takes me out of my own world for a brief pause, and then when I reach the end of another chapter and go back to normality, I always seem to make a better judgment, because nothing is really as bad as you think it is."

Unexpectedly, Noma is somehow crying and saying how much she needed to hear that because she's going through a divorce at the moment and everything feels so impossibly hard to navigate and a moment of respite is exactly what she needs – and she knows exactly which book she needs to read tonight before bed to give her some clarity, and the moral of this story is that I've got the job and I start on Monday.

★ ★ ★

George asked to meet up and have a chat before he went but I couldn't bring myself to go. I knew he'd cry, and I'd cry, and I might even end up getting on the plane with him, and I knew that wasn't the person I wanted to be. I kept thinking about the conversation we had standing outside the lift, on the night we should have flown together, and him saying to me, "I'm sure the sandwich shop will take you back," as if I'd done something wrong. The bits of bread and cheese and salami, they'd take me back, but he wouldn't. Maybe I was reading too much into it all, but the only thing I did know was that I couldn't talk about it right now without getting emotional. He said he'd go to New York and start his job, and once he was settled we should talk about what we're going to do, and whether we thought we had a future. Once *he* was settled. Not me. Him.

I saw a picture he uploaded on Instagram of the apartment. The wallpaper wasn't as nice as I remembered from the estate agent's pictures, and George had captioned it underneath with the hashtag InstaGay so I immediately unfollowed him.

Dylan wanted me to come and move back in for a bit, but Axel has signed a contract so there's no getting rid of him for at least a year. Plus, I don't think being in that house would be very good for me right now. Niamh thinks I'm mad for accepting a new job that will tie me down here, when everything could be patched up with George before I've even completed my first shift, but I just know deep down that I can't come back from what's happened, even though everything in me is screaming to forgive him.

I'm standing in the spare room at Zachary and Steven's and although this isn't quite the American dream, it feels like a pretty good way of starting again. Zachary has suggested taking us to a bar they like in Soho tonight to celebrate my new job as a glasses-wearing Waterstones employee, and I'm French-tucking a new shirt I've bought especially for the occasion.

I look in the mirror and the person staring back at me looks haunted. Usually, I'd avert my eyes from any mirror in the house. I'm like Nicole Kidman in the film *The Others*, running around and covering every window and mirror with a dust sheet so I don't have to look at myself. My hair, which used to be dark brown is greying by the day, my hairline receding quicker than the recession. My green eyes that used to make

George wilt, now look reptilian and small, mainly due to the bags carved under them. I'm 5'11 but always say I'm 6ft. My love handles, which usually hug the corners of my t-shirts, have shrunk a little from The Heartache Diet, but I know they'll return soon, grumpier and stretchier than before. I've got one tattoo, on my ankle, a singular letter G, which for obvious reasons will need to be covered up for the foreseeable. Dylan suggests I could add the letters A and Y after it, but I fear that's too on the nose.

I look very unremarkable actually.

The sort of man who you wouldn't remember. Who you wouldn't notice. And although this man in the mirror has now got a job that he actually wants — that isn't spreading pesto into a baguette for minimum wage — he still can't seem to smile. His mouth is too full of teeth from the years in which he should have worn a brace but was too scared to go to the dentist. I think about the impending night out with my confident friends, my beautiful, confident friends.

I feel the wings of nervous butterflies in my tummy. They flap and flap until I run to the toilet to gag.

CHAPTER FIVE

When I was six years old my goldfish died. I had two at the time. The slightly larger one was called Scampi and the other I obviously named Chips. I came home from school one afternoon to find Scampi floating at the top of the tank, translucent and bug-eyed. I cried for three whole days and with my head teacher's blessing even had an afternoon off on the Friday. When my sobbing showed no signs of relenting, Mum bought me a replacement fish, which I named Scampi Two. Three days later, the pump malfunctioned and somehow managed to suffocate both Chips and Scampi Two in a double homicide. I cried some more. The next day the pump had been sellotaped and two new fish appeared. They lasted a paltry sixteen days before joining their sisters in the big toilet bowl in the sky. I wept – snotty and furious at the injustice of the aquatic world – until I gave myself a headache. Mum sat me down and said not only could she no longer afford to buy me any more maritime pals, but she quite frankly couldn't be bothered to deal with my emotional fallout afterwards. "Nothing lasts forever," she said, spooning spaghetti hoops onto a piece of toast for my dinner.

★ ★ ★

I've been up and down this street in Soho probably a hundred times in all the years I've lived in London and I don't recognise half of these bars. I've never really needed to look inside them. We had some pre-drinks at Zachary's – which consisted of espresso martinis made by Steven, and something called sloe gin. Despite its name the effects are anything but slow – my fingers feel wobbly, my heart is racing, and I sang a word-perfect rendition of 'Black Horse and the Cherry Tree' by KT Tunstall on the Bakerloo Line. A lady two seats down even applauded.

Niamh needs a wee so we've taken a pitstop in a bar where everybody inside has the same beard.

"Is this where you usually come?" I shout over the music to be heard.

"Sometimes, darling, depends on my mood."

Zachary is wearing a black skintight jumpsuit and there's a slick of silver running through their hair. They look like a modern-day superhero.

A gentleman with a half-empty pint of beer winks at Dylan. Dylan smirks. The disco lights are picking out little bits of my friends and shining on their most glorious features: Dylan's eyes, Zachary's jawline, Niamh's long, elegant neck. I pull at my shirt, untuck it from the front. Dylan looks lovely this evening – polished but casual at the same time. His white vest is tucked into smart blue jeans, with what looks like a new pair of colourful trainers providing the spring in his step. His fingers are littered with silver rings of different shapes and sizes, and he's done that thing with the middle curl on his forehead that makes him look like Zach Efron in *Hairspray*. He's clearly after some attention tonight and I know he'll attract plenty. A pang of loneliness spreads down my body.

"You're telling me you've never been in here before, Charlie?" Niamh pulls a clump of mascara from her eyelash and discards it onto the floor.

"No, never. I thought we went out all the time, but never here."

"You just went to posh Couple Things."

There's a slight note of resentment in this retort from Dylan, but I'll put that down to the martinis.

Since everything happened I haven't heard anything from any of the couples we used to hang around with: Alex and Matt, Kate and Lolly, Tyrone and Sash. We used to double date and do weekends in the Cotswolds and play squash. I realised that I can't remember the last time I had a night out with My Friends.

"I want a shot. I'm getting us a round of shots," I declare.

Niamh gives me the side-eye.

"You always say . . ."

"That shots don't constitute a round on a night out, I know, I know, but I'm offering so either have one or piss off."

"As if I'd turn down a kind offer like that."

I float my card around at the bar. I won't have a payday coming for at least another month but I feel buoyed by being with the others, and the music is good and the gin has seeped into the part of my brain which says Fuck It.

All the barmen are topless. They're all shapes and sizes but they are topless. I wonder if that's part of their interview process. I imagine if I'd have had to take my top off when I first went into Waterstones. I can picture Noma in my interview running and screaming, throwing books at me to protect herself from Mary Shelley's newest disgusting creation.

I order four shots of whatever the barman can recommend. He grunts in response. He has a tattoo on his left bicep which says Melanie encased by a thinly drawn heart. He's either a mummy's boy or straight. If he is straight then I think him working here is cheating. I want to be able to know that I could shag him if I wanted to. I realise I'm thinking all of this whilst staring very intently at the trail of fine hair on his abdomen, completely unaware that he's waving the card machine in my face. Mortifyingly I think at one point I might have even licked my lips.

"£28 please mate."

The machine asks me if I want to give a tip. I find myself punching in ten pounds. I consider it an investment in my potential future happiness. I wink at the bar keep. He doesn't notice. He's moved on to a blond-haired twink at the other end.

I dish out the little glasses of precious nectar and we cheers to the night and knock the clear liquid back. It tastes like someone has shoved a lit candle covered in paraffin wax down my throat. I immediately order four more.

★ ★ ★

I'm swaying dangerously in the toilets – the little blue urinal cake has become my target and I shower it with piss. The colour of it reminds me that I absolutely need to drink more water. I wash my hands and give the toilet attendant three pounds from my wallet in exchange for a quick spritz of Jean Paul Gaultier. He smiles at me as I'm handed a paper towel to dry my hands.

"Busy night?"

The man grins in reply, showing off three glistening silver teeth.

"I haven't been out in ages so I'm absolutely fucked to be honest. Thanks for the spray. I was starting to get a bit of a whiff-on."

It's nice to make friends on a night out. Despite having no verbal communication with the kind soap dispenser, I pay him a further fifty pence for the trouble.

Back out in the hazy bar I find myself unable to lock eyes with anybody I know. My friends are nowhere to be seen.

I stumble to a corner of the bar next to a battered air

conditioning unit and allow the breeze to lift the sweat from my hair. A gentleman wearing tightly circled tortoise shell glasses and a denim shirt nods his head in my direction. I raise my beer towards him, immediately staring at the floor afterwards. Taking a couple of deep breaths, I roll my shoulders back and try to remember that I'm supposed to be having a good time. I am having a good time. This is what gay single people do. They drink to excess, and dance in order to seduce. I look back up, but the man with glasses has disappeared.

There's half a Red Stripe on the windowsill next to me. I make an executive decision not to finish it off. I remember everything we did at school about drug awareness.

"Hey!"

A man – only slightly shorter than me – is standing to my right. Where he's come from is anybody's guess, but he appears to be talking to me.

"I'm Ollie."

"Hello. I'm Charlie."

He clinks his bottle with mine. Streaks of chipped purple nail varnish decorate his fingers haphazardly.

"You on your own then, Charlie?"

"No, I'm here with some mates, but they're off having a nice time."

"And you?"

"Well, I'm having a lovely time, yes. Just went to the toilet and lost them, but no rush."

"You can always put a call out – ask the DJ."

"Really?"

"Fuck no, you'll be lynched."

There's a mischievous glint in his eyes that matches the rebellious nature of his shaved head. A single silver hoop pierces his left ear.

"I actually saw you dancing with your pals earlier, when I got here."

60

"Oh. Are you here with anyone?"

"Nah. Just fancied a bevvy after work."

The confidence to be able to walk into a bar when you aren't meeting anybody! I try to get my head around it, but the thought of it makes me feel incredibly anxious.

"What do you do then, Ollie?"

"I'm a legal secretary."

"I don't know what that is."

"Neither do I to be honest, pal."

I'm detecting a southern Irish drawl to his voice, but it's loud in here, and my geography is terrible, so to save myself from offending I won't bring it up. I don't want to scare away the only person saving me from my social anxiety.

"You been here before then, Charlie?"

"I like the way you keep using my name."

"Well, it's a nice name, Charlie. Why wouldn't I say it?"

"Ollie's a nice name too."

"Then feel free to use it as much as you like."

"Thanks. Ollie. I will. Oliver!"

"It's Ollie though."

"Oh right, no I meant Ollie, sorry."

He laughs. Drains the dregs of his beer and offers to buy me another. I accept. Ollie couldn't be further away from George in terms of looks, but his aura is magnetic. I've only known him a few minutes but I don't want to leave his side.

"So you having a good night so far?"

"Aye, I am. Work was hell this week. Clients being arse-holes. My boss is a Grade A prick. If you want to grow and work in the legal sector then here's some advice for you; don't fucking bother."

"Good to know."

"I never asked, what is it you do?"

I consider lying, but my inhibitions are at an all-time zero.

"Nothing at the moment actually."

61

"A man of the earth. I like it."

"I start a new job next week."

"Nice man. Congrats."

Ollie and I continue talking for an insurmountable amount of time. The clock seems to stop. His beard isn't like the rest of the clientele – it's more artfully unkempt, and I find myself drawing physically closer as he talks to me about his weird manic depressive housemate, and the way his father talks to him, and how he's thinking of moving to the coast one day.

I want to ask for his number, but I don't know how to phrase it, even though his flirting is abundantly clear. He's spoken to me, and only me, for what feels like at least an hour, but it suddenly seems as though for the first time in my life, I'm not going to be the one doing the hard grafting.

"So yeah, I was wondering if I could ask something actually," he says, picking at the label on his beer. I move a fraction closer. He's looking right into my eyes now – there's a visible spark between us.

"Yeah?"

"This is embarrassing really."

"Why? What is it?"

My lips begin to tingle. If he wants to ask me out I'll confirm my interest with a kiss. Bold and brave, that's the mantra I need to follow. It's what the rest of my friends do, and as the phrase goes, 'the best way to get over someone is to get under someone else'.

"Well, the guy you're with – the one all in black with the streak in his hair. Is he single?"

My tummy does one single somersault.

"Oh Zachary ... erm, they're not single actually, they're engaged but in an open relationship. And they go by they/them."

"Oh, sure, sorry, I hate to do this to you, but any chance you could introduce me to them?"

"Er yeah, when I find them."

"Thanks, they're really hot."

"Yeah, yeah they are."

"All your mates looked fit to be honest, you lucky bastard."

That's me. One lucky bastard.

* * *

I'm sweating so profusely that I fear I may never separate this shirt from my back ever again. I have become one with the shirt. I am the shirt. I no longer know where I stop and the shirt begins.

Dancing is hilarious when you think about it. It's just a group of people throwing their limbs around. There's no pattern or shape to it. It's very neanderthal. Zachary is in a total trance. Their long, pale arms outstretched towards the ceiling – they've barely said two words to Ollie since I introduced them. They move around each other simultaneously, communicating without words. Just a pattern of extreme eye contact interspersed with their lips meeting. It's passionate and nauseating at the same time. Niamh is being playfully spanked by two girls who I don't know – both are wearing very little. Dylan is nowhere to be seen. I am dancing like my life depends on it. The floor is so sticky I lost a shoe somewhere during Little Mix's 'Shout Out to My Ex', but I don't care because I've found the beat and I'm screaming along like this is my pop concert and the world is my backing dancer.

I tell Zach I need to take a breather outside, but they don't hear me. I need fresh air but apparently you can only get that in the smoking area. I think of what Niamh would say, but her spanking has progressed to some feverish three-way tonguing. Squeezing through a sea of tangled bodies, all talking animatedly, I nestle myself in the furthest corner.

You can never really see any stars in London at night. Squinting, I try to find Orion's Belt or the Plough but all I can make out is the blink blink blink of a plane disappearing into nothingness. I think of New York and it makes me screw my face up.

My thighs are chaffing. I reach into my jeans and pull the legs of my boxer shorts down. I've been dancing so ferociously that I'm surprised the friction hasn't started a small fire, although there is a small hole appearing in the crotch. I've already had Zachary sew these up twice.

I scan the smokers and am surprised to find that there's only a couple of people actually with cigarettes. Grandad told me that when he was younger everybody smoked, so to fit in he used to light up and then twirl the dwindling stick between his fingers until it had turned completely to ash – never once letting it touch his lips. It was an expensive lie but nobody was any the wiser – he still looked sociable and according to him, it Kept the Cancer Well Away. It seemed fruitless to point out to him the perils of second-hand smoking.

I wonder how many of these people in this little pocket of earth knew each other before they came here tonight.

There are boys with thick wavy hair, and boys with piercing green eyes, and boys with pecs neatly outlining their t-shirts, and boys with snug round bottoms, and boys with large peachy bottoms, and boys with neatly-trimmed moustaches and tanned biceps, and boys in slim-fit jeans, and boys in Doc Martens, and boys with meaty calves, and boys with cultivated beards, and boys holding hands, and boys smiling and snorting with laughter, and boys kissing like the rest of us out here don't exist. I catch a glimpse of myself in the window of the shop opposite. I feel a wave of loneliness. I press my thighs together and feel the searing pain of raw skin touching raw skin. George always joked about me not going to the gym, but when was the last time I did any exercise? I feel like I've turned up to a fancy dress party where the theme is Hot and Available but I didn't get the memo.

64

I open my phone to flick through Instagram. Dylan has put up a picture that we took at the start of the night. Niamh, Zachary and Dylan look effortlessly cool – like they're in a new campaign for a reboot of *Skins*. I'm not sure I'm qualified to be in the frame with them. I thought I looked alright before we left but that must have been the gin talking. I look superimposed. A stranger amongst their beauty.

I try to push my hand through my hair but it's clumped together with sweat and won't do what I want it to do. A cloud of someone's smoke wafts past me. I feel bloated.

In the other corner of the fenced-off area I can see Dylan talking with a tall man. Dylan is moving his mouth and the man is roaring his head off with laughter. I don't know who he is. Dylan has always had the ability to strike up comfortable conversation with just about anyone. I want to go over there but my feet are stuck to the freezing floor. I wish I'd at least tried to find my lost shoe. I watch Dylan and feel such a deep sense of emptiness that I blink back a tear.

At university in our second term Dylan and I had met at a meeting for the student newspaper. I fancied myself as a hot-shot reporter because I had a morbid fascination with Fiona and Eamon on *GMTV*, and Dylan was there because he wanted to draw little political cartoons for a hobby.

We'd actually met the night before in the union through a mutual friend and egged each other on to go to the paper the next day and sign up as contributors. I wasn't sure he was going to turn up, but when he walked through the doorway with his little brown satchel I felt my cheeks flush. He was very unconventionally handsome and he had some extremely interesting things to say about pop culture and the Labour Party. I wasn't sure if he was gay, but I liked myself when I was around him, and we spent every day together for the next fortnight.

We both loved Saturday night TV, and reading books, and grating extra cheese on our Sainsbury's Basic pizzas and he had a PlayStation with *Crash Bandicoot* in his dorm room so it was the perfect friendship. One night, when we'd gone out dressed as Tinky-Winky and Po from the *Teletubbies* – and dragged a large Dyson around with us to be our Noo-Noo – I'd laid down on Dylan's bed and had this rush of warmth around my body knowing that I'd made a friend for life. He'd been flirting with me all night – constantly touching my face and looking for me whenever we were accidentally split up by the throngs of other partygoers.

When we got back I threw my purple handbag down and was so overcome with love that I rolled over and kissed him. Dylan immediately pulled away, and said he wasn't sure that's what he wanted. He really liked me, of course he did, but he wasn't Out Yet, because he knew his father wouldn't approve, and he'd slept with a girl on his course last weekend and he didn't want to confuse our friendship. We clung onto each other until he fell asleep, my arms enveloping him all night. I didn't sleep a wink. We never mentioned it. Not the next day. Not ever. Our friendship took over and became so strong that the foundation upon which it was based was easily forgotten. When I remember that night, it's as if it's other people and not us.

I come back down to the smoky earth to find myself staring at Dylan and this man kissing. They are moving their lips together tenderly at first, Dylan's hand brushing the side of this man's face lovingly, and then as the pace increases and they start to mash their mouths together I admit defeat and cast my friend out into the darkness of the night. I've lost him for the evening now. I am on my own.

★ ★ ★

It's five in the morning before I finally get home. I bang on the window to stop the birds from chirping their happy tunes.

I passed Steven going out to work on the way in. He gave

me a pint of water and a sachet of rehydration powder. What he thinks that's going to do that this twenty-chicken-nugget-sharing-box can't is a mystery to me. I climb into bed and stare at nothing. Dylan went home with that handsome stranger and Niámh went on to a female-only queer night. Zachary and Ollie helped me into an Uber but got out at Waterloo to go to the sauna Pleasuredrome. Good for them. I'd never have the guts to go in there.

I've never felt more alone. I am Chips after Scampi first departed this cruel world. I thought tonight might be the start of my reign as King of Singledom, men falling at my feet. Instead, I spent the last half an hour slipping over on the wet dance floor of the pub, with nobody to pick me up this time.

I throw my clothes in a pile on the rug. I only bought that shirt yesterday but I know I won't wear it again. I go to take my pants down and then notice just how sore the top insides of my legs are. I slather them with Vaseline and then face-plant the bed – spreadeagled to provide extra coolness. I look at the nuggets on the bedside table. I push the full box onto the floor. I'm not very hungry anymore.

CHAPTER SIX

Mum orders a large skinny latte and a slice of salted-caramel flapjack. She doesn't ask me what I want, so I make a separate order. A green tea.

"Why aren't you getting any cake?" She barks at me from the collection counter.

"I don't want any."

"Oh great, well make me feel bad for wanting some why don't you?"

We sit in a window seat overlooking the platforms. People swarm like ants out of opening train doors and push their way through fellow commuters. Mum and I stare out at them. She gently picks at the oats and syrup, then plays with the crumbs between her fingers, her bright-red nails becoming glazed with sugar. To break the silence I tell her that I'm getting my G tattoo covered up with a new design and I've booked to jump out of a plane. She asks me if I have terminal cancer.

"No, Mum, I'm not ill, it's just everything's a bit stale and boring, and I want to ... I don't know, just *feel* something different."

"I don't know what you mean."

I sip my tea. She sips her coffee.

"And George won't take you back then?"

"Mum, I don't want to talk about George."

"Well I've been emailing him on The Facebook and he's really missing you, you know. God knows why."

I put my cup down on the table and pick the bitter mint leaves out of the gaps between my teeth.

"Has Leanne got a job yet?"

"Leave your sister out of this."

"That's a no then."

"She's doing fine, working for Paul."

"Hanging out all day at the market doesn't count. She should have finished her A-Levels."

"Well, we can't all be clever enough to go to a university can we? She can make just as good without it. All that work and money spent on your English degree and what has it got you? A job at some posh library."

"It's Waterstones. It's not a library."

"Well whatever it is, it isn't what you should be doing with those qualifications, so you can stop putting your sister down because you've no two feet to stand on."

I stare at the barista cutting a slice of walnut and coffee sponge. The icing fluffy and cappuccino coloured. I lick the corner of my mouth and my stomach pangs. I haven't eaten since yesterday lunch time; a limp salad. The feeling of being out of place at the nightclub the other day has completely ruined my appetite. Suddenly, being single means I have to care about what I look like again, and unfortunately my usual three chocolate bars a day aren't going to help with the overhaul needed to be desired again. Food is not my friend anymore, hence the green tea. Zachary swears by it, because Victoria Beckham swears by it, so now I swear by it. Really, I want to just swear at it, because green tea tastes like shit.

"So that's it then, you're just going to let George move to New York without you and you're not even going to try."

This isn't a question. It's a statement.

"I said, I don't want to talk about it."

"I just can't believe it. A month he's been out there and you've been sitting on your backside doing nothing."

"I've just got a job, how is that nothing?"

She isn't listening anymore. There's a currant stuck in her upper front teeth. She looks like a rabbit. The flapjack is completely destroyed. Torn apart savagely. She always eats like this. Breaking food up into smaller pieces as if to disperse their calories. I am my mother's son.

"And where are you living then?"

"I'm with Zachary and Steven in their spare room, but I've started looking for a place."

"You know Dave Owen has just opened his own mechanic business down the road from his mum's? And Rosie, you remember Rosie, she just had another little girl. So that's two grandchildren Sophie's got now."

My hand clenches around my cup. Mum always does this – plays Whose Life Is Better with random people from my school year group. People that I can't even remember.

"And Hannah, you know the Fountain girl – lovely, bright thing she is – she's the receptionist down at the doctor's surgery, and she's put down a deposit on a flat with her fiancé. Right by the woods. Huge garden. And what are you doing? Drawing pictures on your ankle and heaving yourself out of goddamn aeroplanes."

I push my fingers into the hot ceramic containing my tea, my skin searing.

"George cheated on me, Mum. He slept with somebody else, so stop going on about him like he's this untouchable angel because he's not."

Mum scoffs. The currant finally topples out of her mouth like a rotten tooth finally giving way.

"Well maybe you should have tried a bit harder to keep him interested in you then."

My first week at Waterstones was everything I'd dreamt it would be.

I was given a tour and taught how to use the computer to search for titles, and even asked to write out a little card to be displayed talking about one of my favourite books. I picked *Everything I Know About Love* by Dolly Alderton – despite coming to the recent revelation that I know nothing about The L Word. Niamh had bought it for me a couple of days after The Wall had ruined my life and I devoured the entire memoir in one sitting – I suddenly had quite a lot of spare time on my hands after I finished work. The best thing about the job is being surrounded by literature all day. The smell of a new book is like nothing else; it makes me feel utterly calm.

The reading glasses have become a bit of a strain, and I find that by the end of a shift my temples are screaming, so I've ordered a pair of plain-lens ones from Amazon. Nobody will be able to tell the difference.

My boss, Noma, has invited me to her birthday party in two weeks' time and I think I'll go. I asked Steven if he'll help me bake something to take with me. Zachary's been away for a work event for the past week on some new LGBT+ cruise ship, so I've become pretty close to Steven. He's only mildly irritating now.

It's day five and I'm stacking piles of the new Candice Carty-Williams paperback when a hand taps me on the shoulder.

"Excuse me, do you work here?"

No, I just like stacking the books for fun.

"Yes. How can I help you?" I say, without looking up.

"I was wondering if you could recommend a book for me please."

"Certainly, what are you in the mood for? Fiction, Non-Fiction?"

"I love original stories. Mainly love stories."

"Right, in which case then, you'd probably really enjoy this one here, it's a new-ish classic."

I hold up a copy of *Queenie* and my autopilot fails. I falter slightly and my mouth dries. The angel standing before me has taken my breath away. Soft brown curls frame a delicately shaven face. He has the fullest, pinkest lips I've ever seen. I try and rally.

"This is one of my favourite books from the past couple of years ... because ... erm ... Carty-Williams' characters are so well crafted, you can really see parts of you ... parts of yourself in all of them."

"Oh right, well that sounds quite good. And it's a love story?"

"Of sorts, yes."

"Thanks very much."

He takes the copy from me, and my hand lingers a little bit too long on his. As he begins to move away I find myself not wanting this conversation to be over, so I shout across the shop floor.

"You're a romantic then?"

He turns back to me. I wonder what my breath smells like after the cheese and onion sandwich I had for lunch. It most definitely smells of cheese and onion. And I forgot to go into Boots and put on one of the aftershave testers this morning. I'll have to keep at least one metre away to avoid putting him off.

"I guess you could say that," he says, pushing a curl behind his ear. "I just like escaping into something that's different from real life, you know? And what's better than something romantic? This book sounds like a great recommendation, thanks."

A church bell chimes in my head and I think I see a flock of doves passing in the shape of a heart by the window.

"That's exactly why I love books!" I splutter, somewhat desperately. My tummy hurts and I realise that I'm sucking it in.

"I guess you need to love books if you work in a book shop, right?"

I laugh, over zealously. It's really not that funny a quip. In fact, I think he meant it entirely sincerely. Oh God, is this what my flirting technique is like? The Giddy School-Girl?

I escort him over to the counter to pay, but Farrah, a colleague who joined Waterstones on the same day as me, is behind the till. She's a student, working here weekends and evenings to pay for her studies. Her brown hair is always wrought into submission by a colourful hairband that looks as though it's been on her head so long you'd need a surgical operation to remove it. She reminds me a little of my sister.

I say it's time for her break, even though she only started her shift five minutes ago and because she's easily confused and hasn't read the rota properly she gladly disappears into the staff room. I pull the lead out of the chip and pin machine with my foot, so that I can look at his card and enter it manually into the computer instead – Poirot eat your heart out. The card says it belongs to a Mr Constantino. It sounds good rolling the vowels around my mouth. Except I've said his name out loud.

"Yes?"

"Oh sorry, just . . . that's an unusual surname."

"It's pretty regular. Us Constantinos are everywhere."

"Are they!" My top teeth protrude over my bottom lip as I say this. He furrows his brow as though I'm mocking him, "Because . . . I've never met one before."

"Has the payment gone through?" He says, looking over his shoulder. Of course, somebody is probably waiting outside for him. A husband or a lover. Or a wife. Jesus, how do you know if someone is gay? I hadn't even considered that he might be straight. You can't just come out and ask someone their sexuality. I know that from the training we did on Monday, even though thirty seconds before it started Farrah asked me if I had a boyfriend.

"Er, it's not actually gone through . . . I'm not sure how to do this . . ."

I try to plug the machine back in discreetly, but it starts bleeping loudly. An error warning flashes up on the screen. I have visions of the shop going into lock-down. Bars appearing from nowhere and barricading us in. My face starts to flush.

"Oh God, OK, erm, so just have the book."

"Really?"

"Yeah, fuck it, just . . ."

What am I doing?

"Just have the book! On the house!"

"If you're sure."

"Yep I certainly am. So, here's a bag, just take it and go."

"A free bag too?"

"Yes, yep, it's your lucky day, apparently."

"Thanks, Char-lie."

He sounds out my name like a child reading their first book. "How did you . . . ?"

He points at my name badge. I ache for a moment alone to melt into a puddle of self-loathing.

"Let me know if the machine is ever down again. I'll be back for more free lit!"

He folds the bag under his arm and floats out through the doorway. I can't be sure but I think I saw him give money to the poor and cure malaria on his way out.

★ ★ ★

Niamh is swirling a cocktail stick around a plate of hummus. The stick did have a little sausage on the end of it, but that's long gone. I arrived fifteen minutes later than I should have

74

done because my induction at the gym ran over, so by the time I got to her she'd already had a pre-starter, starter.

"Why are you dressed like that?"

"Like what?"

"A massive bell-end."

"I told you I was joining the gym today."

She clicks her tongue on the top of her mouth. "Great, another one."

I scan the menu: everything is fried. I look at the salads but quickly veto them. I've eaten almost exclusively salad and vegetables for the past three days. Sergio, who did my gym induction, did make me run for a whole twenty minutes on a 1.0 incline, so I've earned something more substantial than a soggy piece of lettuce.

"I just want to get myself back into shape, Niamh."

"You've never been in shape."

"That's the point."

"Janet at work goes on and on about the fucking spin class she goes to. I'm sick of hearing about it. I get enough of a workout running around after the little bastards on the playground all day. Tommy McNally did a shit on the hopscotch at morning break. It was carnage."

"Once you get exercise into your routine though it just becomes part of your every day."

"With all due respect, Charlie, you've been to the gym once, you're no gladiator."

She's got me on that one. I'll have the soup of the day.

"Excuse me, what's the soup of the day?" I ask the passing waitress.

"Minestrone."

"Oh, erm, I'll just have the cheeseburger then I think."

I tell Niamh about the guy from the bookshop. I didn't sleep last night trying to find him on Instagram. There were over one hundred people called Matthew Constantino to trawl through. At around 4 am, after a brief nap, I found him. There's not a lot I can see from his profile. He went to Kent Canterbury University and he's well travelled – in his profile photo he's smiling next to a temple with a small monkey on his shoulder – and on the 16th of November 2015 he posted a picture which included a translucent template of the French flag with the caption, I Stand with Paris. In the picture he is swigging from a bottle of vodka on a beach. I'm not sure if he was standing with the people of Paris or if it was potentially more of a sway. He has 8,054 followers. I scoop some sleep out of my tired eyes in case I'm reading that wrong. How on earth could he potentially know that many people? I ponder whether he is a minor celebrity. He is 31 years old and goes to lots of gigs of bands I have never heard of, but one of his favourite movies is *Hook*, so at least we have one thing in common. He's well read, well travelled and is extraordinarily photogenic.

Niamh tells me I am a psychopath.

"I'm not, because I didn't follow him."

"You didn't press the button that says follow, but you are for all intents and purposes following him."

I mean, I thought about clicking the button,\ but instead settled for writing him a message saying Candice Carty-Williams is doing a book signing in our store in two weeks' time and he should bring his copy back to meet her. I hovered over send for a few seconds and then as I went to delete the message I pressed send by mistake. Then in a panic I tried to close the window but managed to accidentally press the video call button, which rang for a mortifying five seconds before I worked out how to hang up – so that's that relationship over before it's even begun. And also Candice Carty-Williams isn't actually doing a book signing in a fortnight so that's not ideal either. The waitress brings my burger over, and Niamh asks for more honey-mustard cocktail sausages.

"You've opened yourself up to a world of possibility now, Charles. It's dangerous this dating malarky."

Niamh went home with those two girls from the bar the other night – they were a couple in an open relationship – and she woke up the next morning face down on their kitchen floor with her hand inside a jar of Nutella. She can't remember anything about going back with them, and she'd lost her phone, so it came as quite a shock to her when she walked out of their front door and found out from a passerby that she was in Margate.

"People come in and out of your lives and suck all of your attention like a needy puppy. You have to realise that nobody really knows what they want. That's why I don't narrow down my choices. Why pursue one gender, or one sexuality, or even one person when there's so many different people out there?"

"Do you tell your children this in PSHE? Shag around, don't settle down!"

"Well I think I'm just about to get the OK to do a talk about LGBTQI+ relationships, because all I hear when I'm on crowd control in the playground is kids constantly screaming That's So Gay at everything they don't like or don't identify with."

"How advanced are these five-year-olds at your school?!"

Niamh licks some hummus off her index finger. I've devoured my cheeseburger in roughly three minutes. I'm already devastated that it's over.

"I mean the year sixes. They get packed off to the puberty-reeking corridors of secondary school with absolutely no idea of the horror awaiting them, the poor buggers. There's absolutely going to be some of them that are already questioning their sexuality. At least when we were younger we didn't have social media telling us to kill ourselves, and threatening to expose kids if they so much as mention that they're a boy who likes dancing, or a girl who doesn't want to wear pink."

"They're lucky they have someone like you to guide them."

"Well, the governors don't really like me being so open about my sexuality: apparently it's not appropriate."

"Don't they get taught about ancient Romans and the Greeks? I mean, they were fucking everybody weren't they? Those emperors loved carving a bit of fellatio into their Grecian urns."

"They just don't know what they want us to teach the kids. These kids in year six, they know plenty about sex and sexuality already, but according to the old farts, they're too young to be taught it sensitively and properly. So instead, we just don't talk about it. Section 28 never really disappeared."

We both stick our middle fingers up at the ghost of Margaret Thatcher.

"I mean, to be honest Niamh, I thought by now I'd have been married for years, with two kids in a lovely house in the countryside."

"Who told you that?"

"Well, nobody explicitly," I pick some gristle from my tooth, "but school basically makes it seem like that's the path everybody automatically takes. They don't tell you how fucked up everybody is, and that in order to do the Marriage-Kids-Mortgage thing, you have to basically sacrifice every dream you've ever had and find the most soul-destroying job to simply earn money."

"Are you telling me that if you weren't with George you'd be a famous writer by now? Because I'm pretty sure I didn't see you try to do anything other than work the minimum amount of hours a week possible, so that you could be home to make his dinner every night."

"That's not fair. You know I applied to lots of writing competitions, but it was around the time that Grandad died, and George was being so lovely to me that it was just easier to keep a low profile. Besides, I wasn't feeling particularly creative, Niamh, I was in mourning."

78

"George didn't stop you from pursuing your dreams. You know he would have supported you in everything you wanted to do. You just didn't want to do anything about it."

"Well yeah, if you don't put yourself out there, then you can't be rejected can you?"

Niamh gently touches my shoulder. "But, you're doing better now aren't you? You're enjoying being at Waterstones, and there's room for growth?"

"I'm not sure about that to be honest, I haven't asked."

"You should."

"I've only been there a few weeks, I can't be gunning for a management position yet."

The waitress brings over more sausages, and because they look so delicious I kindly decide to help Niamh out with them.

"I just don't want to be comparing myself to anyone else anymore. It's alright for you and Dylan and Zachary, you've always known what you wanted to do with your lives and your careers, so you're doing that. I don't have a clue. I did English at uni because it was the only thing I was good at, and then when we left and I had to decide what I actually wanted to do with it, I crumbled and just got any job that didn't require me to think."

"Then start writing. You want to be a writer, then fucking write."

"I don't know if I remember how to."

"It's like riding a bike isn't it? You don't do it for ages but as soon as you get back on the saddle your brain just kicks into gear."

"That was almost a bit Live, Laugh, Love of you there, Niamh, are you feeling OK?"

Niamh tells me to piss off and we laugh. It feels good to laugh. I spear a sausage with the cocktail stick and devour it. As we split the bill, both our phones on the table buzz in synchronisation.

"Who is it?" I ask as I count out my coppers.

Niamh looks up at me, fear in her eyes.

"Oh God. Oh no. Oh hell-fucking-no."

"What? Niamh, what? You're scaring me."

"We've been added to a chat called Sarah-Beth's Final Fling Before the Ring".

We both groan. Hell hath no fury like a WhatsApp group full of hens.

CHAPTER SEVEN

There's a line in the movie adaptation of *Matilda* where terrifying headteacher Agatha Trunchbull is giving the class a spelling test. They use a mnemonic to help them remember the letters for the word Difficulty and I've always used it too. "Mrs D, Mrs I, Mrs F F I, Mrs C, Mrs U, Mrs L T Y," they chant in unison. Trunchbull slams the desk and bellows furiously, "Why are all these women married!" When I watched this as a child this scene sailed directly over my head, but when George and I watched it again a few months ago it stirred something inside me. By society's standards Trunch is traditionally unwomanly – she plays sports, doesn't take too much care when it comes to her personal appearance, has no maternal instinct (despite her job with children) and lives alone in a cavernous, untidy mansion – all things I can now completely relate to (well except the mansion). We're supposed to hate her. Obviously she does shove kids into a cupboard lined with rusty nails and spikes and that's not ideal – but I feel kind of sorry for her now. She hadn't managed to find somebody to love her, and the pressure to fit in and have The Normal Trajectory of marriage and babies left her a tyrannical rage-ridden monster. I wonder if, whilst she was growing up, somebody had taught her that she did have worth of her own, then maybe little Amanda Thripp wouldn't have been thrown over the fence by her pigtails.

I decide that the next child who comes into the shop and buys a copy of *Matilda* will also receive a TED talk from me on why Trunch is the real victim of circumstance here. It's amazing how your mind wanders when you're on an eight-hour shift trying desperately not to think about the next seventy-two hours you have to spend in Brighton with a bunch of horny straight women.

★ ★ ★

Sarah-Beth is a Woo Girl. By this I mean that her favourite cocktail is a Woo-Woo and she announces her arrival into every room – no matter the circumstance – with a shrill WOOOOOOOOO! whilst throwing both hands into the air with gay abandon.

Her room was sandwiched between mine and Niamh's at university, and we unfairly got lumped with her for the following three years. SB had a different boyfriend every couple of months and would parade them around our communal kitchen like they were on the *Generation Game* and we were expected to remember their names. Niamh took to calling them all Dave which SB found infuriating and I found hilarious.

There was no question that SB was going to be A Wife one day. She had scrapbooks of dresses and canapés and even a list of potential vicars and celebrants, including one line that just read "The Pope" with a load of question marks after it. I dread to think how giddy she became with the invention of Pinterest.

She might have been obsessed with boys, but she was clever – well, clever enough to study law. Once on a night out she uttered the immortal phrase, But If My Husband Is a Lawyer Too, Then I'm Happy to Let Him Go to Work and

I Can Stay at Home and Make Sure He's Happy. I've never seen Niamh so angry. She spluttered her way onto a soapbox so quickly that by the end of it SB was in floods of tears and Niamh had gone very red in the face and there was a lot of door slamming when we got back to halls. To add insult to injury this all happened in the student union whilst at a traffic light party. Nobody was going home with a potential future husband that night.

Our different approaches to adult life were extremely telling. Niamh and I couldn't have packed our bags and moved any faster to the liberal bubble of London as soon as we graduated, whereas SB went back to her hometown of Suffolk to save money for a mortgage. A mortgage at the age of twenty-one. I didn't even know what a mortgage was. I still don't. But now, eight years later she's finally putting her scrapbook where her mouth is by marrying a lawyer called (ironically) Dave.

Why she's invited Niamh and me to the hen do, I've no idea. Why we're actually going is even more of a mystery.

"If there's a Butler in the Buff then I'm out."

"Niamh, are you joking? Of course there's going to be a Butler in the Buff. The group is called, One Last Fling Before the Ring."

"If only this was *The Ring* and that long-haired girl was going to crawl out of the well and drag us all into eternal darkness. I think I'd enjoy that more."

There's something that doesn't sit well in my stomach about celebrating an upcoming heterosexual wedding in what is arguably one of the gayest cities in the UK. We're staying in a house, twenty-minutes' walk from the seafront. We've all had to pay approximately three-hundred pounds for the privilege of sharing a weekend with a gaggle of complete strangers. This fee doesn't include anything except the four walls, the ceiling and a bed. As the Token Gay/only male, I am expected to be thrilled with the prospect of my own private room – which turns out to be a blow-up mattress on the kitchen floor. I am also unofficially meant to be hilarious the entire time and allow SB's Auntie Maria to flirt with me outrageously and play dumb when she gets handsy after two Proseccos.

The two-night stay has been planned with military precision by the Chief Bridesmaid, Claire, who is giving me a vibe somewhere between Malibu Barbie and The Governess from *The Chase*.

The schedule – which we all had to sign our initials on to show that we understood and agreed to – goes like this: we are up at 7 am on Saturday for yoga, then 8.30 am is breakfast (*bring your own croissant, one single pot of jam will be provided for everyone to share, no double dipping*); 9 am is life-drawing; 11 am is something horrifically titled Fun and Games, which continues on for three painstaking hours until 2 pm where (thank fuck) we're making cocktails (*bring your own spirits, one mixer provided per pair*),;then at 3 pm we have a paltry 15 minutes of free time – which I intend to spend screaming into the void somewhere alone – before we go to the pier at 3.15 pm for a ride on The Crazy Mouse. At approximately 3.30 pm (*queue dependant*) we then head back to the house for a glass of Fizz (*bring your own bottle*) before getting ready for a three-course Chinese meal at 5 pm. Which is laughable when we all know a Chinese dessert is a single segment of orange and that does not a course make. This is followed by karaoke (*nobody can sing Girls Just Want to Have Fun as SB has specifically requested to perform this number*). After this there's drinking games, where we are encouraged to tell our favourite funny story about SB – I simply don't have anything to contribute apart from the argument she had with Niamh in uni – and then at 8 pm we have exclusive V.V.VIP entry into a club where it's a fiver to get in and our wristband gets us one free shot of something called Aqua Bite which I'm certain is a brand of mouthwash.

I can't wait.

Niamh is pulling awkwardly at her hair. It's poker straight for the first time in years. Her nails have gone from glittery to plain red. It's unnerving. I don't want to say anything but it reeks of straight-washing.

"I look like shit."

"No you don't, you always look lovely."

"I mean, I look like shit compared to everyone else."

"Since when do you care about the way you look in comparison to other people?"

"When I'm the only girl on this hen do who doesn't have a baby or a fiancé."

She slides a clip into her fringe, clearing a pathway to her forehead to apply more foundation.

"You know it's not fancy dress don't you? You've done Donald Trump already."

"Fuck off."

I narrowly miss a flying comb.

"It's like being away with fourteen different versions of my mother. All asking me why I'm single, and do I want children eventually. I'm going to start saying I've got polycystic ovaries just to shut everyone up."

"That's the spirit!"

Niamh breathes a long, deep, loaded sigh. She swivels on the plush stool to face me.

"This club tonight is going to be so heterosexual."

"I know."

"I bet they'll play the Grease Megamix at the end."

"There's nothing hetero about musical theatre."

"Don't you get pissed off with these things, Charlie?"

"I've only ever been on a couple, and never anything of this scale."

"I just don't get it. Since when does 2025 still involve

willy straws and running around a bar trying to find a man with green underwear to have a photo with? Can you imagine doing that on a stag do? You'd be fucking done for assault."

"It's all harmless fun isn't it really? If it makes SB happy . . ."

"Charlie, it only makes her happy because she thinks that's what she's supposed to do."

"You've properly got a bee in your bonnet about this haven't you?"

"Yeah, it's just bullshit, and I know you agree with me."

I look at my ankle in the mirror. I'm getting my tattoo covered over tomorrow so I'm making a mental note of how it looks now. Just a silently grimacing G. It's been a couple of months since George left for New York; it's the longest we've gone without speaking in a decade and I feel a horrible ache in my stomach to reach out, but I can't because I know when I do that it'll be the last time we properly talk. The closure conversation will be the end of the book and I don't want to read that chapter yet. His mum called me last week to see how I was doing. I don't know what George had told her, but she said she missed me, and she hoped I was Getting On. I don't know what that meant, but it was nice to hear her voice. His dad was pottering in the garden, she said, so couldn't chat. He was usually always happy to talk to me. Is this what happens in the first weeks after a break up? People you know only through your ex start to stop wanting to speak to you, and slowly but surely you have to accept that you're breaking up with his family too.

"Jesus. Our generation is just one big mess isn't it?" Niamh says, smudging a peach colour on her eyelids.

"Well, I mean the world is a mess."

"But specifically, we are, because the generations before us were bought up on going to dances and making a family and a home, and the generations beneath us are all independent and strong-willed and moving away from the norm, and we're in this muddy middle ground of trying to have both."

"Yeah. I guess."

Niamh swigs from the bottle. We don't know whose it is, but we took it out of the fridge before coming upstairs to the bathroom. I imagine Claire downstairs doing a strip search to find the culprit.

"Sarah-Beth told me after cocktail making that she only met this fella six months ago."

"What?"

"Yeah. They haven't even slept together yet."

"Are you serious?"

"She didn't want to be nearly thirty and unmarried, she said. That's not part of her life plan apparently."

"Do you think it's different for us?"

"Because you like dick and I like anything that I can get my tongue around?"

"No, I mean living in London, being away from all the traditions of home."

"Aye, we've had a lucky escape."

I think of when I came out to my mum and the first thing she said was, I'm Just Sad I Won't Have Any Grandchildren. I explained that even if I was of the straight persuasion, children might still have been off the cards, but she didn't understand. The Point of Life Is to Continue the Circle she muttered grandly, which was uncharacteristically profound for her but then I remembered she'd bought Leanne a pirate DVD of *The Lion King* from the market the day before. I told her that expectations are failings just waiting to happen. In response, she turned the TV up a little louder.

"Do you reckon she's happy?" I ask Niamh as she finishes drawing her characteristic heart-shaped beauty spot on her left cheek with an eye pencil. At least something of the Niamh I know has remained for tonight.

"Who, SB?"

I nod. Niamh looks at me in the mirror.

"I dunno. Is anyone?"

★ ★ ★

I'm full to the brim with sesame prawn toast and sweet and sour pork. As we pile into the nightclub, a scantily dressed girl – who can be no older than my sister – struts past, holding a magnum above her head anointed with a flaming sparkler. Niamh rolls her eyes and I squeeze her hand in response. Sisters are doing it for themselves tonight.

The steady onslaught of all-day drinking is beginning to light a fire between my temples. I'm a man, dancing amongst a group of women clearly on a hen do, in a predominantly straight club. I catch the eye of a trio of imposing-looking boys, all wearing beige chinos and too much Lynx Africa and my energetic dancing falters. They're talking about me. I know it. I tug at my shirt: it's too loud and colourful and I'm drawing too much attention to myself. I want to take my Bride Tribe sash off but it'll upset SB. I feel like I'm back at the school disco again, desperately trying to dance without my wrists flicking, or my hips wiggling. If the boys in my class had caught even one whiff of rhythm in my body I'd have been lynched. Marched around the playground, tarred and glittered, my masculinity unravelling. Perhaps that's why Mum was so openly rude to me, she'd had to watch me grow up subverting her expectations, when all she wanted was for me to be on the Stag Dos one day, never the Hens.

One of the imposing-looking boys comes over. I think he's headed for me, but he slides past me and starts dancing with another one of our party. So maybe they weren't looking at me. Jesus, not everything is about you, Charlie, for fuck's sake. Then I imagine George. What we'd be doing if I were in New York right now. I wouldn't be feeling like an imposter that's for sure. We saw loads of same-sex couples holding hands on the street, so surely everyone in this club will have seen them too – on a daily basis – so what am I worrying about? I regret eating that second helping of chow mein. My waistband is tight. I'm the least good-looking person in the room. I'm the least good-looking person in my entire friendship group. When people see us they must know that. Even Dylan and Zachary, they must know that. They'll discuss me. Pick me apart and talk about how they feel sorry for me. Maybe even George told them the same thing – that he knew he was better looking than me, but wanted to help me. Like sponsoring a lame donkey for three quid a month. I'm pathetic. Thinking I deserve to go out and be looked at – be desired by others. What a joke. Mum knows it too. Now that George is out of the picture I don't stand a chance. I should have gone with him. I should be in New York now. Why did I get so angry about him and Axel? It's just sex. And didn't I think Axel was hot anyway? And if I was attractive and Axel wanted to sleep with me, wouldn't I have let him? I'm a hypocrite. I'm just jealous that it wasn't me who could pull someone as beautiful as Axel, and now I've let the only thing I had going for me go. I can feel my mind wandering down and down and down, like Alice, further into the rabbit hole of despair, and then a horrible thought winds me – that this is how I'm going to feel forever. I am not good enough for anything or anyone. The cards have been dealt and I can't change them.

I drink as many Aqua Bites as the bar will give me.

★ ★ ★

The sound of cackling can be heard in the living room. Chief Busybody Claire steps over me, her Kentish tone clipped and dripping with disgust.

"You need to get up Charlie. The Butler in the Buff is here, and I need to get breakfast ready for him to serve."

89

As she pointedly unloads mini-multipacks of Rice Krispies and Cheerios from the cupboard – that I've paid at least a tenner for as per the invitations request – I try to wash away last night with some water from the tap. I've no idea how we even got home, but I'm still fully clothed. My chest feels as though somebody is sitting on it. The last thing I need to see right now is some muscled jock being fawned over by a bunch of rampant women. I peer through the door. He is really fit though. I get out my phone, zoom in and take a photo of his bottom poking out like a ripe peach from his tiny apron. Upstairs in the bathroom I masturbate into the sink. Afterwards, the tightness in my chest is replaced with all-consuming shame. The testosterone released so quickly that now the void is wider and emptier than before. I've not even said hello to the poor guy and I've just imagined doing all sorts to him. He's probably not even twenty yet. I clean myself up and stare out of the window, the sea glistening in the distance.

This can't be normal adult behaviour.

* * *

Sarah-Beth thanks us all for a wonderful weekend. She's touched that Niamh and I came, especially as we haven't really seen each other for two years. She apologises for not reaching out when she heard about George and me. It doesn't feel right to ask who told her.

She tells us that she and Dave are only having a small wedding and she hopes we won't be offended but there isn't space for us on the day, which is why it was so important for us to be here this weekend. My bank balance and I breathe a sigh of relief. I think I see Niamh smile for the first time this weekend, but she did also say she had trapped wind this morning.

Later, Niamh tells me that last night one of the brides-maids she was sharing a room with told her that she'd got changed in the bathroom last night before bed because she didn't want Niamh to see her naked, and that she hadn't felt comfortable sleeping next to her. Niamh's response was, If You Think You're That Fucking Irresistible Then I'd Strongly Suggest You Get Yourself Some Better Glasses Sweetheart. And this girl – called Kayleigh – had cried and cried so hard that she'd made herself sick and then told Niamh how her marriage is boring and she thinks she might be attracted to women.

"I'm understanding, you know that, and everyone struggles, but I don't need her trying to make me feel bad because she's feeling ashamed of herself," Niamh says as I lay my head back into the tattooist's chair.

"So what did you say whilst she was crying all over you?"

"That she needs to talk to her husband and maybe take some time away and work out what will make her happy. And then she tried to fucking kiss me! I mean, for God's sake, if I'd needed the drama I'd have stayed at home with *Casualty* on. It's like they don't realise that just because I'm pansexual that doesn't mean that I then fancy every single person I ever lay my eyes on. She's straight, so does that mean she fancies every man in the entire world?"

"You're preaching to the choir here, honey. A very nervous and terrified choir."

The clashing of needles roars in my ear. The only thing I could think of getting to cover the G was to turn it into a flower. There's no real reason for it, I just wanted it gone.

"You sure about this?" Niamh asks with a sadistic smile.

My fist clenches and I brace myself for the pain. I picture George shaking his head at me.

"No, sorry, stop. I don't want to."

"I bloody knew it."

"I need a bit more time to think about it, I think I'm being rash."

The tattooist tells me that it's still going to cost me sixty quid even if I don't have anything done.

"You're not being rash, Charlie, my darling."

"But it's only been a couple of months."

"I know, but you seemed very certain about it yesterday."

"I'd drunk a lot of Prosecco yesterday, Niamh."

"Exactly, and that's when we always make our best decisions."

We laugh. The tattooist looks at the clock.

"Niamh, I just feel like I'm spiralling. One minute I'm screaming from the top of my lungs in a nightclub that I'm feeling so much better, and I can't wait to find myself, and that being with George was . . . I dunno, stunting my individuality or whatever, and the next minute I'm unblocking him from Instagram and posting pictures of my now slightly toned arm to try and thirst-trap him into taking me back."

"It's not about him taking you back, Charlie, it's about figuring out whether you'd even want to be back with him in the first place."

"I also can't stop thinking about how he's your friend too, Niamh. I know I can't force you to cut him out of your life, but I really seriously want to."

"That's very natural, and I have to say, you've been extremely gracious about it all – you haven't bad mouthed him to us even once. And you can you know, because we bitch about you all the time."

"I fucking knew it!"

"I love you, Charlie. We all do. And it makes me sad that George treated you that way, when you don't deserve that cruelty, but maybe, eventually, this will be the best thing for you, and you won't end up like Sarah-Beth, married to a random Dave. You deserve more than just a Dave, my love."

The tattooist begs me to make a decision, and in that moment I know that I need to remove one relationship from my body in order to cement another.

Niamh and I end up having matching rainbow flags – a reminder that we came away on a heterosexual hen do in Brighton but managed to maintain our homo and pansexual persuasions. I split the cost of Niamh's tattoo with her: An Early Birthday Present, I say. Her birthday isn't for another eight months and she'll have forgotten this gesture by then. I'll write it in her card, to remind her.

Outside, the clingfilm on my ankle comes unstuck on one corner and flaps in the breeze; I look at it in the sunlight for the first time, the G now masked with the colourful stripe of the flag. Niamh bends down and sticks it back on for me and says the words I've been waiting for all weekend.

"Shall we go home, Charles?"

CHAPTER EIGHT

Steven is certainly no Paul Hollywood, but he is bossing me around the kitchen with a certain tone I don't appreciate. Although, I am enjoying exclusive use of their KitchenAid. There's flour everywhere and half an hour ago I lost part of my right fingernail whilst finely grating cooking chocolate. I hope nobody at Noma's birthday party gets a crunchy bit when they bite into my brownies.

"You'll over-mix the batter, Charlie, look, have you not remembered anything I've said?"

I turn the switch off and ask Steven to repeat what he was saying, whilst licking fudge from a spatula.

"You only need to *fold* the chocolate mixture into the beaten egg and sugar. What recipe are you using?"

"I'm not."

"Oh cripes."

"If all else fails I can just get some ready-made ones from the supermarket and put them in a cake tin. Nobody will know."

"But you'll know."

I fail to see his point.

I spot a piece of eggshell bobbing amongst the mixture and pick it out with my wounded finger.

"So we only have the pleasure of your presence for two more nights then?"

"Yeah, there's a guy at work who suddenly has a room going in his place. He owns it so he said I can move in for a three-month sort of probation period, and then if we're both happy I can sign on for longer."

"Well that's lovely news, I'm very happy for you, Charlie."

Last night I heard Steven and Zachary having sex. I had to strain to listen – but without knowing who is the top and who is the bottom I couldn't complete the picture in my head of what they were getting up to. Last weekend when the weather was nice, we'd sat outside and drunk Pimm's out of old jam jars, and Steven had complimented me on my newly trimmer physique (I'd actually decided to stick to the gym for longer than just the two-week free trial). It gave me a little thrill. I never used to fantasise about passersby in the street when I was with George – let alone my friend's partners – but now I find myself doing it on a daily basis. There's a point in most conversations where I suddenly imagine the person that I'm speaking to naked. I've resigned myself to the knowledge that it must be What You Do When You're Single – because almost everyone you meet is a possible shag. Not that I would shag Steven, I'm not a home wrecker, but since living here and getting to know him, the things that I would have once perceived as annoying, I suddenly find endearing.

The brownies take thirty minutes to bake. That's just enough time for me to stare at my clothes and panic that – despite having eight different kinds of plaid shirt – I have nothing to wear.

★ ★ ★

Noma lives five miles from Zach and Steven's place but I have to take two buses and walk for twenty minutes to get there because that's how far everything is in London when you don't have a car. It's warm on the top deck, and I'm already regretting my outfit choice. This is the first time I'm seeing people outside of work so it's vital I make a good impression. The Tupperware box is sticky in my hands and there's condensation beginning to form inside. I hope the brownies aren't mutating in there. Only a few of them caught at the edges.

I check my phone for the address three times as I walk along the road. I know it's number eighty-nine, but every time I lock my home screen I feel the need to swipe it open and check again just in case it's suddenly changed. I'm still not used to turning up to a party alone.

A conversation with Noma in the staff room last week suddenly hits me with such force that I freeze on the pavement. Christ, I totally forgot she's vegan. There's definitely quite a substantial amount of butter, chocolate and eggs in these brownies. I consider throwing them in the bin but don't want to appear rude by turning up empty handed. It's Sophie's choice. And I am Sophie a thousand times over.

★ ★ ★

"And they're completely vegan?"

"Yep."

Noma places one between her teeth. My pulse quickens, but she sighs warmly.

"They taste amazing! Usually the ones I make are so dry and tasteless. You never let on you were such a good baker, you sly dog. You must give me the recipe."

She signs for me to come in, and I put my four fingers to my chin and pull them away sharply to sign Thank You in Makaton sign language. Noma's been teaching me little phrases here and there at work and I'm trying to use them as much as I can. I watch her take another bite and her front teeth turn brown as she pays me more compliments. I slowly acknowledge that I'll probably have to resign first thing on

Monday in order to pack my suitcase in preparation for the train journey directly down to hell where I now belong.

"Can I get you something to drink? There's a couple of people here you'll know. Lana and Tim are outside, and Farrah is going to pop in for a bit, but she's got a bit of revising to do today."

I ask for a glass of white and scan the garden. My armpits are clammy – I have to nod my head down towards my hand in order to sip so I don't reveal my sweat patches.

How on earth do you start a conversation when you don't have a plus one? I should go and say hello to Lana and Tim but they look deep in conversation on a bench by the patio. Lana is the equivalent of a supervisor at work, and it's Tim who has the spare room coming up at the place his parents bought him. I was surprised to find out that some parents can afford to buy their children a house. He lets the other three rooms out to people and pockets the (relatively) cheap rent to fund his lifestyle – which appears to mainly consist of flying to different continents to go to music festivals I've never even heard of, called things like Electric Daisy Carnival and Lollapalooza. He's part-time at work, but I enjoy his chilled nature and his pop culture references. He seems like the sort of person that I'd live with and never really see, which feels quite appealing. I've worked a couple of shifts with Lana and she seems nice enough, but for some reason she stares intently at my hairline whenever I talk to her. It's given me a complex.

I find myself wishing Farrah was already here, even though we don't have much in common. For some reason, even though we started working at Waterstones at the same time, she keeps asking me questions and for permission to do things as though I'm her boss – which I very much am not. Who am I to correct her though – especially when it makes my imposter syndrome slightly quieter when she's around.

The buffet is uncovered but nobody is touching it. The

social etiquette of when it's appropriate to start eating is something I struggle with. I scan the garden, but nobody has a plate.

My brownies sit pride of place at the centre of a small table – the Judas of desserts – winking at me with their glutenous Death to Vegans goodness.

I think I feel my phone buzz in my pocket, but on inspection it's just wishful thinking. There's nothing interesting on Facebook. I pretend to be on a phone call for a few moments, but feel silly. I should have asked if I could have brought someone – a friend – Dylan is the perfect person to bring to these sorts of things, he's so charismatic and talks to anybody. The type of person that mums love. George's mum loved him and would message him all the time. I briefly wonder if they've talked lately.

An older lady in slippers shuffles towards the food. She looks like she could be Noma's mum – they have the same eyes. I advance too – I haven't eaten all day and I feel slightly foggy – but she's only getting a napkin to blow her nose. Lana and Tim are still unaware of my presence. I'm now in garden limbo. For something to do, I crouch down and sniff a bed of unidentifiable flowers. My hay fever will thank me graciously for this later.

"Waiting for someone to make the first move?"

"Sorry?"

A man holding a thimble of brownish liquid indicates the table. I steady myself with my hands so as not to fall into the soil, knocking over my wine glass onto the lawn in the process. He doesn't seem to notice so I straighten my legs and slowly push the glass under some daffodils with my foot.

"You know . . . the food? It's always terribly boring waiting for somebody to pluck up the courage to pick up a plate."

"Oh no, I was just looking to see what there is."

"Right."

"I'm vegan so . . . just checking what the options are."

What am I saying?

"Well Noma's a vegan so you've got it pretty well covered there."

"Fantastic. Go vegans! Vegans unite!"

The man smiles gently, his mouth curling in sympathy.

"I'm Otis. I used to work with Noma."

"Ah, at Waterstones?"

"Oh no, no, long time ago, a boring office thing."

I'd put him at about mid to late forties. His face looks wizened but not craggy. A tweed flat cap casts a shadow that stops just before his kind eyes.

"Do you work with Noma?"

"Yes, I do, sorry, I'm Charlie."

"Lovely to meet you, Charlie."

Otis holds out his hand and I shake it. It's strong; his knuckles are cracked, worn. They remind me of my grandad's.

"She's a bit of a hard task master isn't she? Well she was at the office. I assume she hasn't changed since moving into the rousing world of retail. That sounded sarcastic, I apologise."

"No, not at all. I like working for Noma."

"Ah I've just twigged, Charlie – you only started a little while ago, didn't you?"

"About five weeks or so, yeah."

"She mentioned you actually, said you made her cry in your interview."

"I didn't mean to."

"No, she loves you, goes on about you a lot. She said you were going through a divorce too?"

"Oh erm, not a divorce, we weren't married, we were just sort of together, for like ... a few years ... well nine years ... but it's really only a few years, you know."

Farrah walks past with a bottle balancing underneath her arm, and three full glasses.

"Oh Farrah! There you are! Thanks for this."

I take one of the glasses.

"I'll come over and talk to you in a bit. Bye Farrah!"

With bewilderment she saunters away. Otis looks at me. He sips from his glass, so I sip from mine. The wine tastes of soured gooseberries.

"It's been nice to talk about stuff with Noma, especially when you're also going through it ... not that a relationship breaking down is anywhere near comparable to divorce ..."

"Hey now, heartbreak isn't a competition. I'm sorry to hear you've been going through that."

I don't really want to spend the whole party talking about George, so with the subtlety of a freight train I move in slightly closer to Otis and say, "So, are you here with anyone, or are you alone?"

I suddenly become aware of my free hand so use it to tuck a piece of imaginary hair behind my ear.

"Just a couple of other mates from where we used to work. You?"

"Not really, well, there's some of my colleagues over there from the shop."

I point towards Tim and Lana, and then wave at them energetically; they wave back. Farrah, who has joined them, shrugs her shoulders at me and gestures to the bottle she's holding as if to say Why Did You Take That Glass from Me? I clear my throat and pretend to swot away a fly.

"So, what do you do now? Are you still in the same office?"

"God no. I work in television. A bit of commissioning. Family entertainment, quiz shows and stuff."

"That's cool!"

"It can be. There's only so many different ways for someone to win a couple of thousand pounds."

"I bet you've had some awful ideas!"

I go to apologise but Otis doesn't seem to be phased. In fact, he's grinning.

"Oh, you have no idea."

We talk about diva contestants and terrible celebrity hosts, and what we'd do with a million pounds. This time, I don't say I'd buy a house with my boyfriend.

By this time the garden has filled with guests and to my dismay I notice the buffet table is nearly empty. I check my watch and Otis and I have been talking for nearly an hour and the sun has started to disappear behind some clouds. On the fence a row of little fairy lights in the shape of bumble bees start to gently glow.

"Oh no, I'm doing that thing again. I'm chewing your ear off, aren't I, Charlie? Terrible habit of mine, my friends rib me for it constantly."

"God no, not at all, I just realised how long we've been chatting and there's no bloody food left!"

Otis has topped up my wine three times during our conversation, from a much tastier bottle that he bought along. My head feels warm and sunny.

"I'm sure Noma has got some more. She's a feeder. One sec. Don't move from this spot."

Otis strides across the lawn into the kitchen, his long legs making easy work of the journey. There are a couple of butterflies flitting around the flowerbeds. Tim waves me over but I'm having such a nice time that I pretend not to notice. Luckily I see Farrah intercept his hand.

"Here. I found a bag of salt and vinegar in the cupboard. Don't tell anyone."

He twists the bag open and we tuck in. The salt fizzes on my tongue. I like that the crisps are our little secret.

"Do you like the theatre, Charlie?"

"Erm, I don't really go to be honest."

"You live in London and you don't go to the theatre? It's one of the best things about this bastard city!"

I laugh. A small piece of crisp gets lodged in my throat and my eyes briefly water.

"I just, well, my boyfriend – ex-boyfriend – didn't like it, so we never really went. Plus it's expensive."

I wash down the crumbs with a large slog of wine.

"Not if you look in the right places."

"Oh, in the know are you, Otisssssss?"

I wink a bit too hard like I'm from a *Carry On* film.

"Well yes, as a matter of fact. I love going, so I know the best place to get ticket deals. Plus if you say you work in television it's amazing how many actors can get you company deals."

The wine fogging up my brain contributes to my unnecessary howl of laughter in response, and I touch his arm. A spark visibly crackles between my fingers and his bicep. I don't know what I'm doing, but my technique is improving.

"What are you doing on Thursday?" he asks.

"Thursday, Thursday . . . erm, I'm not sure, I think there's something . . . trying to wrack my brain. Thursday . . ."

Obviously I'm doing fuck all on Thursday but I listened to a podcast about dating the other day and the host said playing hard to get and appearing to be unavailable is key to attracting a mate.

"I'll have to check my diary."

"OK, well it's fine if you're not free, but I've got a couple of tickets for something at the National Theatre and . . ."

"Yes!" I say animatedly, causing a drop of wine to swill feverishly onto the grass. "Thursday, I am free actually, yes. Thursday. Lovely. Perfect! Thursday!"

"Great, I look forward to it."

We sing Happy Birthday to Noma, and she thanks us all for coming. I get a small mention for bringing my chocolate brownies and now every fucking vegan from here to Stratford wants the recipe. I finally talk to Tim and Lana about some boring rota stuff and manage to swap my Thursday evening shift with a reluctant Farrah, who has somehow become my guardian angel for the evening.

Otis sends me a text after the party is over. It says, 'C U Thursday. You can bring the crisps this time,' followed by a winking emoji. The bus lurches forward. I'll take a sharing bag.

★ ★ ★

I've never been to the National Theatre before. I have to look up how to get there on Citymapper. It's near Waterloo station. Otis says the play we're watching is by a French writer. Surely it should be called the International Theatre if that's the case.

Everyone in the audience is old and white.

As the lights start to go down I remember the crisps. The woman in front of me turns around and stares at me as I open the bag. I offer her one, as a joke, but she just scowls. Otis whispers in my ear that we should eat them in the interval. He says it kindly. I remember George shouting at me once on the way out of the theatre after watching *Mamma Mia!* – a Christmas present from his mum and dad – because during 'Voulez-Vous' I opened a bag of Minstrels and dropped them all over the floor. I'd bought them for him. He told me I was an embarrassment. The next year his parents bought us tickets for something at Shakespeare's Globe but I said I couldn't go. The shame of my chocolate drop still lurked in the dark recesses of my head. Niamh went with him instead.

I don't really understand what this play is about, but people laugh, loudly, throughout. I politely force a smile on a couple of occasions to let Otis know I'm enjoying myself. As the evening goes on I allow my shoulder to fall more and more into his. He doesn't move away.

The play is four and a half hours long, with only one interval and lots of drawn-out battle scenes. Three people die during the performance. One of them is unfortunately an older patron in the front row.

★ ★ ★

We're at Zachary's but Dylan is making himself some coffee. He's been on four nightshifts in a row this week so I've barely seen him as he's been sleeping all day. Despite being over-worked, he's got a glow about him, he's growing more and more handsome with age. I mean, he always was pretty, but there's something distinguished about him that I'm noticing more and more. Maybe it's the grey flecks appearing at the side of his hair. The salt and pepper looks good on him.

"So was it a date?"

"I don't know, Dylan. We never really discussed it."

Zachary's eyes light up, "Ah, but did you get the vibe it was a date?"

"Zach have you got any sweeteners? Sorry, Charlie, what did he say when he asked you out?"

Zach points to a kitchen drawer. Dylan roots around noisily.

"I told you, Otis just said to me at the party, 'do you want to go to the theatre on Thursday?'."

"That's a date!" Dylan says as he clicks two little white lumps into his mug.

"Well not specifically," Zachary interjects, "Steven, when I first asked you for a drink it wasn't a date."

"What was it then?" Steven protests from his stool at the kitchen island.

"A drink, darling."

"Which is a date!"

"Did you and Steven kiss at the end of the drink?" I ask, picking at some warm soda bread Steven produced earlier from the oven, "because that would make it a date."

They both say no.

"Exactly! Otis and I didn't kiss. We just both went straight home. Although I think that might have been because the play was so fucking long."

"I texted Zachy after our first date and said, 'was that a date?' and he replied saying 'no'."

104

"Because it wasn't. It was a drink."

"I think if you ask somebody to go and do something – just the two of you – it's romantically inclined," Dylan pipes up.

"So what do I do now?" I say with a mouth full of crumbs. Steven rolls his shoulders around and sits up straight.

"Have you arranged to see him again?"

"No."

"And have you texted him tonight to say you got home OK?" Dylan asks, sipping his coffee.

"I'm not his fucking nanna."

"Well there's your way in. You message now and say that you just got in, then you thank him for the evening and say that you'd like to treat him to something next time."

"Dylan, I can't afford to treat anybody to anything. I've just forked out for a bloody deposit."

"You can date on a budget."

"Economy dates attract economy men," Zachary says, sipping in judgement, seemingly rather pleased with that unhelpful quote they've just made up. I make a mental note to get it printed ironically onto a piece of driftwood so they can hang it up in the kitchen.

"This is all so stressful. Why can't it just be obvious whether I was on a date or not?"

"That's half the fun of dating."

It is evident that Dylan and I have very different opinions of what is fun.

Later, lying in bed, and having stared at my phone for a full ten minutes, I eventually give in and text Otis saying that I enjoyed the play and I thank him for painstakingly explaining the plot to me afterwards, and say that he should let me know when he's around the following week for me to return the favour, with an activity that I'll organise.

I try and stay awake for a response but my eyes are heavy. I fall asleep with my phone in my hand.

Now, I'm not saying that I'm overtly superstitious, but when I opened the bedroom curtains this morning I saw a single magpie sitting directly outside the window on the roof of the house opposite. I let out a sigh. The dice have been loaded and rolled and according to my fine feathered friend, today is not going to be a good one. I pray that I'll get splashed by a passing car or Chipotle won't accept my discount code at lunch or that it'll only be me and Farrah on the shop floor today – anything to take away the bad luck that has been bequeathed to me by the sight of a single, lone, black-and-white fortune teller. I look at my screen. Please, don't let the curse be Otis. Please.

According to WhatsApp, Otis was last online at 10.03 this morning. My message sits patiently with two grey ticks. I keep my phone unlocked and in clear view as I shower.

At work Noma asks me how my theatre trip was. She also begs for the brownie recipe. I tell her it belonged to my gran and I'll have to get her to write it down for me next time I see her.

The message is stewing. Still unread. I pick the onion out of my burrito and watch the screen for five minutes as I silently eat. BBC news sends a notification and I nearly choke on a piece of red pepper.

I accidentally knock a book out of a customer's hand as I feel my phone vibrate in my pocket. It's Niamh asking if anybody wants to come over tonight. Zachary replies and says yes. Niamh texts me separately and says Axel is away for the week and I should come too. She's cooking nachos. I reply and say you can't really cook nachos because they're just crisps.

I send Otis a smiling emoji.

I text saying, "Are you around tonight? Fancy a drink?"

Five minutes later I send, "Oops, sorry that wasn't for you! Hope you're having a good day!"

Otis was online at 16.57. My first message is now ticked blue. How can he read the first message and not the other three?

Under the counter, I read an online article about being ghosted. Is this how it feels? I start to wonder what I said during the interval of the play. Was I being ignorant or stupid? Did the crisps offend him? Maybe he was embarrassed. Oh God, I've embarrassed him. I've done it again. He'll be telling his friends that he took this uncouth, uneducated ruffian to the theatre. Noma did seem a bit off with me this morning. Her question about my night did seem pretty loaded. I can't focus. It feels like somebody is sitting on my chest.

I am convinced I have clinical depression. Or at the very least some psychotic tendencies. I barely even know this man, but I did picture how he would fit in with Niamh and Dylan. I thought that perhaps he'd get on with Zachary the most. PR and TV go quite well together. Mum would also like him because he's handsome, like George.

I send Otis the ghost emoji – the one that has its tongue sticking out – because obviously he's ghosting me. If he doesn't understand its connotations and replies normally then I'll just pretend it was a quirky way of winking at him.

All the messages are now blue ticked. They turned that way approximately twenty-two minutes ago. A lady buys a copy of

Romeo and Juliet. I clutch her hand and tell her love is a social construct. She hurries away looking terrified.

It says 'Otis Is Typing' at the top of the screen. I hold my breath. Nothing happens. It changes back to Last Seen Today At 17.32. It absolutely was the crisps. I shouldn't have got them out, I just knew it. He was joking and I took it too literally. I am doomed to live a miserable life alone. A small child comes up to the counter with her father. She looks up at me and immediately bursts into tears.

I'm about to finish my shift when a notification flashes up. It's from Otis. The preview shows me the first line. It reads, "You're welcome! Would love to hang next week but if I'm honest . . ."

I don't open the message to read any more. My tummy rolls over like a washing machine for the entire forty-five-minute bus journey home, and long into the evening.

CHAPTER NINE

Now that my tumultuous one-day-relationship with Otis is officially over I'm relieved to be able to turn my attention onto moving house and moving on.

Because I had enough of dragging my suitcase around two months ago, Dylan kindly offers to drive me and my meagre belongings to the flat, which is a good fifty minutes away. It's been ages since we spent any real time together. I've missed him.

"Sorry about the Otis thing."

"Oh, it's fine."

"I mean, you spoke about him quite a lot before you went on the date, and then afterwards you were quite intense about it all."

"I wasn't intense was I?"

"I don't mean intense, I just mean you were obviously thinking about it a lot."

"Yeah well, all this dating stuff is very new to me."

"I know. You're doing brilliantly though?" Dylan makes this sound like a question, when I think it was meant to be encouraging. The radio crackles – somebody has been in an accident at work and didn't realise they could claim. Dylan turns the dial all the way to the left. Silence.

"How do you feel about George now?"

I shift in my seat, pushing away the fern leaf that's tickling my neck from the backseat – a moving in gift from Zachary and Steven.

"Fine now."

"Are you sure? Because you know I'll listen if ever you need to just talk."

"But you're always working so hard, I don't want to be any bother."

"I'm your friend, I want to be here for you."

He indicates right. We turn out of the tree-lined suburbs and into the busier main road. Dylan takes a loaded sigh.

"I was always a bit worried about you and George."

"What do you mean?"

"You always did so much together, you were inseparable."

"No more than Zach and Steven are."

"That's not true – we hang out with Zach loads without Steven."

"Well Steven's a bit older so it's probably that he doesn't want to come out with us."

"He's forty-one, Charlie, he's not in a fucking care home!"

"I don't mean that, but you know, George went to uni with us, so why wouldn't he always come out with us all? It would have been weird if he didn't."

"George went out without you."

"I guess, but not loads."

"Yes he did! I was always coming home from a shift to find you on your own in your room watching *Big Brother* without him."

"Well that's only because if you missed one episode then it was difficult to catch up in time because it's on every night, you know that."

"Charlie, don't make a joke out of this, I'm trying to say that on reflection your relationship was a bit one sided at times, and – FUCKING HELL."

110

We screech to a halt to avoid hitting a little van that's pulled out in front of us. I lose a small amount of my Orange Fanta onto the dashboard. Dylan winds down his window and yells a bunch of obscenities into the street. A lady waiting at the bus stop shakes her head.

"Sorry, Jesus. Why can't people drive properly? Anyway, what were we saying?"

"That I'm pathetic because I was always sat at home whilst George went out, apparently."

"I didn't say you were pathetic."

"Well it's what you're insinuating."

"Didn't you notice over the last few years that you stopped doing any of the stuff that you liked to do … like going to author readings and doing the quiz night at The Wheatsheaf with me? It sounds weird to say but, even though we were living together, I missed you. It was like you started copying George's hobbies."

"No I didn't. I did have my own stuff. I played squash."

"George played squash."

"We both played squash."

"Oh come on Charlie, you went because George liked it, and you didn't know how to be by yourself."

"You literally just said you used to come home and find me watching telly on my own, so which is it Dylan? Was I following George everywhere or sitting miserably at home pining for him?"

Dylan stares at the road. I fish a sweet out of my bag like an old grandma and offer one to him but he doesn't notice. His anger from our near-miss seems to have permeated into our conversation. For a moment I don't know what to respond with. We are two cats down an alleyway, backs arched, quietly hissing.

"I did plenty of things by myself, Dyl."

"Like what?"

"Loads actually, and I don't need to justify them to you right now."

My brain whirs. I know I did things by myself. It was nine years for Christ's sake, of course I did. There was that time I went to the cinema every Thursday night … but, that was around the time that George started working late, and I usually left a film halfway through as soon as he texted to say he was finished. Ah, but there were the trips to the little bakery on the high road, where I'd go and read my book on my day off … but, I think I only did that because George was away with work and I didn't like being in the house for too long without him. Have I really spent nearly a decade of my life following somebody around like a lost puppy? I hated squash. But I went every single week without fail because George did. I could have done anything in that time. Learnt how to sew, or been in a band, or brewed my own bloody beer. Instead I learnt how to be average at squash.

"Well, come on, I'm waiting," Dylan says.

The boiled sweet catches in my throat. I choke and spit it out into my hand. It lays there, useless. The red mist subsides and this time the sweet makes way for a lump to catch in my throat.

"Did you all talk about me?"

"Who?"

"You and Niamh. Zachary. Steven?"

"In what way, Charlie?"

"That I'd just become this fucking boring old housewife, who you didn't recognise anymore."

"You weren't boring Charlie, but you just sort of became an extension of George."

I want to hate Dylan for saying that. I want to hate George for making me do everything to please him, but I only hate myself.

We sit in silence for the remainder of the journey.

★ ★ ★

My room at Tim's is cosy. And by cosy I mean I can touch two opposing walls at the same time with both my arms and my feet – and I am not a flexible person. It was described to me as a Box Room but an actual cardboard box would be more luxurious.

I picture George in the apartment in America. The revolving door. The panoramic city-skyline views. The basement pool doesn't look so terrifying anymore.

I snap back to reality. There's some damp in the corner of the ceiling. My room is directly above a chicken shop – and not even the good kind like KFC or Chicken Cottage. The smell of cooking oil wafts in through the air vent. It makes my stomach pang.

Tim is twenty-six. His other four housemates are all around the same age, mainly graduates. A small elfin-looking girl is smoking a joint on the sofa. She's introduced as Cookie. Dylan begins to tell her the long-term effect weed has on the brain. I push him out of the door and he fixes me with a look and says that I'm welcome to come back and stay at the house in his room whenever I need to – for as long as I want. We awkwardly hug and I say goodbye, even though I really don't want him to leave.

"I mean it Charlie. I hope I didn't offend you in the car. I just . . . well, we care about you. And maybe this will feel too soon, but you should take the opportunity now you have your own place to let yourself have a little fun, you know? We live in London – a city full of beautiful men. Maybe you should think about inviting a couple of them round?"

I sit on the bed in my new room – the first new bedroom I've had in years. Mum calls to tell me gran is in the hospital after having a fall but I needn't visit. I make a mental note to get that vegan brownie recipe from her just in case she's on her way out but then remember that I made it up.

I gaze at the four white walls that surround me. Considering the compact size, it feels utterly deserted.

CHAPTER TEN

I haven't had sex in three months.

The last time George and I Did It was a week before our leaving party. We were both a bit tipsy. George came all over me and a little bit of sperm flicked into my eye, requiring me to spend the following hour trying to remember where we'd packed the eye bath. My unelected abstinence has now gotten so bad that the slightest touch from another man sends ripples around my body. Yesterday, a guy on the tube grazed my crotch with the corner of his newspaper and I nearly fainted. I fancy everybody. Every single man I look at is beautiful. I imagine having an orgy with the three baristas in my local cafe – when they froth the milk for my latte I actually have to look away. Even things I wouldn't expect to find a turn on are becoming a problem. Tim was in the lounge watching a documentary about turtles the other day and when they started mating I had to put a cushion over my lap. I've masturbated twice over Vernon Kaye. I think I am addicted to the pursuit of sex. Everybody with a pulse is wank-bank material. The end of my penis has become slightly inflamed and yet I still muster bravely onwards. How do single people do it? I need to have sex and I need to have it now.

For the first time this week, none of my five housemates are home. I open Grindr, which has lain patiently dormant, knowing that one day I would return. I message No Fats No Femmes Jacob. He's not online and even if he was, last time I fell asleep, so he's probably not going to be interested. I scroll through the headless torsos and blank profiles saying Hello Handsome How're You to anybody who looks vaguely online.

A man sends an unsolicited picture of his scrotum. His profile says he Doesn't Travel. That's a Shame, I write to him, There Are Some Gorgeous Places Around the World, for Example I'd Love to Go to Asia. He calls me a Time Waster. I remember Jacob calling me that when we met. I'm about to link this scrotum to an article about the best times to visit Japan but his profile suddenly disappears off my screen, re-placed by an advert for Viagra.

Another user asks me how much for a massage. I'm pretty good with my hands, so I suggest a tenner. He replies, No, on What Planet Would I Massage You for a Tenner and calls me a prick. Looking for sex is exhausting so I make a cup of tea and eat two chocolate digestives. Invigorated, I continue my quest.

One guy asks if I fancy coming over for a cuddle. I imagine this to be code, but it turns out he does just want a cuddle. I decline. Intimacy is not what I'm craving right now. Dylan made out this was much easier than it is. I don't know how he does it. I wonder if there's a course you can go on: The Art of the Hookup.

A rather lovely, toned and hairless chest sends me a message. He's free now and wants to come over. The only stipulation is I have to wear a blindfold. I don't own one of those, but I do have a very thick scarf from Burton. This seems to please him. He wants me to wear the scarf whilst he ties me up. My pulse beats a little bit faster.

The most sexually adventurous thing George and I ever did was in May 2015 at Zachary's murder mystery party when

116

George fingered me in the bathroom between the starter and the main course whilst we were dressed as 1920s flapper girls. That was a brilliant night – more so because I happened to be the murderer and Steven died first.

I agree to being tied up by the Headless Torso and wearing the blindfold as long as I can see a picture of his face. He says No. There's something exciting about the way he's taking control. If I don't say yes now, then I could lose him and I'll be facing an evening of emptiness and more biscuits. I send him my address, and then he asks if he can bring a third person with him. He sends me a picture. This guy is handsome, preppy – to be honest, he looks like he has a pulse so I'm past the need to filter.

I type Yes, Bring Him, Just Hurry Up and Get Here.

He's on his way. I write a quick note to Tim in case he arrives home to find my slaughtered corpse.

"Sorry, needed sex." I place it under the pillow.

★ ★ ★

I'm on all fours over the bed with the scarf tied loosely around my head – I do wonder whether going from sex with only one person in nine years to full bondage with two strangers is a bit fast moving but hey, You Should Do Something Every Day That Scares You and there's nothing more terrifying than potential sexual humiliation or even murder. I barely hear my front door open over the noise of my heart hammering in my chest.

I wonder if Dylan has ever done anything this risky. As soon as this is over with, I'll have to call him and confess all. We haven't spoken too much since he moved me in, so this would be the perfect anecdote to get us back to normal. He'll be proud of me, I think. Now I'm picturing Dylan on all fours wearing a blindfold – it's somewhat comforting. I try to push the image from my head, but it lingers.

This guy – whose name I don't know despite asking – told me to leave the door on the latch. I hope it's him I can hear coming up the stairs now and not a passing neighbour checking we've not been burgled because they'll get quite the fright.

Heavy breathing announces my guest. There's a hand on my thigh. It makes me shudder. There's another hand around my neck. I can't work out if these hands belong to one person, or two people. A mouth presses against my ear and tells me to Kneel Up. I am equal parts shaking with fear and trembling with lust.

My hands are pulled behind my back roughly, and I feel a piece of thin rope begin to bring my wrists together. At the same time a hand moves across my torso and up to my head. So there *are* two people here – I'm quite the detective. I start to imagine I am in porn and make a low moan as this other hand rips my head back with one sharp movement. The moan becomes a yelp.

"Ouch, sorry, can you just, be a bit more careful—"

Another hand presses my mouth closed. There is no verbal response from my lovers, but the hand moves away from my head – presumably with a clump of my hair attached – and suddenly the rope is being fastened around my shoulders. For what feels like a good fifteen minutes the rope continues to circulate around the entire top half of my body until I can't move even an inch. I realise how incredibly dangerous this is – I can't reach my phone, nobody is home, and I only know what one of these people looks like. Although how do I know that the picture Headless Torso sent of the other guy is real? It could be anybody. I try to struggle but it's absolutely no use. This guy must be ex-military – these knots are so tight. Either that or he's spent a substantial amount of time watching YouTube tutorials.

I'm manoeuvred to the end of my bed, where I lay on my back. I picture what I look like. I'd have never done anything like this with George. I couldn't imagine myself ever needing to be strung out so brazenly.

I can hear kissing, but it's not my lips that are moving. These two are getting off with each other whilst I lay here like a joint of trussed up gammon waiting to go into the oven on Boxing Day. I squish my face to try and move the blindfold up so I can peak out of the bottom. I can just about make out two people in boxer shorts, and one of them looks like the Headless Torso. This is reassuring news. The pair of legs that doesn't belong to Headless Torso start to bend and I get a flash of blond hair as he comes into my vision properly. I relax a bit now that I've had it semi-proven that one of these sexual archangels is who I believed them to be.

I'm not entirely sure what I'm supposed to get out of this. I cough gently, hoping to remind them of my presence, but the blond head is going up and down on this other gentleman's penis and I am helpless. I close one eye to try and see a bit more clearly but I've been rumbled – a hand reaches over and pulls my blindfold down. Any erection I had hoped of sustaining has now completely disappeared. I begin to wonder what I might have for dinner.

After what seems like a good thirty minutes – but it could have just been ten – four hands are suddenly on my body. It shocks me back into life, rousing me from the gentle nap I'd fallen in to. There are tongues and mouths all over me, and as my legs are being raised into the air and something – which I hope is a penis – is being slipped inside of me I start to laugh at the complete absurdity of the situation. I'm laughing but also bloody hell it feels good and laughing isn't a good thing to do during sex, so I concentrate on the feeling good part.

This is the first time I've ever had sex with somebody not called George in nine years, and I can't even see them Doing It. The other guy who isn't inside of me is stroking my face and Jesus Christ it feels amazing and now I am saying Harder, and

I hear a voice say I'm Going to Come and then I'm begging Come Inside Me, Please and then with a jolt and a judder he collapses on top of me and as he does my face flushes and I shudder into an orgasm harder than I've ever felt before.

Dylan said I never did anything for myself, so I wonder if bondage could count as a hobby.

★ ★ ★

Despite hoping for a full post-coital reveal, I have to wait for the front door to close before I can take off the scarf – these were strict instructions from Headless Torso whilst he was untying the rope. I peel down the blindfold. There are two red burn marks around my wrists. I'll be wearing long sleeves for the next couple of days at work.

The smell of sex lingers in the air, masking the wafts of fried chicken coming from downstairs for a brief second. I pick up my phone to text Dylan, but it's late.

Sitting on the floor, I start to think about the fact that people do this kind of stuff all the time – rough play and toys and whips. Zachary even said they'd been with Steven to a place called the Torture Gardens. I didn't want them to expand on that at the time, but maybe now they should.

A breadcrumb from the toast I'm inhaling falls into my belly button – I forgot how Really Good Sex makes you Really Bloody Hungry. I fish the crumb out and wonder why I don't feel any shame in what I've just been complicit in, and I realise, it's because I couldn't catch a glimpse of myself during the act – I couldn't look at the stretch marks on my thighs, or ask him to slow the pace to not let my tummy flap too much. George never drew attention to my wobbly bits, but he unintentionally referenced them every time we were naked together because he was so toned, so streamlined and so perfect. My mind couldn't help but go there. I know that wasn't George's fault, but these are things I now need to think about if I want to have a healthy, explorative sex life. This time I had nothing to look at but darkness. I just got to feel the pleasure instead.

I wonder how I'm going to tell every sexual partner from now on that I need to wear a blindfold at all times. I am a therapist's dream.

CHAPTER ELEVEN

Niamh has asked me to come in to school and help her with an assembly she's doing for year six about sexuality. I hate public speaking. I've had sleepless nights thinking about it, but I know this means a lot to her.

It all seems to have been spurred on by our rainbow flag tattoos – kids were asking questions about why she'd had it done and she didn't want to lie to them. She's promised me I don't have to say much – just introduce myself and be a Physical Embodiment of a Gay Man. I ask if I can enter the hall to 'I'm Coming Out' by Diana Ross. She says No.

I'm wearing a white t-shirt that has 'Love is Love' emblazoned across the front in rainbow colours. A man sitting opposite me on the train raises his eyebrows at me. I pull my jacket further across my chest and slump down in my seat until we pull into the station.

Walking into the corridors sends me immediately back in time. The smell of something baking in the Food Technology Room and PVA glue mix with the sounds of jovial screaming on the playground. It's a little time capsule. I wonder what ten-year-old me would have thought of an assembly about sexuality. I probably would have missed it, seeing as most of my school days were spent in the first aid room pretending to feel sick. I didn't know it at the time, but my entire school life was interwoven and riddled with anxiety. I couldn't play sport, I wasn't good at maths and I didn't say very much. Compared to all the other children in my class I barely participated. I found an extract from my diary a couple of years ago on a rare visit to Mum's. I'd written that two boys had called me a 'lezzie'. I didn't even know what that was, but they said it with such disgust that I knew it wasn't a good thing. I'd told my teacher but she responded by drearily remarking that I was to just ignore it, which was a bit difficult when they'd also written it in thick red pen all over my homework diary.

For a short period of time Grandad used to take me to school. Mum had just had Leanne and wasn't coping very well, so I had sleepovers with him and Gran. One morning I was so angst-ridden at the thought of another day in class that I got up early and made my own vomit out of chopped carrots, mayonnaise and ketchup. I smeared it all over my face, threw a large puddle all over my sheets and then clung to my mattress as though I'd been shot. It was the stuff of legend in my family – an award-winning performance. Grandad found me and I remember him calling Gran – who'd already left for work without checking on me – and saying, It's Like the Exorcist in Here – followed by – But There is Quite a Lot of Carrot in It. I'm not sure when I admitted that I was fraudulent, but it was one of my grandad's favourite tales of deception. He always brought it up at family parties and I even told the story as part of his eulogy. I often wondered why we never discussed the lengths I was prepared to go to in order to miss just one day of school. My truancy became an anecdote, when it probably should have been a cause for concern.

Niamh has invited three other people to join us on stage: a bisexual friend, Sammy, who she met whilst travelling a few years ago; a transgender woman, Kayo, who teaches at the neighbouring secondary; and Coco, who works at the pub round the corner from my old house with her girlfriend and always used to help Dylan and me cheat on the pub quiz.

I immediately regret wearing my t-shirt. It's a bit on the nose. Zachary was supposed to join us too, but had a last-minute PR disaster. I imagine them running around with a bottle of Bollinger to try and appease whichever celebrity has had a meltdown.

We are already on stage. The hall – which smells of freshly iced buns and chicken nuggets – fills with noisy children, fresh out of their morning break time. They form neat little rows and sit cross legged, expectantly. I try to swallow but my mouth is bone dry. I picture miniature versions of Dylan, Zachary, Niamh and myself sitting in these school uniforms, wondering what we'd have made of what Niamh is about to talk about. Niamh stands behind a podium. She touches her right ear lobe a couple of times, her usual dramatic makeup tellingly muted. I can tell she's nervous.

"Settle down year six, your break is over now, quiet please."

It's always a bewildering treat to see a friend in their place of work. You suddenly realise you know nearly nothing about them at all.

"Now, I know you don't normally see me outside of the reception classrooms, but I'm here with some very important friends of mine to talk to you about a subject that is very close to my heart."

Her voice is soft. Niamh breathes out sharply and her breath reverberates around the wooden-clad panels stuffed with pictures of tree-rubbings and hanging papier-mâché planets.

"How many of you in here know what the word 'Gay' means? No calling out, just raise your hand."

A few hands timidly appear. There's a bit of chattering. One of the teachers at the back puts up his hand. The teacher next to him nudges it down.

"OK, good. And how many of you have heard of the word 'Lesbian'?"

Again, there are a few movements. One girl at the front folds her arms across her chest. Scowling.

"What about 'Bisexual'?"

This prompts some titters of laughter. To be fair I laughed at the word 'Bum' in year six. I think hearing something with the word 'Sexual' in would have sent me into a coma.

"Thank you, year six, settle down. Now, how about 'Transgender'?"

The hall feels like a desolate wasteland. Nobody moves. Kayo fidgets in her chair.

"OK, that's OK. Now, last one; 'Queer', has anybody ever heard that word on the television or in the playground?"

Still silence, but Niamh is getting into her stride now.

"So all of these words that I've mentioned all belong to the acronym LGBTQ. Now, the L, G and B are all to do with who we love. Put your hands up if you've ever been in love before."

A sound of comedy disgust echoes around the hall.

"Good, because you're all only eleven years old so absolutely none of you should have boyfriends and girlfriends. Now, if you are a lesbian, then you are a woman who loves somebody of the same gender. My friend Coco here is a lesbian. She has a girlfriend called Tina. Please say good morning to Coco."

"Good morning, Coco," the children chime in unison.

"If you are gay then you are a man who loves a person of the same gender. My friend Charlie here is a gay man, so he loves men. Please say good morning to Charlie."

"Good morning, Charlie."

A little cherub-faced child with blond curtains in the second row calls out, "Does he not have a boyfriend like Coco has a girlfriend, Miss?"

"No calling out, questions at the end, please."

There's nothing like sixty pairs of eyes burning into your

skin with pity. Little bastard. A handful of girls at the back say, Awwww and I accidentally scream SETTLE DOWN YEAR SIX and a few children look like they might cry. Niamh gestures for me to be quiet.

"B stands for bisexual, which means you love people of both genders. Sammy here has had both a boyfriend and a girlfriend at one time in his life."

The children greet him. The girl with her arms crossed is now leaning in and listening to Niamh so intently she's in danger of falling into her own lap.

"The T stands for transgender, and that means that the gender you are assigned at birth feels different to the gender you feel inside. Kayo here, who is a very good science teacher, and somebody who you might meet when you move up to Redbridge Academy next year, is transgender. Kayo was assigned the gender of male at birth, but felt as though their gender identity was more aligned with being a woman. So now she lives her life as a female."

I become painfully aware of the clock ticking on the back wall. I want to stand proudly but my shoulders are rounded. My three other co-volunteers are beaming with confidence.

"Now, just to confuse you there's another word called 'pansexual' and this means that you love people who might be LGBT or Q. And that's me: I'm queer. I might love any one of these people up on this stage with me, because it doesn't matter to me who they are or how they identify. So, do you think any of what I've explained is a bit strange or weird or confusing?"

A number of heads turn around and swivel side to side, to see if any of their classmates are going to say anything.

"And now you know that about all of us up here, does it make us seem scary or different in any way?"

You could hear a pin drop.

"It's OK if you do think that."

Nobody moves.

"OK then, let's put it this way, if you don't think differently about any of us then put your hand up."

A sea of palms raise up.

"Good, that's nice. Thank you. Hands down. So Sammy here has travelled to over one hundred different cities around the world just for fun! And Coco owns her own online ethical clothing company alongside working full time in a pub. Charlie gets to surround himself with books all day in the shop he works in – and gets paid to read! And Kayo has been nominated for the Teacher of Physics Award on three different occasions. They are all superstars in their own right, and who they love has no effect on the things they can achieve. And me, well I get to teach the next generation of superheroes. All of you sitting in front of me right now might be just like any of these wonderful humans sitting up here, and that's just fine. We are all unique, which is what makes life so incredibly exciting, and you should never judge or be mean to anybody who is different from you, because you too are different from them. Love is a very wonderful thing, and when you find it with somebody – whoever that is – it's a cause for celebration and not for censorship. Each of you has feelings, and we could all do with being a little bit kinder towards each other."

Niamh continues on with her speech for the next five minutes. She's warm, enlightening and above all the children are transfixed, and so am I. She explains how the need for this assembly came from a group of kids who were using the phrase That's So Gay on the playground, towards a boy who had a worn a pink t-shirt on a non-school uniform day. Niamh phrases things in such a profound way that I feel as though I'm learning something too. I imagine the difference a conversation like this would have made during my time in education. Perhaps I'd have actually stayed for an entire day of lessons.

At the end, as the children noisily digest what they've

heard and make their way back to class, a little boy comes up to me and tells me that his dad is gay and sometimes people shout things at them in the street and it makes him feel sad. He wraps his arms around my waist – causing me to hold my hands above my head and squirm like a car has just driven through a muddy puddle and splashed me so that Niamh can see I've read the child safeguarding policy she sent through. It's very sweet though.

On the second of my three trains home, I muse over how Niamh spoke about me. Usually when I mention to people that I work in retail they ask me what I want to do next – what career progression I want, or whether I'm applying for anything else. Mum acts as if I'm wasting my days, and I catch myself at work sometimes feeling sad for no reason, but Niamh made my job sound awesome. There was no measuring of success against the others on stage – although they were all infinitely more inspiring than me – I'm just a gay man, working in a book shop and living in London with incredible friends and that's my life right now. Why do I necessarily have to be looking for something more?

★ ★ ★

There is a baking competition at work. Noma is furious that I haven't entered my vegan brownies. I couldn't bring myself to make anything for fear of landing myself in another awkward situation. I whisper to her that I knew I'd win if I entered, so it was only fair I ducked out of this one. This seems to placate her extremely well. Tim has made a Battenberg and Lara has brought cupcakes. Farrah's entry is a coffee cake that looks suspiciously like a Taste the Difference one from Sainsbury's. Nobody wants to accuse the 19-year-old student of cheating, and it clearly tastes nicer than the rancid marzipan that Tim is offering, so Farrah wins a £10 book voucher. I wonder whether this constitutes theft.

As I finish my shift my phone rings: it's mum.

"Leanne's been by Gran's side constantly since she fell again last week, why haven't you been to visit?"

"I have a job to go to, Mum, and you told me not to come."

"Well I didn't mean it. Family should always come first, Charlie."

"I'll come up the next time I have a weekend off, and I'll call Gran later."

"No, you need to come up now."

"Why, what's happened?"

"Just stop wasting time and get here."

I wrap up a couple of slices of Farrah's sponge for the journey and head home. Well not my home, but *home* home – where I grew up – to *Bas-Vegas*. Basildon, Essex.

★ ★ ★

The ward smells of antiseptic with a side of death.

Gran has always been slight, yet in the waves and folds of the blanket she somehow looks even smaller. She's asleep, whistling through her teeth. A lady in the bed opposite is shouting something about her dignity being taken away, and I'm pretty certain I can hear someone else behind a curtain in the corner shitting into a bedpan.

I ate my piece of cake on the train, so I leave the second piece on the table. There's some pale orange liquid in a clear plastic jug. I've never really been in a hospital that much before, but I used to watch a lot of *Holby City* with George hungover on a Sunday, so I pour Gran a glass and place the straw inside her mouth, encouraging her to drink. Her eyes flare open and she clutches at her neck.

"Are you trying to kill me?! Nurse! Nurse!"

"Gran it's me, it's Charlie."

"What are you trying to do?"

"I thought you might be thirsty."

129

"I was asleep you little bastard, I don't need a drink when I'm asleep."

"Sorry."

"Could have fucking drowned."

For someone so petite she's certainly always had a mouth on her.

"Anyway, what do you want?"

"I've brought you some cake."

"I don't like cake."

"Right, well, I wanted to check in and make sure you were OK."

"I slipped on the stairs."

"Mum said. Did it hurt?"

"Of course it hurt, have you ever heard of anybody falling down the stairs and not hurting themselves?"

I've never tripped down the stairs, but I did fall off a statue on Clapham Common once. We'd had way too many vodka Red Bulls for Dylan's twenty-fourth birthday, and feeling invincible I climbed to the top of this stoney figure. All I remember is one minute being vertical, and the next being horizontal on the pathway. Dylan tells everyone that I'd actually only climbed as high as the man's legs, so my fall was only very short, but I distinctly recall looking directly into the statue's cold hard eyes and my life flashing before me. There was a very large bump on the back of my head for two weeks. I don't think Gran would appreciate me saying that I can empathise with the large bruise that I now notice is spreading across the side of her face.

"Have you made any friends in here, Gran?"

"Of course not. Everyone is bat-shit crazy. That one won't shut up about wanting her own private room and saying she can't sleep because it's so noisy, when she's the one making all the bleeding racket."

Gran waggles a bony finger at the lady in the bed opposite. They scowl at each other. Gran rolls her eyes.

"Where's your sister?"

"I don't know."

"She's a good girl, that one."

I audibly sigh. All the times I've driven Gran around to various appointments, made sure to call her every other day for a chat so she's not alone, ordered online food shopping and helped her buy Christmas presents – for other people, never me – yet it's Leanne who is the Good One. Leanne who once made Gran go with her on a night out because she'd bought a new coat and she didn't trust the people in the cloakroom, so she made Gran sit in the corner of the British Legion holding it all night. She was seventy-three at the time.

"Mum tells me your boyfriend left you."

"We spoke about this on the phone, Gran, a few months ago."

"You never told me."

"I did tell you."

Facts and information slip in and then straight out of Gran's brain at a remarkable speed these days. It's sad. I can feel the cold grip of mortality constantly trying to take over my thoughts whenever I'm with her.

"No, you never told me. I'd remember. It's a shame, I liked him, handsome he was."

"Yep."

"Lovely chap, was so helpful with me, always happy to drive me around and call me up for a chat. He did my online shop sometimes too."

I can't be bothered to tell her that George couldn't drive, didn't have her phone number, and in all the time we were together only visited her house with me a handful of times. Come to think of it, he always had something suddenly to do on the weekends I'd go to visit her. I always cleared my diary for his family trips, even though his grandad consistently taunted me by calling me Charlotte.

"Now he's gone what are you doing with yourself?"

"I'm working in the book shop, aren't I?"

"What shop?"

"Waterstones."

Gran tuts. Her jowls tighten and then loosen. "I get everything from Woolworths, it's cheaper."

"That closed down years ago, Gran."

"Oh don't start." She unwraps the napkin around the cake. "What's this?"

"It's the cake that—"

"Your sister must have bought this for me whilst I was asleep. Bless her."

I'm constantly surprised by my resilience in these situations. The way she and Mum talk to me makes me want to walk away and never look back. Never again subject myself to their torrents of hatred towards me for reasons that I can't work out. But Granny and Mum are peas in a pod, and so is Leanne now. They think the same, and talk the same, and I stick out like a sore thumb.

Gran takes a large chomp of icing and rolls it around her mouth. She holds it like a praying mantis torturing its victim, then swallows it down with a nauseating gulp. Her nose wrinkles.

"I hate chocolate."

"It's coffee flavoured."

After clearing her throat into a tissue, she settles back into her orthopaedic pillow, her hair wispy and fair, fanned out around her face. Her eyes turn into beads, scanning my entire body.

"Are you eating properly?"

"Oh, well I am actually, despite the circumstances."

It's unlike her to tell me I look slimmer.

"You can tell, you've got chubby around the neck."

There it is.

"There's too much choice with food now, all this fattening stuff. All I had when I was your age was a bit of meat and some veg and that was my lot. None of this sugary shite."

She takes another bite, "eurgh, I hate chocolate," then spits it out into her hand and scrapes it onto the table. It lays there glistening with saliva. I look at the plastic plant in the corner to stop myself from retching.

"You need to eat well if you want to make sure somebody else will find you attractive. Maybe that's why George ran off in the first place. I was on a diet for my entire life to keep your grandad interested. Never weighed more than 112 pounds. You have to be presentable if you want to be looked after. Although I'm not sure which way round you do it when you're both men. Who stays at home and keeps everything in order?"

"It's not like that anymore, Gran."

"There you go. There's your problem – too feisty. Too ambitious. He'll be needing somebody to look after him properly."

I change the subject in order to quell the sound of my rising heartbeat. "Are the doctors and nurses nice?"

"No, they're fucking horrible, what are you asking me about them for?"

"I've come to see you! Not talk about me."

"Oh well fine then, sod my advice, is that it? I've been around a lot longer than you."

And I'll be around for a lot longer after she's gone. Which reminds me, I must thank Gran at some point for voting Leave in the EU Referendum.

"Charlie, you'll never be happy if you don't sort out your priorities."

"I'd better be getting off now, I've got lots to sort out back at the flat before work tomorrow."

Gran grabs my arm as I start to stand. Her hand, almost translucent, clutches at the sleeve of my jumper.

"Don't be one of these people who thinks they can do it on their own. Humans weren't born to be alone. It's miserable. Your grandad has been gone for six years now. I know what alone is. When he was gone what little happiness I had went with him."

If I'd have stayed with George forever, and carried on living my life under his shadow then maybe Gran lying in that bed would have been me one day. I want to tell her that if she'd made efforts outside of her marriage then maybe she wouldn't spend all day sitting in her armchair and waiting for me to call, or for Mum and Leanne to go over for five minutes every other day, but that's not what you did in Those Days. I often wondered if recent technology scared Gran, or whether it made her sad – to see how easy it was for us to connect with people now, and stay in touch, and that this technology had left her trailing behind in a bewildered loneliness.

As I walk down the corridor – the shouts and screams of the ward fading with every step – I wonder who would visit me at the age of seventy-five when I've broken a hip. I smile. My friends would.

★ ★ ★

Outside the hospital I call Mum.

"Why did you tell me I had to get here now, like Gran was dying? She isn't, she's fine."

"She's not fine, Charlie. Her dementia is getting worse. She's so frail now. She's one fall away from a fatal blow."

"That's a bit dramatic, Mum."

"What would you rather I said when I called you; that we don't think she'll be around for much longer?"

"I'm an adult, I can decide when I want to come and visit my family, I don't need to be coerced into coming."

"Here we go, using the big words to make me feel stupid."

"Do you like me, Mum?"

134

Her breathing into the receiver quickens. "What a stupid question, you're my son."

"Yes, but do you *like* me?"

"I'm not doing this now, Charlie. If your Gran passes over tomorrow I'll be sure to wait until it's a convenient time to let you know, so you can decide if you're too busy to come and help us arrange the funeral."

I squeeze my fist tightly around my phone, as an ambulance comes tearing into the car park.

"I don't know what I've ever done to upset you, but for years – ever since I've been with George – you've treated him like he's your son. Before I was with him, I was lucky if I even got a birthday card from you. I thought before George that it was because you didn't like that I was gay, but if you loved George so much then that can't be true. You can't be homophobic – so it must be that you simply don't like me, and I'm sorry if you don't but I don't think I can go on much longer with you, and Leanne and Gran talking to me the way you do."

The dial tone rings out. I think for a second that she's hung up on me, but then realise, as my rage subsides, that it was me who in fact hung up on her.

★ ★ ★

Later, back home in the flat, I take out my phone and begin to write an email. It starts with two simple words that I've been unable to contemplate writing up until now, but the sudden need is overwhelming. My fingers tap out a sentence on the screen.

'Hi George'.

CHAPTER TWELVE

Dawn is breaking over the Manhattan skyline. I can see the Empire State Building from the bathroom window. I stretch my legs and my toes fall out of the end of the duvet. I've always been too tall for this bed.

I can hear the sound of a food processor in the kitchen and the smell of citrus fruit drifts underneath the door. I pad across the rug, slide into my dressing gown and tie a loose knot. We didn't get much shut eye last night but I'm in no way complaining.

George stands at the breakfast bar, his hands berry-red. I pick a stray seed from his cheek. He pours two glasses of smoothie and pecks me on the lips.

"Good morning, handsome. Strawberry, banana, açaí and a dash of lime."

He sits on one of the bar stools, picks up the *New York Times*, and settles into our familiar routine.

"There's coffee too if you want it."

I've never liked coffee, but here it tastes incredible. I crave it every morning. I love the way it sours on his breath. I sit across from him. My leg instinctively reaches out and tangles with his. His calves are warm, the downy hair comforting.

"What will you do today?" he asks me, his lips rouged from the fruit.

"I'm going to take a walk downtown, there's some groceries I need to pick up."

"Make sure you take the company card."

"Oh I will."

I smirk. We haven't paid for any food since I arrived. George's bosses were so happy he wasn't moping around anymore that to celebrate me joining him, they've given us a weekly shopping allowance. I go to Whole Foods every Monday after he's left for work and buy large tubs of natural peanut butter and fresh apricots, and wholemeal flour to make bread and jars of delicious honey and spices. I buy new spices every week to add to the rack. Our spice rack! I have become quite the cook, counting Thai fusion and neatly rolled sushi as some of my best dishes.

George opens a large window and the sounds of the busy street rushes in. I feel safe here. He looks different to what I remember. His hair is fairer, his torso just that tiny bit fuller – he puts that down to the heartbreak. His appetite has improved even more greatly now I'm here. I run my hands across his chest and he kisses me so deeply I feel as though I'm falling. Everything else melts away.

I hear a door open and turn to see Axel in an identical dressing gown to mine walking over to the breakfast bar. I instinctively pull the drawstrings across my stomach tighter.

Axel picks up my untouched coffee cup and sips it appreciatively. George lets go of my waist and suddenly his lips are on the back of Axel's neck. Axel purrs in delight and turns his head to catch George's mouth. George peels himself away slowly and faces me.

"I know we said we'd do dinner later, but I forgot I'd promised Ax that he could have tonight with me, is that OK, baby?"

I find myself nodding.

137

"You'll find something to do, won't you?"

My head nods again. Axel looks straight at me. Takes another sip of my coffee.

"Actually, baby, would you mind if Axel and I used the main bedroom before I go to work? I could really do with some me and him time this morning."

Even though this question is rhetorical – and despite all my willpower – my head is moving up and down giving permission, and I watch as Axel takes George by the hand into my bedroom and closes the door.

I step backwards, trying to put as much distance between myself and them as possible. I don't want to hear those moans again. So far, I've managed to avoid it whilst I've been here. I push further and further away from the bedroom. The door is already gently banging against the frame. I put my hands against my ears and press hard to block out the noise. Dust is crumbling from the wall as the door smack smack smacks against the frame, and a tiny crack starts to make its way down from the ceiling. I press my fingers harder into my ears and they begin to feel warm. Blood trickles down my wrist and onto the varnished timber floor. As I'm stumbling backwards – desperate to get away from the muffled noises – the door flies off its hinges and I see their naked bodies are intertwined in such a way that I fear they may never come apart. George fixes me with this wild look. His eyes are completely overtaken with lust. My fingers push all the way into my canals but I don't feel any pain. As I take another step back I fall through the open window and watch the apartment disappear from view. I don't feel sad at the thought of the inevitable. The wind rushes past me, and despite the pain in my ears, it's deafening. I wait for the blackness to envelop me but it never comes. The ground is there but I can't reach it. I'm falling, continuously. Falling. I can still hear Axel and George, their voices almost becoming one and then the smell of chicken permeates the air. I sniff. It's definitely chicken. As I'm falling into never-ending death? Odd choice.

Then my eyes open. I've sweated straight through my bed-sheets. I hear Tim flush the toilet and climb the stairs back to his room. I rub my face, check that my ears are intact. My phone tells me it's 3 am. Another night's sleep cut short by George and Axel.

★ ★ ★

I'm sitting on the sofa in our living room. I mean, Niamh and Dylan's living room. It's only the second time I've been in the house since I left – and the first time Axel was out of the country. This time he's only at work. I feel as though I'm dicing with death. Niamh is propped up against the door, sitting in the chair yoga pose: I've no idea why and I can't be bothered to ask. Her legs are shaking. Dylan is wrapping up a bottle of Sainsbury's finest pink fizz, in preparation for Zachary and Steven's engagement party.

"Do you think they'll close their relationship back up when they get married?" Dylan says with a piece of tape between his teeth, "or will they keep seeing other people?"

I say nothing, staring intently at the front door for any sounds of approach. Niamh lets out a large puff of struggled breath. Dylan throws a cushion at her, and she topples to the floor.

"You bastard, I was nearly onto a personal best then."

"Which is?"

"Thirty seconds."

"Quick, I'll call the *Guinness Book of World* records!"

"Piss off," says Niamh as she walks into the kitchen.

"I asked you a question," Dylan calls out to her.

"I don't know, why don't you ask Zach?"

"They might not want to talk about it, so I'm asking what you think."

"It's Zach and Steven, who are both happy to talk about anything, sometimes to their detriment, and why did you throw a cushion at me, and not at Charlie? He didn't answer you either."

I want to tell them about the email I typed to George, but I'm enjoying the patter between Dylan and Niamh. It's hasn't changed much since we were at uni; it's comforting knowing that despite growing older, that same sense of humour is there. Niamh returns from the kitchen with three pale ales in colourful tins.

"Three for two at Marks and Spencer's, don't get used to it."

It's bitter but warming on my tongue. Dylan wipes foam from his top lip, "God, if I have to hear one more conversation from Steven about what they're planning to do . . . you know he wants them to get married in Cannes. Fucking Cannes. How are any of us supposed to afford a weekend in Cannes?"

"Maybe that's the whole point. We can't afford it, so they don't have to invite us."

Dylan and I stare at Niamh, quietly shocked at her comment.

"Niamh, why would you say that? Of course we'd be invited. We're Zach's best mates."

"Dylan, come on. Charlie's spent most of their relationship calling Steven boring."

"And I agree with Charlie, Steven is boring."

I can feel myself being hoisted onto the fence without permission, "Well, I did think that, but whilst I was staying with them it made me realise that Steven is actually really nice, and I think I was probably just jealous of him somehow, I don't know."

"Why would you be jealous of Steven? That's weird." Dylan finishes covering the bottle in paper and places it on the coffee table. It looks like it's been wrapped by a six-year-old.

"I don't know, I guess, he's got a brilliant job, always seems

140

super stable and he knows who he is . . . and I guess now I look back and can see that I didn't have a fucking clue who I was, and I still don't. Plus Zachy loves him, so I love him."

"You've changed your tune!" Dylan sips his ale pointedly, "They can get married abroad if they want to, I just think it's really selfish of Steven to expect us all to be there."

"I don't know why it's bothering you so much, Dyl," Niamh says, sitting down next to me.

"Because it just feels really fucking sudden that's all, and I thought you'd agree with me Charlie!"

I don't say anything during this exchange. I wonder how many conversations have been had on this very sofa over the past eight years with the names Zach and Steven exchanged for Charlie and George. Grandad once told me if we knew what our friends said about us behind our backs we'd never have any.

"It's only sudden because we're all single. Marriage feels unachievable at the moment because it's so far off the cards; we're all playing with a different deck. I'm the only teacher in lower school that's a Miss. And I'm the eldest! The children in upper school are doing *Great Expectations* at the moment and one of them asked me if I identified with Miss Havisham. The fucking cheek of it!"

Dylan puts down his beer and leans on Niamh's knees, looking up at her from the floor like a puppy dog.

"Any more news on that school complaint?"

"What complaint?' I ask.

"Oh, some bastard parent of one of the kids has written a letter about my assembly, saying the content was inappropriate and that I've put ideas into their kid's head because this boy went back home that night and told his mum that he thinks he's gay – like it works that fucking way! Poor little thing. I don't know if he is actually gay, but it doesn't matter, she should listen to her kid and not dismiss what he's said.

141

Anyway, because it's a formal complaint it's got to go to the governors etc. etc. It might just disappear, but the parents at this school – once they've got a bone to pick they don't let it go."

"Fuck, I'm sorry Niamh, that's bullshit," I say, squeezing her leg. "And is your senior leadership team being supportive? I mean, what have they said?"

"It's something they need to take seriously, apparently, which is code for, we're homophobic and didn't like the assembly either."

"FUCKING REFORM VOTING BASTARDS," screams Dylan, raising his can.

Niamh and I follow suit, raising our cans, and together we shout it as loud as we can.

"FUCKING REFORM VOTING BASTARDS!"

★ ★ ★

We pass around half a bottle of warm Blossom Hill rosé on the tube to Zachary and Steven's house. Since moving to London I have been to roughly twelve of Zachary's flat warming parties. I have taken houseplants to seven of those. There are no New Home designs left in Card Factory for me to choose from – Zach's had them all – so it was a welcome change to pick out an On Your Engagement card for this occasion.

The flat is pristine as usual and smells of Jo Malone. There are lots of people milling around the kitchen, talking loudly and expressing views on political topics. I don't recognise anyone else here. They must be Zachary's colleagues who we've never really met. Zach very much keeps business apart from pleasure. Dylan started a rumour that Amanda Holden was going to turn up, but this has been heavily denied by Zach, and according to Holden's Instagram story she's in Sicily with Alan Carr so we've concluded that she's not coming.

However, somebody has bought a cheeseboard which looks very expensive. I love people who work in PR with disposable income.

I take a cup and head to the living room, having already lost Niamh who is holding court with three people in the kitchen, and Dylan who is chatting to a strikingly handsome chap wearing a blue boiler suit and a beret. It would be nice to actually spend some time with my friends when we go out, instead of immediately being discarded by them in their quest to make connections with strangers. Is that what I'm supposed to do in a new location – scout out the talent from the second I've stepped over the threshold?

Despite being amongst three of my best friends, it's amazing how quickly the loneliness sets in. It only takes one fleeting thought of remembering you're single and whoosh, there it is. Crushing, destabilising loneliness.

I'm flicking through the Spotify playlist on Zachary's iPad, skipping a couple of songs that I don't know, when a voice shouts over from the other side of the living room.

"Oi, DJ! Are you gonna choose one song or is it a mega mix?!"

I've never seen this guy before. He's wearing the same fake glasses I wear for work. The fraud.

"I'm trying to find something good," I offer back.

He shrugs and rejoins his conversation. I hate people who work in PR.

Dylan is still with The Boiler Suit. He's doing that thing he does when he finds someone attractive; touching his tongue to the corner of his mouth. Either that or he's getting a cold sore. I wonder if he's still got that satchel he used to bring to uni. I loved that bag, I used to use it to pull him backwards in the corridors so he'd bump straight into me – both laughing, the smell of his aftershave pouring straight into my nostrils. He still wears the same one now. I don't know what it is, but it's his scent. If I smell it out and about somewhere I'll search for him in the crowd – furious at a stranger for making me think I was about to bump into my favourite person in the world. I wonder if it had never been George and I, then might it have been Dylan and I? If Dylan was out when he was at uni, would he have been more comfortable getting to know me in that way? What would I have become then with someone like Dylan by my side?

I pour another can of beer into a glass, to stop myself from daydreaming and gravitate towards the sofa. Steven beckons me over at one point but I smile and wave him away. He's having a lovely time celebrating with his friends, and I feel like I don't have anything to contribute tonight. I haven't got the willpower to make the effort with anybody I don't already know.

The doorbell goes and Zachary makes a fuss pushing their way through everybody, loudly declaring, I Wonder Who's Next Over the Threshold to nobody in particular.

I hear a man's voice from out in the hallway say Hey Guys and the clinking sound of bottles jostling in a bag. A few people turn and greet him back. I notice Dylan do a double-take. His tongue retreats away from the corner of his mouth. The Boiler Suit may be up for relegation.

Zachary comes in and hurries over to me.

"Darling, I'm so sorry I had no idea he'd be able to make it."

I'm about to ask what they're talking about when I see Axel standing in the doorway. He's wearing a simple plain white t-shirt, sculpted around his neat pecs, and skinny black jeans which perfectly cup his peachy bottom and muscular thighs. He couldn't look more picturesque.

"I felt mean not inviting him when he lives with Niamh and Dylan, and he said he was working so I didn't think it would be a problem, oh damn, it's insensitive of me really, I'm sorry."

144

The beer answers for me.

"It's fine, Zach, really. I've got to get used to seeing him at some point."

"If you're sure? Let me get you a glass of Bolly, that'll do the trick."

Dylan looks over at me and mouths Are You OK and I nod; he smiles half-heartedly. He turns and waves at Axel, then turns back to The Boiler Suit. Niamh hasn't noticed, she's deep in conversation with a few others.

Axel looks over and smiles. I have absolutely no idea what my face does in response, but it must have been something welcoming as he responds by making his way over.

"Yo stranger."

Stranger! Fucking stranger! I want to reply – You've Had Your Penis Inside My Boyfriend, I Think We're Very Much Acquainted, Thank You Very Much – but instead I interrupt my inner monologue to say, "Hello, Axel! Hi! How are you!"

Oh right, I'm coming from the In Complete Denial school of thought for this encounter, that's good. Axel leans down and plants a quick kiss on my lips, something I'm discovering is his trait.

"You're looking well, Charlie baby."

Now, when somebody says that, what they usually mean is, You've Put on Weight or You've Got a Bit of a Tan and I haven't been abroad recently so no need for the jury to deliberate on the subtext of that one. I hug a cushion into my chest, spilling a bit of beer in the process. If Axel notices he doesn't say anything.

"You look lovely too."

"Thanks, man. When are you gonna come over and see your old place?"

Is he taking the piss? I mean, he must be aware of what he's saying? He knows that I saw him and George together. Hang on. Does he know that I saw? Why would he? Unless Niamh or Dylan have said something, and they wouldn't because it would make living with him too awkward.

"I'm really busy with work at the moment so I'm not sure."

"Oh yeah, Dylan said you're working at this really cool bookstore. Congrats."

So Dylan and Axel talk about me? Why would Dylan make conversation with him when he's supposed to be my best mate? But then, they do live together, he can hardly just ignore him can he?

"Thanks. It's a nice shop. Very full on, but nice."

"Things at work are just crazy at the moment for me. It's just non-stop but TGIF y'know?"

"Ah right. Yeah, George said it was always a busy office. How do you cope?"

"A lot of fucking cocaine."

I can't tell if he's joking. He's still standing over me. His skinny jeans are so tight. I wonder how it feels to be between his thighs.

"So, is that your . . ."

I point over at the man he came in with, who is holding court in the kitchen. He's taken his denim jacket off to reveal the sinewy beauty of his lean arms. A thick tuft of dark hair escapes over the curve of his fitted polo shirt.

"Ah no he's not my boyfriend, we're just fucking."

The audacity of the Beautiful People. A bead of sweat follows the line of my sideburn. I dab it away.

"I'm not looking for anything long term at the moment. I'm young and free and living in such a great city so why be tied down, you know?"

I suddenly feel ancient – like Gran in that hospital bed, but instead of that lady opposite shouting about dignity I've got an American waving his dick in my face.

"Listen man, obviously I heard about you and George."

I shift in my chair. I desperately try and make eye contact with Niamh or Dylan. Axel takes my silence as an invitation for him to sit down uncomfortably close to me.

"I feel awkward because of what happened at your leaving party, and I totally wouldn't have gone there, but earlier that night George said you guys were open so … I hope I wasn't the straw that broke the camel's back you know, because I heard that you broke up the day after we hooked up."

My head is swimming. Every word I know is drowning completely. My mouth falls open, limply.

"I've been with guys in open relationships before and it's always weird when you hear they broke up not long after, because then you're a bit like, 'was it my fault?' y'know. Not saying that I'm some kind of like, Sex God, but the timing was a bit odd I guess."

I want him to immediately stop talking, but apart from shoving this glass down his throat I'm not sure what else I can do.

"It sucks that you didn't get to go to America with him, but it sounds like he's having a bit of a shitty time out there so maybe it was a lucky escape for you, man."

He and George still talk? George isn't enjoying himself? This is too much information to take in at once. I think I'm just staring at the wall. My eyes, glassy, are starting to dampen. I try with all my might to keep the ensuing flood at bay.

"Anyway, I just wanted to make sure there were no hard feelings between us. You're a nice guy, and I'd love to hang out sometime. Hey, you should come to the cinema with Dylan, Niamh and me next time we go. We spoke about going next week on Thursday to see the new Marvel, so let's all go together if you're down?"

It's like I'm at the end of episode one of *Doctor Foster*, except I don't have to open the boot of Bertie Carvel's car and expose all of my friend's secrets because Axel is doing that for me.

They all go to the cinema together? My friends and this man? And George told Axel we were in an open relationship?!

"Just let Dylan know and we'll book you a ticket. Anyways, I'm gonna grab a beer, you want one?"

Axel jumps up from my side and I shake my head. He pats me on the arm and leaves. I watch that bum wiggle away. That bum. Dylan and The Boiler Suit have disappeared. I can't even focus properly to look for Niamh. I don't want to ruin Steven and Zachary's night so I stumble to my feet. That voice from earlier calls back out across the room.

"You're not going to change the song again are you, pal?"

I steady myself against the wall. I feel like the ugly duckling learning how to walk for the first time when everyone around me seems to be flying. I try the bathroom door unsure if I'm going to be sick or if it's all just in my head. It's locked – and I hear Dylan call out from inside, Someone's in Here, followed by the sound of giggling and then, slurpy, passionate kissing. The beret lays discarded just outside the door.

I am so weary.

★ ★ ★

On the way home, I rack my brain for anything that will confirm or deny that George and I were in an open relationship without me realising. George worked away a lot, but I never had any suspicions that he was seeing somebody else. We slept in the same bed together every night, so I would have known. His phone was always buzzing with texts but I never even looked at his screen let alone read any messages because I didn't feel the need to.

I go to the draft email section on my phone and look at the message I typed to him last month. I never sent it. I couldn't bring myself to do it because I didn't know what I wanted from a reply, but now Axel has told me that George isn't having the best time out there then maybe I should. Is he not enjoying the work? Or being away from his family? Or is it . . . ? I can't bring myself to even contemplate that it might be down to me. The idea that he's wallowing and weeping in the apartment because I'm not there brings an immediate lump to my throat. I want to shout to the driver, Take Me to the Nearest Airport! but then remember I'm on a bus not in a taxi.

If he was missing me that much then he would have contacted me, or reached out to say he was thinking about us, and that he'd realised he'd made a terrible mistake. My mind is so clouded with thoughts it's giving me a headache. There's a man chatting vapidly on the phone in front of me and I want to scream at him to shut up – shut up because my ex-boyfriend is a liar and yet I want, no *need,* to know how he is. I need to hear his voice. I thought I was doing OK. I thought I was getting better.

I add another line to the email. It reads, 'How are you?'. It sticks out like a sore thumb amongst the outpouring of grief contained within the rest of my words. I select the rest of the text – except this new sentence – and hit delete. And then to my own amazement, I hear a whoosh as my email hurtles across the pond and into George's inbox.

★ ★ ★

I spend the rest of the evening frantically trying to find how you can recall an email after you've sent it – but it turns out you can't.

Niamh calls me and leaves a voicemail asking where I am. They're all going on to a bar around the corner from Zachary's. I can hear Axel shouting in the background. In the WhatsApp group that I have with her and Dylan, I text that I left because I'm on an early at the shop tomorrow. She replies with the painting nails emoji.

I can't get the image out of my head of the three of them hanging around with each other at the flat. I'd never even

149

considered it – thought they'd just be co-inhabiting and nothing else. Sharing milk not sharing secrets.

I text Otis and ask whether he wants to get a friendly drink next week. In the text he sent after the theatre, he did say he enjoyed my company and that even though he didn't see me romantically he was happy to have a platonic hang out. It's already 9 pm so I know he's not going to reply, and even if he did, would I even want to go? I click onto Matthew Constantino's Instagram page but he hasn't replied to my message from months ago about going for a coffee.

I tap bondage man on Grindr. He was online ten minutes ago. I think a couple of the girls are in upstairs, but we've barely spoken, except in passing on the way to the bathroom, and Tim's away at another festival for the weekend.

Those beers have gone to my head a little bit. It would be strange of me to get in touch with Noma this late; although I've been to her house before for the party, we're very much colleagues rather than friends, and I don't have Lana or Farrah's numbers and even if I did, I wouldn't have anything to say to them. I even contemplate calling Gran, but she'll be asleep now. Leanne told me that Gran's out of hospital and back at home. I can't phone Mum because we haven't properly spoken since I put the phone down on her – it's just been the odd perfunctory Facebook message. I stare at my phone looking for some sort of connection with someone but it doesn't offer me anything. It's funny, I know so many people, yet sometimes I just don't know who to call.

The damp on the ceiling in the corner of my room has spread slightly. I hung a pack of battery-operated fairy-lights around the window to try and distract from the patches of black and green, but instead they just seem to illuminate the mould.

Sarah-Beth has put some pictures on Facebook of her wedding. She looks beautiful. I sit in the dark and flick through all 320 photos in the album. So many smiles. There are some snaps of her getting ready in the morning – her hair piled high on her head whilst a makeup lady artistically dusts her face with a brush. Her house is exactly what I'd expect – there are inspirational quotes everywhere you can see. Her mirror has glitter around it. I want to pick at more things but I can't really because she looks happy, and what's the point in hating someone who I don't even really know anymore?

When George first found out about the job, we went to IKEA to pick out furniture – just like in *500 Days of Summer*. We knew the apartment would be fully furnished, but we wanted to add a few little touches of our own – a plant, a picture frame, His and His dressing room tables. George sat on a stool in a plush lounge and he held my head in his hands and said One Day I Will Marry You. We had meatballs and lingonberry jam afterwards and they'd never tasted so good.

I am the only unhappy person in the world. Except then I think of those who are homeless or living in war zones or dying of incurable illnesses and all I'm sad about is not having a boyfriend to spend eight hours building a DOMBÅS wardrobe with. This vicious circle of sadness and shame spirals continuously until I can see the sun coming up through the curtains. I'll dream of George and Axel again tonight. I know I will.

★ ★ ★

At work the day after the engagement party I am useless. I'm so tired my hands are shaking. I convince myself I have developed early-onset Parkinson's. For a good hour I hide in the health section devouring book after book and page after page looking for evidence of my symptoms. Every ten minutes I check my email inbox. Each time I'm not sure if I'm relieved or deeply saddened to find it empty. No reply from George.

I try to think of things I have to look forward to, but can

think of nothing. I call Gran on my lunch break but she doesn't answer. Yesterday, Leanne put up a picture of them at a garden centre with the caption, Me and My Best Gal. I notice Mum has commented with an angry face reaction.

Noma is walking around near the Brand-New Fiction section. I know she's looking for me – it's my turn to be on the tills but this is not the face of customer service. I'll tell her that I'm not feeling well and should go home. I pinch my cheeks and consider putting my forehead against the radiator for a few minutes in order to feign a fever. This is primary school level stuff, yet here I am nearly thirty-one and up to the same tricks. If children knew that things didn't really change that much when you get older there would be riots.

I'm preparing my best I'm Poorly voice when I see Matthew Constantino walk up to the counter with an armful of books. There's nobody there to greet him. I can see Noma now over with Farrah helping an elderly customer up the stairs to Poetry and Drama.

I duck down and hide behind the slim stand holding stacks of greetings cards. I push them around for no particular reason. Please Noma, spot him and run over – but no, they are taking this customer up every single stair, excruciatingly slowly. From where I'm hiding I can't see the tills fully. I'm about to attempt a slow crawl through the aisle towards the staff room when I feel someone standing behind me.

"Excuse me, am I able to pay for these please?"

I look up. His expression changes. His mouth turning into this big smile.

"Oh, I'm glad I've caught you again, am I going to get another freebie this time?"

"HELLO!" I yell, way too over enthusiastically.

"I came in a couple of weeks back but you weren't here. Thank you so much for that recommendation, I loved *Queenie*, I devoured it."

I gather myself off the floor, pretending to stock a couple of greetings cards in the process and make my way over to the tills, with Matthew following me. He's wearing a very cute buttoned up blue jacket, with a neatly tied neck scarf poking out around the collar. A black beanie hat sits on his head, with some flicks of blond hair sneaking out of the bottom and decorating his forehead. Rolled up black jeans and desert boots complete his artfully dishevelled look.

"I only just saw you'd sent me a message on Instagram. Sorry, I'm hardly ever on there. Thanks for letting me know about the Candice Carty-Williams talk, I'm gutted I missed that. Is she doing another one any time soon?"

"Erm, no, she's not."

I start to scan the books: it's a mixture of new and classic, and a variety of genres. He's attractively well read.

"So, do you message all of your customers with bespoke recommendations of events, or just me?"

I don't know what to respond to this. I can see Noma coming back down the stairs, if she comes over and hears that I've messaged him then maybe I'll get into trouble. There's probably some GDPR rules against this. Perhaps I've committed fraud. I can't lose this job, it's the only reason I've really got to get out of bed in the morning.

"Sorry about that, you just . . . you came up as a Suggested Follow, on Instagram but, yeah I probably shouldn't have done that."

"No, no, I'm glad you did. It's why I came back in today actually."

"Oh?" I pack his haul into a paper bag and slide it across the counter.

"Yeah, you probably get this all the time, but, do you fancy going for a coffee sometime?"

I never get this all the time, and I don't fancy a coffee – because coffee is disgusting – but I do, very much, fancy him.

153

CHAPTER THIRTEEN

In year eight at school we had this Geography teacher, Mr Brawn, who used to get these chronic headaches in the middle of a lesson, and to get rid of them he'd dry swallow paracetamol whilst sat behind his desk. I used to watch in horror as he placed the pill in his mouth, gulped like a fish on land struggling to breathe, and then used his fingers to stroke his throat and help the relief slide down. Every time he did it, it would make me gag in sympathy. There was something about the way he clawed at his throat that made me decide I would never ever take pain relief, or pills of any kind. Mr Brawn didn't realise it, but he'd given me the best Anti-Drugs lesson by complete accident. Aged 10, Hannah Fountain once offered me a little blue pill on a Beavers and Guides joint camping trip in the woods not far from where we lived. I refused, and then watched aghast as her and several members of our party took loads of them each in secret. They writhed around on the floor, screaming about being visited by the devil like they were in *The Crucible*. After a swift interrogation by the Brown Owl it was discovered that they'd all been a victim of Blue Smarties and an Overactive Imagination. In comparison, I was such an angel I wouldn't even pretend to smoke the

White Candy Sticks that everybody in the playground rolled around their fingers to look cool. I was a hypochondriac. I just knew that I would be the one child who overdosed the first time they sniffed a Pritt Stick and would go to my grave being known as the troubled kid with an early-onset drugs problem. I'd be the kid with no dad, no prospects and no future – It Was Inevitable, the town would whisper at my funeral.

★ ★ ★

My lower back is hurting because in three days I will turn thirty-one years old.

It's the beginning of June and we're on our way to Niamh's family cottage in Wales. In a complete moment of rare serendipity, all four of us are free to go at the same time, so we've crammed into Niamh's Ford Fiesta and all forgotten to wee before we left.

Mum's contribution to the birthday weekend was to send a tenner towards petrol and a card that still had the fifty-nine pence price sticker on the back. In comparison, for Leanne's nineteenth birthday Mum paid for her to go to Disneyland Paris.

We're only a quarter of the way into the seven-hour journey and already I've begun to drone out the sound of Zachary monologuing. At one point Niamh did an emergency stop when turning into a service station and for three blissfully short minutes Zachary stopped talking whilst we all listened to Niamh trying to educate three teenage boys on why they shouldn't cross a dual-carriageway. It ended with one of them calling Niamh a Boring Old Grandma so I'm fairly certain they'll reoffend. As soon as we're back on the move Zachary strikes up again.

"So, darling Charlie, how do you feel about officially being in your mid-thirties?"

"I'm turning thirty-one, so that's still early thirties."

"No it's not," says Zachary, "Thirty is early thirties, thirty-one to thirty-five is mid thirties, and thirty-six to thirty-nine is late thirties."

"That is utter bullshit, don't listen Charlie!" says Niamh, looking at me in the rearview mirror, "thirty-one is early thirties, you don't hit your mids until you're thirty-three."

"I think Zach's right, you're in your mids baby!" Dylan pokes me in the ribs, teasingly.

"Ow, Dyl get off! You've literally just made that up Zach."

"No, it's Niamh that's making it up. I speak the truth, and only the truth."

"Stop it or I'll pull over and you can all walk."

Zachary turns around from the passenger seat and peers over the top of their designer sunglasses.

"Darling birthday boy, tell us, any new dates or love life titbits?"

"Well it might be nothing, but remember that guy I told you about Niamh, who came into the shop and I sort of broke the card machine and ending up giving him a free book?"

"Oh, the one who you stalked on Instagram."

"I didn't stalk him, but yes, his name is Matthew, and ... well he came into the shop the other day and asked me for a coffee."

Niamh slams on the brakes, her second emergency stop in under twenty minutes.

"Charlie! That's amazing!"

"You don't even drink coffee," muses Dylan.

"And get this, he asked me by saying, 'I bet you get this all the time, but would you like to go for a coffee with me?' ... I never get this all the time, but he thinks I'm one of those people who gets this all the time!"

"Oh he is into you," Zachary accompanies every syllable with a click of their fingers.

"We haven't arranged a time yet, but he gave me his number and we've been texting a bit."

"You never told me this," Dylan says slightly sulkily.

"Well, I didn't want to jinx it by talking about it too soon."

I open my second bag of Percy Pigs, offering one to Dylan, who takes one and uses it as a conch to take over the conversation.

"Speaking of dates, well it wasn't a traditional date, but last night this guy came over from Grindr with his mate and they tied me up and made me wear a blindfold, whilst they both took turns fucking me. It was so hot."

Because my mouth is full of Percy I say absolutely nothing. Nothing at all. It couldn't be, could it?

"Yeah, and don't I know about it," Niamh says, rolling her eyes dramatically, "I had to turn David Attenborough up to maximum volume in the lounge."

The notion that the same penis has been inside both Dylan and me makes me feel really weird, but also strangely excited. I pull at my seatbelt. Dylan touches my arm.

"Oh, and I'm going to meet up with Zachy's friend Idriss, from the engagement party again next week."

"Is that the one who was wearing a boiler suit and a beret?" Niamh asks.

"God no, he was a terrible fucking shag. Three minutes we were in the toilet for, and two of those were spent trying to get twenty bloody buttons undone. No, Idriss was the gorgeous one, turned up a bit late, he was wearing a lovely three-piece suit as he'd come from a wedding reception. This guy, look."

Dylan shows me a picture. I don't recognise him. I was most likely well into my Axel-based meltdown by the time he arrived. In fact, I'd most definitely left.

My best friend's ability to pull two different people on one night is baffling. It's like being on *Mastermind* and your specialist subject is *Eastenders* but you've only ever watched

Coronation Street, yet you're still able to answer with confidence about the private lives of Cat Slater and Alfie Moon between the years of 2002 and 2010. I am envious of his apparent ease when it comes to meeting new people, but this weekend isn't about boys, it's about friendship, and that is a much easier thing to navigate.

"Oh by the way, I bought some weed, I know you've never tried it properly Charlie, but it's your birthday, and you need to properly chill out this weekend," says Zachary waving a bag from the front seat.

Oh fuck. I think of Mr Brawn, addicted to his painkillers. I'm too young to die. I'm not even in my mid-thirties yet.

★ ★ ★

We arrive at our destination, fatigued but happy. We've shared many a weekend here over the course of our friendship – always sponsored by copious amounts of homemade rum punch and gentle arguments about which pathway to take up Snowdon.

The cottage has been left behind in the seventies, but it couldn't be more inviting. There's a circle of mismatched armchairs, piled with knitted cushions and various multicoloured crochet rugs. The stone floor cools the bottom of my bare feet, which dependant on the time of year is either a blessing or a curse. Cobwebs drape over ornate vases and ceramic plates which litter every available surface. It could be something out of a Victorian horror, but its back-to-basics charm is a refreshing change from the pace of modern London.

Dylan lights a fire whilst Niamh mixes Captain Morgan with fresh chunks of pineapple and orange juice. Zachary comes in from the kitchen looking agitated and looms slightly over Niamh.

"I left a bottle of Veuve Clicquot here last time, at the back of a cupboard, and it's gone."

158

"I'm making rum punch aren't I, you don't need any bubbles."

"Well it's just the principle of it."

"Why did you leave it here?" Dylan says as he snaps some more kindling.

"I forgot I had it, but I remembered again on the way down so I was looking forward to drinking it, but some pillager's guzzled it down."

"Oi, that's my family you're talking about." Niamh slices into a lime on the dining room table and a small fountain of juice sprays across the cream-coloured doily decorating its centre.

"Well they can pay for a replacement."

"Drink this and shut your gob."

Niamh hands them a glass and Zachary gulps at least two thirds without stopping. These are always heavy weekends for drinking. There's barely any phone signal in the tiny village, which means we're left with only our conversation as entertainment, which seems to flow when the alcohol is doing the same. I'm glad to be cut off from the world for a bit. I'm still constantly checking my email inbox religiously, but there's not even a hint of George, and I don't want him to dominate the weekend. Last year we'd spoken about him taking me to San Francisco for my next birthday as it would be easier for us to get to. I sigh. My chest hurts. I wonder if I'm going to cry later, but then Niamh passes me a glass and bellows around the house, "Here's to the weekend, you beautiful bunch of lovable disasters!"

★ ★ ★

Zachary joins us once they've finally finished hanging up and steaming their six identical black romper suits, and we sit around the hearth, attacking a tub of hummus with batons of carrot and cucumber, passing around a joint. I watch my

159

friends taking in big, long, deep puffs. I'll go very easy; I've never really done it before.

"Is this how you thought life would be at thirty-one, Charlie?" Niamh asks through mouthfuls of chickpea.

The fire crackles, sending happy shadows dancing across the room.

"I don't know really. I was thinking about that on the way up here. I had ideas of what it might look like to be this age when I was younger, but I can't remember what exactly. I remember thinking it all seemed a bit mythical?"

"Isn't it weird to think that when we were at school, our teachers were probably younger than we are now?" Dylan says, his eyes vaguely glazed over and transfixed by the flames.

"Well do you not remember that lecturer I had, Paul, who taught me business studies?" Zachary asks. "Ghastly little fellow. We went to his twenty-third birthday party at the pub when we were in first year."

I do remember that because Zachary tried to take him home, but then worried they were so drunk they wouldn't be able to get it up and Paul would subsequently fail them on their sexual inexperience on their upcoming module.

"Twenty-pissing-three and teaching us what to do with our lives. I'm nearly a decade older than that and I still don't have a clue, and I'm teaching children!" Niamh swigs from her glass and purses her lips at the sharpness of the citrus. She passes the joint to me. I take a puff and immediately cough.

Zachary leans in to me, "breathe in for longer, babe."

I do and fare slightly better this time. It tastes bitter but feels good.

"Steven called me Daddy in bed the other night, the cheeky sod. I mean, he's older than me! He's the Daddy! He's lucky I love him so I let him off."

Niamh tops them up with more of the rum mixture, her voice softens.

"Anything more from Steven's parents?"

"They sent us a letter saying they enjoyed Steven and me visiting for the weekend, and we shouldn't leave it too long again, but it was strangely formal."

"Nothing about the engagement?"

"Nope . . . A union between two men who love each other seems to be too far fetched for them to understand." Zachary puts the poker down, "It's fine. My dad is just wonderful, and if his parents can't support us then I'm not interested in having them there and spoiling the day."

I'd never really considered how Steven and I share similar relationships with our parents. Both of us feel distant and disengaged with our families – although I've always thought the two of us were lucky to have the support of our partner's folks in lieu of our own. I hadn't heard from George's mum since I last spoke to her, just after George moved. I wonder if she'll wish me a Happy Birthday. Niamh squeezes Zachary's arm.

"We'll be there love, and we're the most important people anyway."

"Are you having any bridesmen?!" Dylan says, winking at Zach.

"No no, we want to keep it simple."

"You never keep anything simple! And I would make an excellent Maid of Honour."

Dylan stands and pretends to prance down an aisle, using an empty bottle of lime cordial to form a bouquet. He's obviously done this in a mirror many times before, but then haven't we all.

"I'm sure you'll all be a part of the day whatever we decide to do – and ignore Steven, we're not doing Cannes. I work in PR in London. We can't afford Cannes, and I know you lot certainly can't afford Cannes and you simply have to be there. I refuse to do it without you all."

I sink further, more comfortably, into my chair, and start to think about how a series of chance encounters have brought us to this very cottage. If I hadn't chosen to study at Bristol; if Dylan hadn't wanted to join the uni paper; if Niamh had picked an all-female hall; if Zachary hadn't gone to that party where we met – I could be sitting in a different cottage, in a different country, with three different people, and I wouldn't be any the wiser. One tiny little choice can make us cross paths with a multitude of people, across an infinite amount of possibilities. I'll never even know what those decisions are that led me to be sitting here, but I quietly thank the brilliant universe that I made them.

* * *

After four pizzas, copious amounts of syrupy cocktails and an ill-advised shot of something labelled Homemade Brew that Niamh found under the stairs, we draw in closer to the fire, our tummies heavy and our hearts full. Zachary wraps a blanket around my legs and snuggles in next to me. More joints have been rolled, and we appear to have one each now.

It might be because my head feels fuzzy or I'm in the relative safety of the middle of absolutely nowhere but I feel so completely at peace that I find myself saying something before my brain can catch up.

"George slept with Axel."

I hadn't expected to mention it this weekend, in fact I had every intention of never telling any of them. Not to protect George, or Axel, but because the crushing shame of it still reared its head whenever I was feeling low. I hope for a second that maybe I didn't say it out loud, but everyone is staring at me with very wide unblinking eyes, so I definitely did.

"What do you mean?" Niamh says so quietly I barely catch it.

"The night of our leaving party ... I came downstairs and George and Axel were ... making love ... against the wall."

162

I've never used the phrase Making Love in my entire life, but for some reason it sounds less violent, less of a betrayal. Niamh's jaw is practically on the floor.

"How?" She says, slightly louder now.

"Well, Axel had him lifted up, and George's legs were around him," I say, my voice pathetically small.

"No, I mean, how could he do that to you?"

Her eyes are so wide I fear they might pop out of her head. Dylan breaks the silence.

"Charlie, are you sure?"

"Well he wouldn't just make it up would he?" Niamh snaps back at him.

Zachary squeezes my knee under the blanket – it makes me jump.

"Why didn't you say anything to us? We sat with you at the coffee shop the next day. You had your suitcase with you!"

"I didn't know what I was doing, my head was a mess."

"That's why you were acting so strangely. We just thought you'd lost the plot; Steven did say to me he thought there was something more going on."

Zach leans forward in their chair, it creaks – the only other sound apart from the crackling of the fire. This has all become far more dramatic than I'd intended it to.

"Well as soon as we get home Axel can fuck right off."

"No Niamh, that's not what I want to happen."

"It's what I want to happen, Charlie. I don't want him in our house pretending to be our friend when he's done something so horrendous to you."

"It's not his fault, George told him we were in an open relationship."

Niamh's eyes grow impossibly wider.

"Were you?"

"No!"

Zachary squeezes my knee harder.

163

"You should have told us darling, we can't be there for you properly if you don't open up. I can't even imagine how difficult that must have been to see."

Dylan seems to be taking this worse than anybody else, he's looking up at the ceiling, saying nothing, avoiding eye contact. It's like George cheated on him too, but in a way, I guess he did, and Dylan has always been protective of me.

"I'd been really hard on him before I went to bed, trying to get him to stop drinking when he was clearly having a lovely time, so I don't know really, I sort of thought I deserved it."

"You've been nothing but an incredible boyfriend to that fucker for years," Niamh says, spitting louder than the fire, "the only thing you deserved was love and kindness and respect and if I ever see him again I'll rip his fucking throat out."

That's absolutely the last rum punch for her tonight.

Zachary fixes me with their best therapist look. "Why would you say you deserved it?"

"I don't know really. I was just clinging on to his coat tails to go to New York, and he was the one making all the money, and you all loved him – my Mum idolised him – and I just felt … lucky to be with him I guess. And thinking about it now, I don't know what I physically brought to the relationship, I was just sort of always … there … so maybe it didn't surprise me that much to see him with Axel. Maybe I expected it?"

"I can't even begin to tell you how incredible you are, Charlie," Dylan says, finally looking over at me. His voice waves with emotion, so much so that it takes me by surprise. "And I know you won't want to hear this but I'm going to tell you anyway – you are an absolute catch. You'd do anything for any one of us, and just because you might not have a high-flying career or a body that's toned to within an inch of your life as you comment so often, it does not mean that you are any less worthy than anybody who does have that. Yes,

164

George is gorgeous and successful, but he had *you*. You helped him get to where he is, and become who he is, because you filled him with so much love and support he was able to be the best version of himself. Do you realise how rare it is to find somebody like that? If he's going to do that to you so easily, then he doesn't deserve to call you his boyfriend. George was the lucky one, not you."

Dylan falls silent again and my eyes are damp. I try to say Thank You but I can't make any sound. If I'd have known that drugs would make people say such nice things about you, and make you feel so warm and whole inside, then I wouldn't have been so scared of them. But maybe that's the weed talking again.

We sit in reflective silence for a while. I don't know what I want to say, and the others seem to be collecting their thoughts. Zachary asks if I want to talk about it properly and I don't want to spoil the night completely so I say No. Eventually, we drain the last of the punch and head to our respective beds. Everybody hugs me goodnight. Their hugs are weighty. I feel very loved. Loved and very, very high.

★ ★ ★

I'm sleeping in the small adjoining guest bedroom, situated in a little cabin which you can only access by walking through the garden. I make my way across the lawn – guided only by the moonlight – the sound of the babbling stream at the edge of the darkness piercing through the otherwise still evening. My socks are damp from the dew on the grass by the time I make it into the room. I lay my head on my pillow and start to try and drift off, but it's too quiet outside and my mind is noisily racing. I imagine the three of them convening for a secret meeting in the kitchen, wondering what to do with me – the poor patient. I knew I shouldn't have said anything.

I'm not sure if I've fallen asleep properly or not, but I'm

165

awoken by a soft knock at the door. I draw my legs into my chest and pull the cover over my head – it's obviously a serial killer – albeit a polite one who announces their arrival. A voice whispers, It's Me. I slide open the latch and Dylan is standing there with a glass of water and a packet of Oreos.

"I thought you might want this – to save the inevitable headache in the morning. And the biscuits are for the munchies."

Seeing the liquid makes me realise I am incredibly thirsty and I gulp it down gratefully. We begin tearing through the wrapper, giggling as we split the cookies up. Dylan sits on the edge of my bed.

"Are you OK?"

I shrug.

"Do you want some company?"

The thought of sharing a bed with someone for the first time in months is so appealing.

I push the covers back, and Dylan slides in beside me. We both stare up at the wooden beams. Dylan breaks the silence.

"Remember when we used to share a bed all the time in first year, after we'd got pissed and didn't want to sleep on our own, God, we were obsessed with each other."

"It was very sweet of us."

"I meant everything that I said earlier, you are a catch."

I'm not sure what to say so I find his hand and intertwine my fingers with his. He reciprocates by nestling his head into my shoulder. He smells of hops and toothpaste and his fingers are cold.

"I've missed you," he says.

"What do you mean?"

"Well, we were so super close, like inseparable and then when you met George it sort of became more and more difficult to spend time with you, properly I mean."

"Oh not this again, you've already told me I spent too much

time with George and forgot about you, and forgot about myself and changed my personality for him, I get it, Dyl."

"No, I don't mean all of that."

"You and I shared a house for basically a decade, Dyl."

"Yeah but anyone can just live together. What I mean is we haven't really hung out together like we used to."

"Well, I dunno what you want me to say to that Dylan, I've been busy, and George was my life."

"I know that, and obviously I'm not jumping for joy that George cheated on you, and this is going to sound weird but, selfishly . . . it's been nice to have you back."

"You're making no sense at all. I haven't gone anywhere, and we haven't hung out any more than when I was with George – in fact it's probably less, since I don't live with you anymore."

"Well, you should still come over whenever, you're always welcome."

"Dylan it's not like you've been sitting around twiddling your thumbs. You're seeing somebody new every five minutes, you've hardly got any time left for me!"

"Why are you being so defensive?"

"I'm not, it's just weird that I told you about George and Axel and suddenly you're being all super friendly."

We're arguing but my hand is still in his.

"Fucking hell, Charlie, I'm just being a friend."

My palm is sweaty, or maybe it's Dylan's palm. I can't tell. Is this the weed doing this?

"It's just been hard, you know, going from thinking you were moving to another country, and dealing with the idea of you not being around, and how much I was going to miss you, and then suddenly you weren't going, but you weren't going to be living with me anymore, and yeah, you're right we don't get to see each other as much as I'm used to, and I know you're dealing with a lot and finding yourself again, but I'm

167

just sad that's all. Jesus, I don't really know what I'm trying to say except I really care about you deeply, I always have done."

"I was trying to figure out what I was supposed to do with my life – I still am! I haven't gone anywhere, I'm right here, Dylan. And I'm sorry if my relationship breaking down had a huge effect on you, but you can blame George for that, not me."

"I'm not blaming you for anything, Charlie."

"Well what's the matter then? What am I supposed to say to all this? That I'm sorry that because of circumstances out of my control we don't hang out as much?! We're getting older Dylan; these things happen to friendships. We aren't still at university."

Dylan's breath is quickening. He shifts in the bed.

"I just want you to be OK because when you're hurting, I'm hurting, and ... ah fuck, fuck, fuck! I have to tell you something, Charlie."

He grips my hand tighter. I'm wondering what he's about to say, when suddenly my breath catches in my throat. What if it's the thing that's been at the back of my head for so long – the thing we didn't act on at university. I could tell we both wanted to and suddenly it was too late because George came along. What if everything that's happened up until now has been for a reason? To lead us to this very moment where we finally re-alise that the answer has been, and was always, meant to be us.

"I slept with Axel," Dylan says, so quietly, gently, I almost think I misheard.

"What?"

"I've had sex with ... Axel. A few times."

My heart skips a beat, and my fingers slip away from his. "I needed to get that off my chest, and I need you to know that of course I wouldn't have done that if I'd have known about George and him."

I swallow the rising vomit to keep it at bay.

168

"Why?"

"Why did I sleep with him?"

"Yes, why."

"It was a drunken thing one night and . . . he's in the room next door to me and we were just horny I guess. And then it just kept happening every so often, but it was just sex . . . you know what it's like."

"No Dylan, I don't. You knew he and George kissed!" I'm shouting now. Louder than I want to.

"I know, but don't be angry with me. I didn't know they'd done more than that, but now that I do, I feel guilty as fuck, and I thought it was best to hear it from me rather than Axel, but trust me I won't be going there again, because I care so mu—"

I cut him off before he can finish.

"But why?"

"I told you it was just a drunken—"

"No. Why do you have to sleep with everything that has a fucking pulse?"

It's out of my mouth before I can stop it. We are both sitting up now, staring into each other's eyes. Those beautiful green eyes. His expression twists from shock into sadness. And not just sadness but deep deep melancholy. He's up and out of bed and before I know it the door is closing and the bed it empty again. It's suddenly freezing. I can't even hear the crickets anymore. It's just silent.

★ ★ ★

The sun is blazing through the net curtain. I didn't sleep for what felt like even five minutes. Constantly tossing and turning, going over the conversation again and again, and then imagining Axel and Dylan against The Wall, and seeing George's expression of ecstasy as he gave in to Axel. Every time I closed my eyes it was burning into my retinas.

169

It's just Niamh and Zachary for breakfast, and later on as we're putting our walking boots on, Zachary says we're to go without Dylan as he's not feeling very well. Niamh shouts up the stairs.

"Lightweight!"

We walk for twelve miles, stopping only for a ploughman's and a pint at a local pub but I leave most of mine untouched. The anxiety spilling over from my comedown is horrendous. Our phones get a burst of signal.

I don't have any messages. Or emails.

The fresh air feels good on my skin. I fill my lungs with the cleaner air.

We talk nonstop – the three of us – about politics and celebrities and funny cat videos and traumatic childhood memories and awkward dates and the last time we cried and the riskiest place we've ever had a wank – Niamh, in the staff room, Zachary, in the toilet of a Russian oligarch's private aeroplane. I miss Dylan. I feel responsible for him not being here.

We arrive back at the cottage, weary and desperately needing more alcohol – But No More Weed I cry out internally. Zachary has picked up some wine and fresh sea bass from the fishmongers. We're dining al fresco tonight, they say.

Niamh and I lay the table in the garden. It's my birthday tomorrow. Everybody I know who has reached this age tells me tales of finding themselves and suddenly not giving a shit about anything anymore, and how freeing and adult you feel the more into your thirties you get. I wonder if that all suddenly happens at the stroke of midnight. Or whether I'm the exception to that rule and I'll just turn into a pumpkin and slowly rot. Nobody tells you that actually when you're in your thirties you can still upset your best friend and feel useless about pretty much everything else.

When the food is ready I hardly eat it, but nobody seems to notice because Zachary is on top form – bantering back and forth with Niamh like they're a comedy double act. Niamh clutches her stomach, laughing so hard that I can see right down the back of her throat. I'm glad to have them here, to lighten the mood. Dylan joined us as we were eating dessert, and I try in vain to catch his eye but he won't look at me. I think back to what I said last night, and although it was harsh, it's definitely rooted in some truth. He does prioritise sex above everything else. I wonder if he hates me or himself more.

Later, when Dylan is washing up and I am on drying duty, I take the opportunity to ask him if he's feeling better. I touch his back and he flinches away from me, barely grunting back a response.

I drink more and more wine. We have to go to the local pub and beg them to sell us a couple of bottles because the shops are shut and even if they weren't, we're all over the limit to drive to them anyway. I drink and drink until I can't make out anyone's face any more, only shapes. I'm laughing but I don't know if anybody has said anything funny, and the room is spinning. I fall into the table, and I laugh and laugh but then suddenly everyone is making a fuss of me and I realise that I've put my hand into the fire by accident. It's throbbing, but Dylan is running it under the cold tap: well, I think it's Dylan. And then I'm being carried by what feels like hundreds of hands and arms and I can see the full moon and all of the stars above me, and then I wake up with my hand wrapped in a tea towel and realise that I'm now thirty-one.

★ ★ ★

Nobody else is up this early, so I walk back down to the pub. It's not open but I sit outside on a bench and log on to their Wi-Fi, my breath visible in little clouds. There's a gentle rumbling of birthday posts on a few Instagram stories, and Steven has put a photo of me on Facebook from about three years ago looking horrendous. It's an alright picture of him though. I hide it from my wall. There's nothing from Mum yet, but a voicemail from Gran saying Many Happy Returns and asking me when I'm visiting next; she sounds very weak and confused. I can hear Leanne in the background asking for a tenner and Gran saying there's money in her purse. The side of my hand stings. I feel stupid for being out of control last night. Thirty-one and still none the wiser.

An email pings. My stomach churns. It's from him. I open it already knowing that this could completely ruin or make my day. It reads:

'Hey Charlie ... well not so good really.
How're you? Oh, and happy birthday x

There is a single kiss at the end. I stare at that x for twenty minutes, whilst intermittently pressing down on my wounded hand and ignoring the sharp ache, until the skin becomes raw and agitated.

CHAPTER FOURTEEN

I'm dancing in the shower to a song by the Pussy Cat Dolls because today will mark the fifth time Matthew Constantino and I have had coffee together during our own Private Book Group. The last two meetings involved more cocktails and snogging and less about the latest Bernardine Evaristo but really it's working out fine for me.

Already the pavements are scalding hot and the leaves on the trees are barely moving. We're meeting in Battersea Park for a picnic. I spent an agonising thirty minutes in Marks and Spencer's spending money I don't have on artisan sausage rolls and crumble-topped pork pies and two little bottles of champagne. I boosted my feast with a packet of crisps that have been at the back of the cupboard in our kitchen for the past three weeks and a jar of chutney in the fridge that nobody seems to have touched. Laden with a blanket and a basket – well, a Bag for Life, I'm heading for my Prince Charming in My Sunday Best.

Matthew is an events planner. He does weddings and birthdays. He sends me pictures of him looking frazzled – but still handsome – holding clipboards and seating charts and veils in dining rooms of stately homes. He quotes funny things

Bridezillas and nightmare grooms have said to him, and even sent me a voice recording of a woman yelling at her husband-to-be that the day was ruined because he'd forgotten his black socks. Matthew jumped to the rescue and gave him the pair off his feet – despite how easily his ankles get cold. He is a modern-day Gandhi.

This is the first time we're meeting during the day because he's always so busy. I've told everyone how well it's going. I even told Farrah and she nodded and said she recognised him from coming into the shop. I haven't told Dylan though, and that feels completely bizarre. Things are still strained between us and I want to forgive him, I do, but I can't scratch the image of him and Axel out of my mind.

We've arranged to rendezvous by the little pagoda in the park on the river front at 1 pm. It's 12 pm and I'm already here. Better to be early and have time to breathe, mop the brow and check the pits. I sit and re-read one of my favourite books, *A Little Life* by Hanya Yanagihara, because despite how traumatic life can be, it's never going to be as rough as what the characters in this book go through. I let what little breeze there is flit the pages from one to the next.

I dislike having to stop halfway through a chapter, so when it gets close to our meeting time I continually scan the last paragraph of the chapter I'm on over and over again. I want him to arrive whilst I'm reading. It makes me look intelligent. I place my ankles together. I'm feeling very *Little House on the Prairie* and loving it. Peripherally I can see him approaching but I keep my head in the pages and hope my posture looks nonchalant and alluring.

He greets me with a polite but gentle kiss on the cheek and we immediately fall into book talk. I've spread the blanket on the grass, slightly away from the path so we have some privacy. We discuss female protagonists in literature, and I open the bottles of fizz. He declines my offer of a straw – We Must Do Our Bit to Save the Planet – and we drink straight from the neck instead. A tiny bit comes out of my nose after the first swig, but luckily he doesn't see. He's deep in discussion.

"Do you think the Brontë sisters would be pleased with the idea that their words are still in circulation today, being adapted by all and sundry, or would they be aghast at the idea?" he says whilst removing his sandals. "You often wonder if these authors really knew the impact their body of work would have. Shakespeare would be a bloody multi-billionaire if he were still alive."

His toes accidentally touch the sole of my trainer. I hastily take them off in case he brushes against me again. I've not read any Shakespeare since school and, keen to not unmask my unintelligence, I decide to hastily change the subject.

"Did you watch any of the adaptation of *His Dark Materials* on the BBC?"

"No," he picks at the skin of a cherry tomato, "I prefer to create my own worlds from the page rather than have them painted for me."

I never saw it either. I've been too busy rewatching *Selling Sunset* on Netflix, dreaming of one day owning a multimillion-dollar property on the Sunset Strip. I already know Matthew wouldn't watch anything so brilliantly trashy. It's a show that Dylan and I would always text about, but since my birthday we've not spoken. Niamh's overwhelmed at work with everything that's going on with this parent complaint, and Zachary is well and truly in the throes of wedding planning – so I've felt very much separated from my friends lately, hence spending so much time with Matthew.

How do people get to sound as intelligent as Matthew? It's as though everything that comes out of his mouth is a piece of poetry. I fall ever so slightly, a little – but not very much – in love with him.

After we've finished eating, we stroll along the Thames and cross the water to take a look around the Tate Britain. At one point we're standing so close to a portrait that I think we might hold hands.

"Look at that brush work. It's just exquisite. So much power in one stroke."

I make a wordless noise of agreement. This continues for the next forty minutes. Every painting starts to look the same, but he's enjoying them so I am too. Dylan's voice looms in my head – You Only Liked Things That George Liked – but this is different, Matthew is teaching me about art, and it's interesting to have discussions on things I know nothing about – every day is a school day after all.

There's a special exhibition on Van Gough. The only thing I know about him is that he went mad and cut his ear off. I can relate.

The gallery is busy and for a while we are separated by a large throng of tourists, noisily exclaiming what I think might be joy at anything in their path. One girl stops briefly to take a picture of me staring at a painting. I have become the art.

When I eventually catch up with Matthew he looks weary.

"I find Van Gough's work always makes me emotional. I can feel his pain seeping off the canvas."

I think he's going to cry. A recorded announcement tells us that closing time is in half an hour. Matthew touches my shoulder gently. His hands strong yet delicate all at once.

"I'm just going to have a quiet moment of reflection, do you mind? I'll meet you in the gift shop."

The shop is overpriced. I buy Matthew a fridge magnet with Sunflowers on for £12.99. I agonise over my purchase for a good four minutes afterwards, and I'm just about to return it to the cashier when he appears, his eyes red. I think of suggesting that we find a nice pub, so we can while away the last few hours of our glorious Sunday, but his hand is on my shoulder again.

"Do you mind if we call it a day? That just bought up a lot of unexplored feelings in there for me, and I'm afraid I won't be good company for the rest of the evening. Let's do dinner one night next week instead? I don't have any plans for Wednesday?"

Wednesday is the only night I had made a tentative plan to see Niamh and Zachary at the pub, with a strong chance that Dylan would be there too. It's the only night I'm busy.

"Yeah! Sounds great! I'm free on Wednesday!"

"Great, OK we'll text. Sorry to just . . . I must seem mad," he gestures to his puffy eyes.

"Not at all, I'm pretty tired to be honest."

I force a yawn but it doesn't come. Matthew hugs me tightly. His mouth is close to my ear.

"I adore spending time with you."

He kisses me, gently at first and then more passionately. I am painfully aware that we are directly in front of the commemorative tea-towels and somebody might wish to browse, but he doesn't show any sign of letting off. I think I hear the sound of somebody tutting and I want Matthew to stop but I don't want to come across as fearful. I wish we were doing this back at his house, comfortable and safe in each other's arms. Eventually he pulls away. He touches my cheek and leaves. I want to say that we're definitely heading towards the same tube but he seems to be in a hurry and I rasp a quiet Bye! I look around but nobody is in the shop. Even the person behind the counter isn't there. I touch my lips and feel the sheen of Matthew's lip balm on mine. The fridge magnet remains dormant, burning a hole in my pocket.

* * *

177

Matthew texts on Wednesday morning and asks if we can rain check as something has come up. The clouds are grey and it starts to pour.

I'd already texted Niamh to say I couldn't see her in the end. She'd replied saying it wasn't an issue and they'd miss me being absolutely no use at the pub quiz. I could just as easily now reply and say I Can Come! But something stops me. I read the email from George again. I should reply to that soon, but not tonight.

★ ★ ★

Matthew sends me at least twenty texts a day now. Niamh says I should ghost him, but after Otis did that to me I don't really want to be the perpetrator of something so cruel. Plus he knows where I work so I wouldn't be that invisible. The mental health of his step father is becoming progressively worrying and I get a phone call from Matthew at 2 am one morning saying that he hasn't heard from him all day, and the last text he received from him just said, I'm Sorry.

I take an Uber over to his flat and sit with him until the police telephone in the morning to say they've found his step father in his garage. He'd connected the exhaust pipe to his window. An image of him sat alone in the car rolls around my head, even though I don't know what he looks like. I call in sick and spend the day with Matthew who intermittently sobs and shouts at his mum on the phone, at me, and at the world.

A week later he asks me if I'll go to the funeral with him and I feel compelled to say yes. I've only ever been to one before, and that was Grandad's. Matthew clutches my hand through the entire service and it feels weird for a number of reasons; one, I have no idea if two men are even allowed to hold hands in a church and two, I only started going on dates with this guy a month ago, and here I am literally holding him upright through one of the most traumatic events a person can go through. He introduces me as My Charlie to all of his family and I dutifully smile and nod like a First Lady through a multitude of conversations with various aunts and cousins. It's an out of body experience.

For a moment, towards the end of the wake, I imagine what George would think if he could see me now. I'd always sketched myself by his side supporting him through various family bereavements, and now I would never be a part of any of that. Somebody else would stroke his hair, and wipe his tears, and tuck him into bed afterwards. I suppose if Gran died tomorrow then I could ask Matthew to repay the favour for me, but I already know I wouldn't do that. He would feel like an imposter.

I shuffle around the village hall, collecting paper plates and discarding stale sandwiches into black bin liners. Matthew's mum, Debbie, has thanked me a thousand times already, but I don't know what else to do. I'm sure the step father is looking down from Heaven at his wife wailing on my shoulder and is thinking, Who the Fuck is That Guy? Also, this smart black shirt that I borrowed from Zachary is way too tight – the last mushroom vol au vent was absolutely one too many.

In the cab on the way back to London, Matthew asks me if I can give him some space tonight – he wants to be in the flat on his own to gather his thoughts. I agree and he jumps out a couple of roads before his as he Needs the Air. He doesn't give me any money towards the journey. This entire day has cost me nearly sixty quid on travel alone, but he's a grieving man so I can't ask him for anything.

I don't hear from Matthew for the next few days. Eventually, a week, later he messages to say he can't commit himself to anyone right now, and I should forget about him and move on. It's abrupt, and I can't quite work out if I'm more disappointed or angry.

I send a few messages to make sure he's OK in the

upcoming months but Zachary says he can tell I've been blocked on WhatsApp.

I know they say that people come in and out of your lives for a reason, but who knew you could be a Rent-A-Boyfriend for funerals?

CHAPTER FIFTEEN

We're having a crisis meeting In Nando's. Niamh has poured so much hot sauce onto some chicken legs that I'm afraid she's purposely trying to self harm.

"Can you believe it? Can you abso-fucking-lutely believe the sheer cheek of it? Those miserable bastards."

Niamh plucks at the meat with her fingers, playing with the bones and then biting into the flesh. I'm genuinely frightened.

After that one parent officially complained about Niamh's LGBTQ+ assembly a few months ago, they've managed to rally more and more mums and dads to make a stand, and now they've all signed a ridiculous letter to demand the school has Niamh fired.

The meat in my burger is spicy but it leaves a sour taste in my mouth. Zachary spears a single grain of rice with their fork.

"Perhaps if I'd have been 'exposed' to LGBTQ relationships then I wouldn't have spent every lunch break at primary school feigning illness so that I could go home and escape the relentless homophobic bullying I received every playtime."

"Zach, I was exactly the same, I mean, I made my own

sick to avoid having to go in. That's how desperate I was to protect myself," I say, wondering if Grandad would still find that story funny now.

Dylan almost leaps out of his chair; it's the first time I've seen him since our argument in the cottage, but it appears that we've come together for Niamh and put that behind us, for now. There's definitely a different vibe between us though – our usual tactile nature replaced with an apology every time we so much as brush against each other.

"Everyone on the playground used to tell me I was gay, but I didn't even know what that was! Imagine if a teacher had spoken to us the way that you did Niamh and just casually let us know that it was OK to be different. Maybe now we wouldn't be continually dealing with the shame of burying our feelings so fucking deeply three decades later."

Niamh's cheeks are growing steadily more rouged, and I don't know if it's the anger, red wine, peri-peri or a combination of all three.

"What are we going to do about it?" Zachary asks.

"They want to picket the bloody playground every evening if the school doesn't get rid of me. It's not fair, none of this is fair."

Niamh looks like she might cry and the waitress is about to come over to ask how our food is but I give her a thumbs up and wave her away to save the awkwardness.

"I just remembered, this little boy came up to me at the end and said I reminded him of one of his dads and he hugged me, and if you don't have assemblies like that where queer people can be visible then it's only going to make children like him feel as though his family is abnormal."

Dylan sighs, sombrely.

"It feels like the day after Brexit again. I'm constantly surprised that we keep losing the battle."

This is the first time I've had alcohol in a Nando's and the rosé is going to my head quicker than the garlic bread is going into my belly.

"We're preaching to the choir here, my loves. We all feel exactly the same about it. What did your headteacher say?" Zachary asks between mouthfuls of halloumi.

"That he's on my side, they can't physically get rid of me for something like that, but it puts him in an awkward position. Parents rule that school by vigilante committee."

I put down my corn on the cob.

"I know what we need to do, Niamh."

★ ★ ★

We look a bit like some weird sort of homosexual *Brady Bunch* straight off the set of the movie *Pride*. A collective of the not weird – just wonderful. Niamh wrote to every single parent who wanted to lynch her and invited them to come into school to meet her and us. 'Us' being Zachary, a happy, successful public relations expert with a well-respected lawyer fiancé; Dylan, a hard-working NHS nurse; and me.

Me, a-fully-functioning-break-up-surviving-working-hard-to-pay-the-bills-like-everyone-else-but-always-trying-to-keep-smiling-constantly-riddled-with-anxiety-about-not-achieving-enough-but-spending-three-hours-a-day-watching-reality-TV cisgender male who just happens to fancy men, and my same-sex attraction and gender identity has absolutely no affect on my work ethic or decision-making or cooking preference or my ability to eat a five-pack of Taste the Difference white chocolate and raspberry cookies in one sitting or that just like straight people I worry I have absolutely no purpose on this planet and I'm just ticking along and in decades to come anything of note I've achieved won't even make the history books because the whole planet will have eaten itself and burst into flames and even David Attenborough won't have saved us, because deep down we're all the same greedy-single-plastic-using

183

neanderthals no matter who we want to lay our head next to at night.

I won't say all that though – it's a bit of a mouthful.

I'm here as a presence, so these parents can see we exist. So Niamh is not alone.

* * *

A smattering of people arrive. They look a bit angry and a bit tired, which coincidentally is exactly how we feel.

The hall is set out with a few tables and chairs. Essentially we're going to be doing the most awkward speed-dating session in existence, and everybody is guaranteed *not* to get a Happy Ending. My idea was that we'll sit face to face with a parent and just talk to them. Unthreatening. Casual. Utterly terrifying.

Niamh thanks people for coming and explains how the hour is going to work and then we're being told to find a table and sit down opposite somebody we've never met before. Kayo from the last assembly is also here, and Coco, this time with her girlfriend Tina, and even Axel has turned up. Him coming was my idea. These parents should see that it's not just in England that we have queer people, but heaven forbid they have them in America too! The troops have well and truly been rallied.

A man hesitantly sits down opposite me. He is wearing a white shirt with little tiny squares on – like a maths exercise book – and a purple tie that's not quite long enough. He looks at me and I look at him. It's as though we are the leaders of North and South Korea meeting for the first time. I shuffle in my chair, then smile. He politely returns the gesture. Niamh announces that we are to introduce ourselves and get to know each other. There's No Hidden Agenda – she keeps saying. We have twenty minutes.

I extend my hand.

"Hello, I'm Charlie."

"Bert."

He reciprocates with his hand. Briefly.

"Oh, is that short for Robert?"

"No."

Everyone else around us seems to be chatting – animatedly even – trust me to get the least enthusiastic partner in the room.

"It's short for Betrand."

"Oh, that's an unusual name. I've never met a Betrand before."

"Well now you have."

He says this with such a straight face that I can't judge his tone. My palms are sweaty.

"I don't really know why I've come here. I thought we'd be talking to Miss McCormack ..."

It takes me a second to realise he means Niamh. I forget my friend has a second name and is seen differently by these people. To them she's a teacher, not a real life human.

"Ah right ... I'm sure she'll say something later."

"So you're a mate of hers?"

He says the word Mate as though it's dirty. I am guilty by association.

"Yes. We went to university together."

Bertrand doesn't appear to have anything to say to this, so I fill the gap with inane details about what we did with our weekends and our favourite chicken shop on a night out, and the time I accidentally printed an interview in the uni paper with somebody called Mr Tuck, but somehow it had changed to Mr Fuck and my editor was a complete stoner and didn't read it properly. I'm trying to normalise my life for him, but Bertrand's eyes have glazed. I imagine everyone else having life-changing debates. My friends sitting around their tables – acting like the United Nations – making a difference, and here I am talking about Mr Fuck.

Bertrand breaks his silence.

"So you're . . . ?"

This hangs in the air. I know what he's asking but I'm not a sentence-finisher. I hate sentence finishers. Actually, George was one of those. I let him get away with it much more than I should. Bertrand looks at the floor.

"I'm . . . what?"

His gaze drifts to almost every single inch of the room – his soul squeezing into the smallest of cracks. Something suddenly lights a fire under him.

"Look, I know what you are and what this is all about and I don't like it. My daughter is ten, she doesn't need to hear about what you lot get up to. She's a child."

My heart is thumping. It's as though the entire room can hear it. The table is vibrating with the pounding of my nerves. I wish I had Niamh's calm reason, or Zachary's quick wit, or Dylan's charm but I don't. I just have shame. And a dry mouth. I find myself somehow muttering, I'm Sorry. And I'm saying it again and again and again to him. I'm apologising to this man that I've never met, because he's telling me his ten-year-old daughter doesn't want to know about my existence and he looks angry and all I can think to say is, Sorry. There's a voice in my head screaming – really screaming – at me, because it knows I should be saying something else but all the words are jumbled and this man has made me feel so small, so tiny and pathetic that my legs are trembling.

"So if I'm supposed to sit here and listen to you telling me that ten is the right age for a girl to hear about a bunch of men sticking their dicks inside each other then you want to have a word with yourself mate, because it's paedophilic is what it is, and you know it is too."

"It's not . . . I'm not . . ." I stumble.

I want to ask him if he knows what Niamh was talking about in her assembly, and how powerful her words were, and what it would have meant to me at the age of ten hearing that I wasn't abnormal, but I'm gasping for air like a goldfish in a thimble of water.

"It is mate. And I'm here to send a clear message that we don't want this sort of thing in our school. How dare you spread this to these impressionable kids when they're in a safe space."

Each time he calls me Mate, it's like a blow straight to my ribs. I'm trying not to be winded, but it's hard.

Niamh looks over and smiles at me. The panic in my eyes must be apparent. She starts to stride over to me but for some reason I shake my head and she halts. I can't be saved. I have to get through this on my own. I take a long sip of water. Bertrand is saying something but I can't make out any words. The wall is going up. The wall that started construction in primary school when those boys called me 'Lezzie', and the wall that gained a few bricks every time my mum ignored me, and the wall that covered itself in concrete after my grandad died, and the wall that has stood, weathered and worn even though it's been pelted with words and shit and shame and guilt and been kicked by people who I love and who I thought loved me, and even though I've never made it to the top of the wall suddenly I want to climb it – I want to climb it so desperately but I'm suddenly aware of Dylan's voice, and it's rising above the others. He's standing up and there's a lady opposite him with short brown hair and glasses; I recognise her as the woman who Niamh pointed out as making the original complaint, and she's shaking her head as a torrent of words are pouring out of Dylan's brilliant mouth towards her:

"I'm tired of saying sorry. I'm so tired of saying sorry. I am a person. A human being with feelings and I should not have to justify my place in this world. Your son is eleven and he is in-quisitive and hungry for answers and he doesn't know who he is yet – even I don't really know who I am yet – but it's OK for him to see that he has options. He can be anything he wants to be and he should have your unwavering support because he is not only your son, but like me he is a human being, and one day it might be your son standing on a stage and telling a group of children that he has been classed as Different by society, and you will want him to feel good about saying that. He should be proud of who he is, and you should be proud of who he is, because the world is shitty enough already, and life is short, but also if you're not happy then it can be exhaustingly long and tiresome. When I came out to my dad, he couldn't look at me for months, he was so ashamed and now, all these years later he's come to his senses but it's too late for us – he and I will never be the same, because he's hurt me too much. He took so long to see that the person behind the news was still his son. His own flesh and blood. So, please, I beg of you to take your archaic views and educate yourself, because the world is still spinning with all of us on it, and people like me? I'm not going anywhere."

He pushes his chair back and the scrape of it on the wood reverberates around the hall which feels instantaneously cavernous. There's no sound except the click clack click clack of his shoes and the door slamming, and then Dylan is gone. The lady with brown hair takes a tissue out of her handbag and blows her nose. Niamh goes over to her and everybody else resumes talking.

I look at Bertrand.

He looks at me.

"Are you lot always that dramatic?"

"Please would you mind not referring to being gay as You Lot. I am my own individual person, as is Dylan."

"So you know who that little Queen was then . . ."

My face is hot.

"Flouncing out of here like that. That's the way to solve an argument isn't it – running away. How very adult . . ."

188

A tiny bead of sweat drops into my eye and it stings. It really stings.

"And that's what I'm supposed to be teaching my daughter is it? That if you don't get your own way then you make some big dramatic scene and storm out?"

"Do you understand how it feels to be told that you aren't allowed to be yourself?"

"And do you understand that you don't have to be gay and rub our noses in your business."

Dylan's outburst fuels me, words are tumbling out without filter.

"I didn't choose to be gay. I wouldn't ask for all this pain, and constant fighting to be heard. I wouldn't wish that on anyone. I was born and for some reason, whatever reason, I happen to be attracted to the same sex, and do you know something? I wouldn't change that for the world. I have a community, and I have friends who love me, and I get to be a part of something that makes me proud. I am so glad to be different. And if you could wave a magic wand tomorrow and turn me straight I'd say no. Absolutely not. Because I have tolerance, and acceptance and understanding and compassion and I am so thankful to have those things, because if I have children those are the qualities that I want them to eat and breathe everyday. I won't teach them hate. I won't. We are extending a hand of understanding here, and you are showing nothing but hatred, and that is a very lonely place to find yourself in. I hope your daughter brings you joy, and I hope she is successful and admired and loved, but that starts with you. And if she just so happens to be a little bit like me, then you're going to lose her one day if you can't be open to difference. Difference is a word. We invented it. We chose it. Just like you can choose your reactions. We don't want much. Just understanding. That's all anybody ever wants."

My voice hasn't raised once. I am calm. I don't recognise

myself. Bertrand is staring at me – his expression one I can't pinpoint. Is he going to cry? Or shout? He rubs his shoulder and goes to speak but Niamh claps her hands loudly and asks us all if we can reconvene. The lady with the brown hair is sobbing, and another woman is comforting her. Zachary looks beaten, Axel is rubbing his forehead, Kayo's eyes look sore. We're tired of fighting. I'm tired of fighting.

★ ★ ★

We've finished stacking the chairs and the hall is spookily empty. Zachary has gone to look for Dylan, outside. Niamh is in a conversation with her headmaster. It looks intense.

The evening became quite heated in the end. After we all came back together to talk as a group it descended into madness. A cacophony of voices in complete disharmony. I didn't have anything else to add to the mix. I felt happy with what I'd said to Bertrand, and when it was time for everyone to leave I made a point of saying goodbye and shaking his hand. This wasn't quite the peace talk that we'd had in mind, and part of me feels guilty for suggesting it, but surely making a bit of noise has done something – even if it's only made one parent feel differently. Niamh's body language tells me otherwise.

Axel wanders over with a black liner full of paper cups.

"The Brits are strong willed aren't they? Jesus that was quite something."

He puts the bag down and hoiks himself up onto a tower of six stacked chairs, something that I've never been cool or agile enough to do, and offers me a chewing gum. I take a piece.

"Is it like that in America?"

"It's worse. We have guns, remember?"

"Were you bullied?" I say, through a mouthful of spearmint.

"Nah not really, maybe I got Faggot every now and then, but I did cross country and stuff so I didn't really get that much shit because I was sporty."

Of course he fucking didn't. Nobody ever dishes it out to the face of an angel. I suspect most of the straight boys wanted a go too.

"But home was a different matter . . ."

"What do you mean?"

"Well, when my parents caught me frenching with my study bud Luca after school one day, they kicked me out, so I lived with my aunt for a bit and then when I was old enough I got as far away from them as I could."

"Where did you go?"

"New York. Somewhere that wasn't a small town with stupid backwards views."

He hops off of the chairs and drags the rubbish outside through the fire exit. Just before he gets to the door he turns to me.

"This was a really good idea of yours, Charlie. I know it got a bit wild, but I'm gonna bet that at least one parent here tonight is going to think differently about us now. And it was a nice thing to do for Niamh, to come out here and support her like that. You're a good friend, Charlie."

I can't help but smile. Who'd have thought this man would ever make me do that. He holds the door open and I see Dylan, smoking by the little bicycle shed, how cliché. He looks pained and restless and heavy. I ache for him.

Zachary appears and says they're jumping in an Uber to Soho with Dylan, but it's a Tuesday and even though I don't have work tomorrow I still feel weird about going out on a School Night. I decide to head home. Niamh and the head-master are still going at it over something so I gently wave goodbye and leave. I'll call her tomorrow. I text Dylan saying, You Were Amazing Tonight. Followed by, And I'm Sorry.

On the bus on the way home I listen to Girls Aloud. I play 'Biology' on repeat.

CHAPTER SIXTEEN

The weeks seem to be blurring into one long stretch of nothing at the moment, and I somehow manage to turn up to work on my day off. We've just had a delivery come in so Noma is glad of the help, and I'm desperate for a little bit of overtime.

"You've been a bit quiet recently, Charlie. Is everything OK?"

Noma is piling books onto shelves in the stock room whilst I scan the new barcodes into the system.

"Me? I'm fine. I've just got lots of things going on."

"Right, OK."

A silence envelops us. There's a different kind of quietness to a bookshop in the morning: it's comforting, still. You can almost hear the buzz from the pages of books wishing deeply to be selected by browsing customers. Pick Me they seem to say, like expectant puppies in a dog home. The store room is even quieter. Just the soft pat of books as we pile them up, or the bleep of my scanner, the only real continued sound is Noma's breathing. Sturdy, dependable.

"I've got a little bit of news actually."

She's either leaving or dying. Nobody ever follows a sentence like that with good news.

"I'm pregnant."

I'm not sure I even knew she was seeing somebody so soon after the divorce, so it's justified that I greet this by dropping a box of books and covering my mouth with my hand.

"Who's the father?"

Not quite the response Noma was probably looking for.

"Well, my husband, I hope."

"But I thought—"

"That we were getting divorced? I know, but just before it was nearly finalised we had a bit of a night together to say goodbye and somehow we ended up in bed, and well, now we're not getting divorced and we're having a baby."

I will never understand straight people, but it's somewhat refreshing to know they're just as baffled when it comes to love and relationships.

"That's wonderful news, it really is."

I'm not sure if it's appropriate to hug your boss, but I find myself drawn to embracing her and we even have a moment where I awkwardly brush her stomach and say Hello Baby in a high-pitched squawk. I immediately apologise.

"When I go on maternity, Lana is going to step up to cover me as store manager, but I reckon you'd be a good shout to cover Lana's senior position."

I go silent. Now I'm aware of how loud my breath is. Raspy, not dependable.

"Only if you'd want to, that is. Most people here are part time, and Farrah wouldn't want the responsibility alongside her studies, and I don't think I'd trust Tim to not burn the place down."

"I'd love that. I really would, I'd love that."

"You'd have to interview for it with someone from head office, and I know you haven't been here too long, but I'd put in a really good word for you obviously, and I'm fully intending on coming back, so Lana would go back to her position when I do, but I think it would be good for you."

193

For the first time, in a very long time, I feel proud. Of myself. I smile and look down and we carry on unloading boxes. Noma tells me not to mention it to anybody else yet, and jokes that I can thank her by finally giving her the recipe for those vegan brownies as she's already getting cravings. Sorry unborn baby, but I can't lie to you too.

I finish helping a couple of hours later and as I'd thought I was supposed to be working all day I spend the afternoon walking through London and looking up. It's so easy to keep your head down when you're negotiating the streets, but when you've got nowhere in particular to be then it's a treat to cast your eyes upwards and see bits of the city that you normally miss; turrets and awnings and blue historical plaques and carvings and signs and birds and people cooking in windows and smoking out of windows and laughing in windows. I picture myself as the supervisor of a busy central London bookshop. A shop which I've wanted to work in for as long as I can remember. This is the first potential promotion I've ever had.

I know a few weeks ago my instinct would have been to call George and tell him the good news, and then I'd face that soul-crushing realisation that he's not that person that I call with good news anymore. This time though there's only one person I want to tell.

★ ★ ★

"You've rung me eighteen times so if you're not dying or already dead then I'm going to be pissed off. I'm trying to watch *Queer Eye*."

"Dylan, we haven't spoken for weeks, and now I don't even know what we're not speaking about and this is absolutely ridiculous and I want to see you, so can I come over?"

Dylan clears his throat.

"You missed something extremely vital out of what you just said."

"I'll bring pizza?"

"Good. Hurry up, I'm only on episode one of the new series."

I order a Veggie Supreme to arrive at the same time as I will and practically skip all the way.

★ ★ ★

We're on our old sides of the sofa in the living room.

"I really wouldn't have slept with Axel if I'd known what had happened. You didn't say anything, so how was I supposed to know?"

"Well, George did tell you that he kissed him, so you've got to cut me a bit of slack here too."

We agree that we've both not treated each other particularly well recently and maintain that the next month is going to be dedicated to a bit more self care alongside each other. The mozzarella from the pizza burns the roof of my mouth. Dylan gives me his glass of cider to cool it down.

"You were pretty cool at that assembly."

"I didn't feel cool. I think it was everything I'd ever wanted to say to my dad. It just came pouring out of me."

"Well, you inspired me."

"I don't really want to think about my dad."

Dylan takes a bite of pizza, then puts it down, wiping his hands on a piece of paper towel.

"I've been sleeping with a lot of people recently, Charlie."

The change of subject takes me by surprise.

"How many?"

"I don't know, I haven't kept count. I think you're right. I think I've got a bit of a problem."

I look at my friend. I wonder who he becomes when he's in the throes of passion. It makes me think how odd it is that we give ourselves over to people in order to have sex with them, and that feels like the most private thing you can do, but really it's just surface-level privacy.

"Do you want to talk about it?"

"Not really. I guess acknowledging it is a starting point though, right?"

I nod.

"Is Axel upstairs?"

"Yeah but he always has his headphones in. I didn't realise but he's a massive gamer. He's up there for hours. I barely see him now, which is good because I can't really look him in the eyes."

"Is he good?"

"At games? How should I know?"

I swallow some more cider, my mouth still irritated.

"No I mean, was Axel good when you two ..."

It takes a few moments for Dylan to catch up.

"Don't ask me that."

"Why?"

"Just don't. Don't do it to yourself."

"Oh God, he was good wasn't he?"

"Charlie, stop it."

We sit quietly, watching Antoni teach someone how to make a simple sandwich whilst Jeremiah furnishes and renovates an entire house.

"Should I be worried?" I say, picking at a piece of red pepper.

"About what?"

"You."

"Maybe. I don't know. Lately I always feel like shit afterwards."

"Really? Why?"

"It's a self loathing thing I think. Or some sort of internalised shame."

"About being gay?"

"I don't know. Maybe. Might be about being a slut too. Society doesn't exactly look kindly on those who sleep around."

196

"Since when have you ever cared about what society thinks?"

"Well, sleeping around is fun when you're in your twenties ..."

"I wouldn't know," I say, jokingly.

"Well, it is, but it's not really a very adult thing to do."

"Maybe just ... I don't know ... cool it down for a bit. Next time you're feeling horny, just have a wank. It's much quicker and you don't feel half as shit. Then call me and we'll hang out."

"Ring you after I've had a wank? Bit weird."

"Dyl, in this house I heard and saw it all."

We both laugh, and then sit in comfortable-friend silence for a few minutes.

"Do you ever feel a bit sad about missing out on all that shagging around that you could have done at uni, or when we first moved to London?"

I look at The Wall.

"Erm, I guess I don't have anything to compare it to. And it's not like I'm going to go out and do all that now."

"Why not?"

"You just said yourself it's not a very adult thing to do!"

"Yeah, but everyone's got to experience it at one point or another. It's a rite of passage."

"I just don't feel ... sexual at the moment I guess."

"Did you sleep with that lunatic who took you to the funeral and then ghosted you?"

"Oh Matthew? Jesus, I'd rather forget about him, but we did bits here and there but nothing like all the way."

"So you haven't had penetrative sex since George?"

I'm about to lie and say no, but it feels like now is the time to stop telling little white lies to my friends to save face. So I tell him all about being tied up by Headless Torso, and he screams a little gay scream and then shows me the guy's profile

197

on Grindr, and it turns out it is exactly the same person, and we laugh hysterically about our shared experience, and he calls us Bonking Brothers, which is ridiculous but also fun and stupid and makes me feel closer to him than ever.

After we've finished eating I tell Dylan about the potential maternity cover at work, and he's genuinely delighted for me.

"Oh, and I'm going to try and write a book," I say.

Dylan pauses the telly.

"Are you?"

"Yeah. I'm around books all day and I dunno, I just keep imagining pulling something I've written from one of the shelves."

"Well good for you. You always said you wanted to. What's it going to be about?"

"I don't know yet."

"Will I be in it?"

"I'm not saying anything."

He rises up onto his knees on the sofa – like a Cobra ready to strike.

"Fuck, it's going to be about me isn't it! You bastard, what are you writing?!"

"You'll have to wait and see."

His cushion collides with my face.

"Well, as long as there's nothing libellous, because we all know a good lawyer that'll have that shut down fast. Oh, and I want a dedication at the front. Those are my only conditions. Then you can go ahead and write what you want. Just make sure I get to come on the book tour with you."

He unfreezes the screen and the Fab Five burst into life again. I study his face for a little bit. I can tell he's had his haircut today – flecks of stray hairs litter the top inside parts of his ears. The glow from the television makes him look child-like with his new short back and sides. The overwhelming desire to nuzzle into him is almost unbearable.

"I really am sorry I said you sleep with everyone."

"Forget it, we both said hurtful things, and as we've now established, I have been sleeping with everyone."

There's no pizza left. I'm about to suggest we get something else, but Dylan has paused the television again. He picks up his phone, unlocks it and then starts flicking through his home screens.

"I'm going to delete Grindr. And all my dating apps."

"Why?"

"Dunno, I just feel like it. Might be good for me to take a break from it all. Focus on myself a little bit."

Dylan and I stare into space for a bit. I glance at The Wall. It tries to catch me off guard and push that image of George and Axel into my head again. Luckily Dylan breaks the silence.

"I think I did spend most of my week hunting for a shag, rather than focusing on anything else, and I'm getting too old for that because it's a quick fix and it used to make me feel really good about myself and like I was worth something, but lately it's just been making me feel sort of sad. I want real human connection now. With people. Not apps and pictures of penises."

"I get that."

"So I'm not doing that for a while."

Dylan smirks at me.

"Charlie?"

"Dylan?"

"Shall we order another pizza?"

"I thought you'd never ask."

★ ★ ★

Lying in bed that night, full of dough and warmth, a Facebook memory pops up with my status from ten years ago. It reads:

'Charlie is feeling excited to make a change!! Joined the gym and can't wait to get beach body ready!!"

I admire the sheer bare-faced lies of my twenty-one-year-old self. I don't remember joining any gym after posting that. Also, I absolutely didn't go on holiday that year, so what beach I was planning on attacking is anyone's guess. I wonder who that status was actually for. Some people underneath have commented how proud they are of me, but I don't recognise half of their names. Maybe people from uni, who I've since deleted or forgotten about. Or maybe they got married, and their new last names don't mean anything to me. I end up spending the next five hours trawling through my timeline, and reading posts from Dylan and Niamh and Zachary – and George. Post after post from George. Funny videos he saw and thought of me. Secret coded messages from when we first dated. It spirals and spirals until I'm clicking through every photo I've ever been tagged in, and my brain is awash with memories and smells and moments where I felt incredible and times that I'd rather forget. I find a picture of me from 2010 at a party somewhere and I look so thin, so incredibly thin, but I can vividly remember looking in the mirror at that outfit and declaring I looked disgusting and huge and fat and subsequently spending the whole evening thinking the most atrocious things about myself, yet here I am in the picture smiling, as though nothing is wrong.

This timeline is going to hang around long after I've died and eventually – when it says Remembering at the top of my profile – people will scroll through and look at this capsule and take it as read, when actually it's a lie. I text Dylan and tell him my Facebook password and that if I do suddenly get hit by a bus tomorrow then I want my profile to be deleted. I'd want people to remember me for what I was actually like – not just how I wanted them to see me. I mean, how many of my eight hundred friends would even come to my funeral? They'd all be too busy getting beach body ready and sharing misinformation about whatever election was happening at the time.

★ ★ ★

Dylan and I spend pretty much every evening together for the next few weeks, breaking only for a stock check evening at work, and a night where Dylan has suspected food poisoning; but even then I pop in and make him tea and tuck him into his bed. I've never really spent much time in Dylan's room before – but it hasn't progressed much further from his one at university. Whilst he sleeps it off I put on a load of his washing and clear the floor of dirty plates and odd socks, and I even light a candle which Dylan finds hysterical when he wakes up.

"Are you trying to perform an exorcism on me?!"

"No, it just smells like shit in here. And, I'm not going to lie Dylan, it's pretty rancid in here. You used to bring boys back to this? I mean, how do you manage that?"

We fall into a comforting, easy pattern – leaving a continuous stream of voice notes to each other whilst we're at work and counting down the hours until we can see each other again. We never run out of conversation. Time with him feels endless yet painfully short, and I find myself wishing that we lived together again – it would certainly cut down on my travel time.

Whenever I see Axel he smiles and asks how I am, and I always politely say I'm Fine, You, and he chatters away about something in American and Dylan makes funny faces behind his back and I don't feel even an inch of anxiety when I'm around him because Dylan's presence is so genuine and so beautiful that sometimes I can hardly breathe. Axel has started seeing a guy called Duncan, who looks remarkably like George, but is also very kind and smart and funny, and always makes the effort whenever we're all in the house together, and I find myself oddly wanting to spend time with them both. I even dare to entertain the thought that This Person, the one that did That Awful Thing to me might actually become a sort of friend.

It's Niamh's birthday and we all sit around their living room table breaking poppadoms together like some weird fucked up family – Niamh and Axel and Duncan and Zachary and Steven and Dylan and I. It doesn't feel weird sharing a Peshwari naan with the Scarlett Woman who topped my boyfriend, in fact, I look forward to seeing him. The feeling of anger towards the situation has ebbed away so suddenly, that occasionally I worry it's going to rear back up again when I least expect it, but for now, right now, here with my friends, I am content enough.

A jar of mango chutney is being passed around the table. Dylan spoons a little on to the side of my plate, being careful not to give me too much as he knows I only like a little. In return, I leave the crispy corners of the tub of pilau we are sharing between us for him, as that's his favourite bit. Steven has a streak of Goan curry on his sleeve, but he's holding court with a conversation about the latest fuck up on the GB News channel. Dylan and I stifle a giggle as Steven imparts the yellowy orange sauce onto everything he touches, including Zachary's cheek and Niamh's new tablecloth.

I am so quietly in love with Dylan that I have no doubt I'll be happy forever with him as my friend, by my side. Just as my friend. Honestly, he's absolutely and completely unequivocally a friend, who I might have thought about kissing once, or twice, or yes OK three times, but there's absolutely no way I want to do The Sex with him because that would just be completely weird, and I know I've imagined him having The Sex with other people a few times but that was only because I wanted to picture the other guy, not Dylan, no no, not Dylan. It's like when you watch Straight Porn because you want to see the Straight Guy being hot and you just concentrate on him to get you off – not the woman. I've never imaged Dylan himself to get myself off. He is my friend. With a capital F. My Best Friend who as I said, I quietly love, and even if he proposed marriage tomorrow I'd laugh in his face. Ha Ha, I would say, laughing so bloody hard in his face, Are You Mad! We Are Friends, You Fool! I want to be at his wedding – his wedding to another man obviously – and support him as he marries someone – who isn't me obviously – and be so proud – and not at all jealous obviously – that he has found someone to love. And when the vicar says Does Anybody Know of Any Reason Why These Two Should Not Be Joined in Holy Matrimony, I will say I DO! But I will be joking – obviously joking – and everyone will laugh at my witty joke that's never been done before. And Dylan, well Dylan will find it so funny that we'll laugh about it until we are blue in the face – like that time during second year Freshers when I jokingly and drunkenly said I didn't want him to marry somebody else, because I wanted him to marry me.

The idea of falling in love with a friend – a best friend – is so poetic and calming that I allow myself for a brief second to imagine waking up with Dylan in my bed every morning.

I realise my leg is jiggling up and down under the table frantically and I don't hear Zachary asking me to pass them the dish of pickles because I am staring at Dylan sitting opposite me, and oh fuck, fuck fuck fuck fuck fuck fuck fuck fuck, I am in love with my best friend.

★ ★ ★

I don't know what to do with myself. I sit at home staring into space – like Judi Dench in *Notes on a Scandal* when she sees Cate Blanchett through the window with that Irish boy – except I am Judi Dench looking through the window at myself being in forbidden love with my friend. I mean, people fall in love with their friends all the time – they spend all that wonderful time getting to know each other without the pressures of dating and then one day, one magical day, they realise cupid has fired his arrow a lot closer to home. Maybe Dylan feels the same. He does seem to want to spend as much time with me as I do with him. But then, if there was a spark of anything other than friendship then I'd feel it wouldn't I? The move wouldn't have to be calculated, it would just happen naturally. I don't remember forcing anything with George. But, maybe Dylan is waiting for me to make the first move because he thinks I'm still grieving? But am I still grieving George? I haven't thought about him properly in such a long time now. Dare I say that I am properly ready to move on with someone else?

★ ★ ★

I have gone insane. I've honestly gone completely mad. I'm analysing everything Dylan says. On the rare occasion we aren't together then I'm constantly checking his social media to see where he is, and who he's with, and if I see he's with a boy that I don't know then my heart sinks. It absolutely sinks to the empty pit of my stomach and I can't sleep until I've spoken to him. I'm in a toxic relationship with him and he doesn't even fucking know it. I can't really talk to any of our friends about it because: awkward. So I'm stuck in the isolation that is my never-ending thoughts. Dylan's taken the day off work to come along to my skydive next week – which I looked into cancelling because I could seriously do with the cash back, but it's non-refundable so that's fun. I practice asking the instructor to not bother with the parachute in order to free me from this unrequited nightmare. Dylan calls to say how much he's looking forward to it, and he's so proud of me, and he's told everyone at work, and his colleague Dr Suzanne, who I don't even know, has sponsored me a fiver and it's all too romantic.

I can't fuck up our friendship, I can't. What if I tell him, or make a move and he's horrified? I'd have lost him and George in the space of a year. That can't happen. Maybe I'm just horny? Yes, that's it, I just need a shag, but not involving a blindfold. No, it's not a shag I need, it's a date! Yes, I need to go dating and play the field and meet new people who will distract me from being completely and utterly head over heels in love with Dylan.

The app store is about to become intimately reacquainted with my thumb print.

CHAPTER SEVENTEEN

I download a dating app on my lunch break at work. Somebody called Jack asks me to tell him something that I've never told anybody before. I think for a second and then type:

'I think about death a lot.'

He blocks me.

★ ★ ★

"Why would you say that?" Farrah asks me as we pull books into the window display.

"He said to tell him something I'd never told anybody before."

"So you decided to tell him you're suicidal?"

"No, no! I didn't mean me. I meant that I think a lot about what death means, you know ... and I worry about losing my friends ... and how I wouldn't be able to cope without them ... I meant it in a sweet way."

"But that's not what you said."

"Well it is."

"You said you think about death a lot."

"Well he didn't give me a chance to explain."

Farrah tucks the jacket of a book back behind its cover. Then fiddles with her nose ring.

"If somebody said that to me on a dating app I'd block them too."

"He wouldn't really think I was talking about myself would he?"

She raises one thickly knitted dark eyebrow and saunters back into the Best Sellers section, which is unusually empty.

"You can't control how someone interprets a message, Charlie," she calls back over her shoulder.

I re-read the message. I can see her point.

"Ah, Jesus, app-based dating is going to be impossible isn't it? This should be much easier than it is."

"I don't know why you're spending so much time on them. You're, like, a really charming man, Charlie. Put yourself out there IRL, don't just confine yourself to a handful of messages with dull men who probably won't catch how witty you really are. Especially when your jokes only land in person."

"I'm funny on the work WhatsApp group aren't I?"

"I'm just saying ... you're better in person. Don't rely on that to be your personality." She taps my phone that I'm now fondling in my hand. "Oh and I'll tell you what's really not funny anymore – GIFs – so stop sending them in the group."

A customer waves Farrah over and she slinks over to them, leaving me looking down at my phone. Is it really that hard for people to see the real me through my messages? If I'm going to make this work and meet any decent potential matches, then I need help.

★ ★ ★

Over drinks one evening with my housemate – on the rare occasion that he's in the flat for longer than a week without a festival – Tim tells me all about this newish app he's been trying. Last week he had four different meetings arranged with four different people, and he's managed to bag a second date with all of them.

Tim explains that its USP is simple; you match with somebody and then you can only chat with them for seven days until their messages disappear, meaning that you have to try and physically meet with them before then – thus saving you weeks of pointless chatting that ends with no meeting.

He's so keen to show me the benefits, he's on my phone and downloading it for me, and before I know it I'm watching as pictures are being selected and stats are being filled in. Each time he swipes through my photo gallery to find appropriate selfies, Tim winces and almost closes his eyes. He says it's in case he comes across anything he doesn't want to see, but unless he's frightened of cupcakes or screenshots of Jake Gyllenhaal, I think he'll be OK.

★ ★ ★

I'm hooked.

At work I find myself flicking through profiles under the counter, despite Farrah's disapproving gaze. I do it on the bus. I do it whilst I'm cooking dinner. I do it whilst I'm on the toilet. I do it just before I go to sleep and immediately as I wake up. There are endless men at my disposal and I want to talk to them all. Even a ten-minute gap is a wasted opportunity. My showers become shorter, phone calls with Niamh go unanswered. I will not stop until every single man in London has been exposed to my textual charms. There are so many conversations on the go that I accidentally ask one gentleman the same question three times. With the countdown clock ticking slowly to the seven-day deadline I begin to worry about who I'm going to attempt to meet up with before my time runs out with each of them. I narrow it down to three potential choices. I have progressed from being Sophie in *Mamma Mia!*, to being her mother Donna Sheridan and it feels fantastic. Everyone was right; your thirties are ace.

★ ★ ★

Date number one is Jack, who is twenty-eight, Welsh and six foot seven. He can't spell the difference between Your and You're but who cares when he looks like he could bench press an entire football team? He's a vet, and even though I'm indifferent towards animals our exchanges are dominated by my sudden apparent desire to run away and own a farm. Jack wants the same. We're going to meet at the pub on Saturday afternoon and have a burger. Then I'm very much hoping to follow that up with some sausage.

★ ★ ★

Date number two is Cathal. I have absolutely no idea how to pronounce his name and can't bring myself to ask, so fingers crossed we don't bump into anybody I know when I'm with him, because that'll make for a very awkward introduction. He-Who-Shall-Not-Be-Named-Because-I-Don't-Want-To-Get-It-Wrong, is also thirty-one, and from Northern Ireland. He works for Apple which is great news because I really need an upgrade on my phone. We're going to have a game of bowling on Saturday evening. He's very competitive and I've managed to tell him that I used to play professionally. We'll have to put the sides up.

★ ★ ★

Date number three is Monty. He's a true romantic, and has a small dog called Bruiser. Monty is an actor which thrills and terrifies me in equal measure. He's just come out of a six-year relationship and isn't looking for anything serious, which is perfect. We work out we only live a couple of roads away from each other and then later realise we've chatted on Grindr several times, which really breaks the ice – particularly as I've seen a picture of his exposed anus. Monty wants to go for cocktails because he's working evenings at the moment. He knows a great underground place in Soho and can do late Saturday night.

I am a dating machine. Is it wise to do a three-date Super Saturday? I text Dylan and ask him and he says I should do it so he can live vicariously though me as he's still off the apps. Which is good news because the thought of him going on a date makes me feel nauseous, but also I need to get myself out there so I can be distracted from being in love with my best friend. I wonder whether he's been on a date with any of my three future lovers. It's a small gay world after all.

★ ★ ★

The pub in Richmond is already rammed by the time I get there. There's a rugby match blaring out of every TV screen. I spot what I think is Jack sitting with his back to me near the patio doors. I catch my reflection in the mirror behind the bar. The wind has done my hair no favours on the journey here. I smooth it down a bit, take out my gum and wrap it up in a napkin before shoving it in an empty pint glass on a table that I pass.

I bound over, taking a deep breath before tapping him on the shoulder.

"Hey, it's Charlie!" I say enthusiastically as he turns.

He looks very, very different to his pictures. Still sort of handsome I guess, but he must have used an older picture because he certainly doesn't look like he plays rugby now.

"Erm, OK, hello Charlie?"

I falter for a moment.

"Sorry, you are Jack aren't you?"

"Nah lad, not me."

210

I feel my face redden and am just about to start apologising profusely when I see the actual Jack sitting three tables over, waving at me enthusiastically. I run over, horrified.

"I think I had some momentary lapse in memory there or something, I thought he looked like you."

"Yeah I saw, mate! I was waving when you first came in, but you just walked straight up to that guy. He doesn't look anything like me."

"I've not met up with anyone from this app before, so I don't know what I'm supposed to be looking for!"

"Well, the person you've actually been chatting to is a good start."

I take my jacket off, hang it over a little stool and sit down next to Jack. My back will be fucked from sitting on something with no backrest but I can't make a fuss after already publicly embarrassing myself.

"Well, I'm Charlie, nice to meet you."

"Yeah, good to meet you."

"Do you want another drink?"

"I'm fine with this one for now. Never like to jump into rounds on a first meeting, you know, makes it harder if you want to make a quick exit."

I laugh even though now all I'm thinking about is him wanting to leave only a few seconds after he's met me.

"Do I go to the bar, or is it table service?"

"I just went up and ordered."

"Ah right, won't be a second."

I bound up to the bar, pushing my way through the burly revellers already a few pints deep. A loud jubilant roar screams out as someone scores a try. I'm not sure what to order. I've got a long afternoon and evening to get through, and I want to be on my best behaviour, but also I think I'm going to need some dutch courage to kick me off. I'm sweating already and my mouth is excruciatingly dry. I can't have wine because I won't

211

make it past date number one, and beer makes me feel bloated. I order a rum and diet coke, with a tequila shot to calm me down. I am not the sort of person who starts a meeting with a shot, but it feels like the right thing to do. I check my phone, Niamh and Zachary are already ribbing me in the group chat, asking for feedback on my initial impressions of date number one. Dylan hasn't said anything yet, but he is on a long shift today, and it's a Saturday so A&E will be heaving. I quickly type that Jack is nice and very handsome and click my phone off, shoving it into a pocket in my jeans.

Back at the table Jack has nearly finished his pint in the time it took me to throw back the shot and get back to the table. I sit down and he immediately says he's gonna grab another. This feels really quite pointless as I could have literally just got him one, but also it's good to start off slow. I'll sip this one drink and only get another if I'm having a nice time.

Another try is scored and the place erupts into a cacophony of cheers, someone slops some drink down my back during their celebratory dance. I try and dab at it with a napkin but it's no use, it's already soaked through.

Jack returns, and he's so tall he has to duck to fit under most of the ceiling beams. I think of all the questions and topics I've been working on whilst I was getting ready.

"What's that you're drinking?" I ask, which is not anything like any of the questions or topics I'd been working on whilst getting ready.

"Just a lager."

"Oh lovely."

I don't know what to say, he's really handsome but feels really young, and I'm aware that my face has a lot more lines than his does. He's wearing a Ralf Lauren polo shirt, with the buttons undone and there's not a single hair on his chest. His tan is even and smooth, and his hair is frosted with blonde at the tips.

"So you're a vet? That must be an interesting job."

"Yeah, it's different. I mean, every day is different."

He seems nervous, weirdly this makes me relax a bit more.

"I have to admit, I'm not a massive animal lover. We never had any when I was growing up, and it sounds strange but I just didn't take much interest in them at school."

"It's a sort of requirement to like animals in my job."

"Yeah, I'm sure."

We both sip our drinks. This is the part where Jack is supposed to ask me more about what I do, but he doesn't. His eyes flick to look behind me. I'm suddenly aware that because of where we are sitting, the entirety of this side of the pub are basically looking directly my way, because the screen showing the match is stuck to the wall above our heads. It makes it look as though everyone has come to watch my first ever app date. Spectres at the feast.

"You a rugby fan?" I ask him, wincing as the commentator suddenly shouts in frustration.

"Kind of. I prefer football really."

I have absolutely nothing to say on the subject of either rugby or football. The banter on our messages was really good, snappy and witty, but just like Farrah warned me – people come across differently online, and I'd been so worried about whether I would be exactly what people expected that I didn't think about the potential for my date to be the one who was completely unrecognisable.

"Have you been single for long, Jack?"

I say his name because his eyes have drifted to above my head again.

"Erm, well I've never been with anyone officially actually. I've sort of not really properly come out yet."

"Oh, OK."

I don't want to be rude, but the thought of helping a partner come out to their friends and family, when it was hard enough for me to do it, feels like something I just don't have in me.

My brain moves away to Dylan, to a night at uni when he told me that he'd had the confidence to come out to his parents because of George and me. Dylan said that seeing us together and happy made him realise that he wanted to be the same. I was so proud of him and I'd only known him for a short while. He called me after he told his mum, he was crying, and I was crying too because I knew how deep that feeling of relief was. I try to imagine going with Jack to tell his parents, but I'm getting way too ahead of myself.

I look down and notice I've already finished my rum. Jack is nowhere near the end of his drink. I look at my watch. It's another two hours before I need to be at date number two.

"Shall we order the burgers then? If you're still up for that?"

"Oh I asked when I got here, and they said the kitchen's closed, they haven't got a chef or something."

"Ah no that's a shame." My stomach growls. "I'll just grab another drink then, and maybe some crisps if you want some?"

Jack says Sure, and I push my way back through the patrons, already wondering what on earth I can say next. If all three dates are going to be as hard work as this, then I am going to need more sustenance.

I order two packets of sweet chilli crisps, a double rum and coke, and another tequila shot.

★ ★ ★

The last time I went bowling was on the Wii at Hannah Fountain's house in 2007. I didn't wear the strap of the controller around my wrist tight enough, and put a hole in the corner of her parent's new twenty-inch plasma screen whilst aiming for a strike.

By the time I left Jack at the pub, I'd had two more double rums. The crisps had mopped up a bit of the alcohol, but they'd done nothing to distract from my and Jack's two hour long on-the-surface chat. I could barely tell you anything about him, and he certainly couldn't tell you anything about me. We left on a handshake and I practically ran to the tube, voice noting the group on the way to say it had been the most boring afternoon I'd ever spent, and that included the time Niamh had tried to teach me how to play Cribbage.

Cathal has chosen the bowling alley at the top of Westfield Shopping Centre in Stratford. The hoards of Saturday afternoon shoppers are doing terrible things for my anxiety levels, and I arrive sweaty, frazzled and looking like I've done three rounds with Mike Tyson. He's slightly shorter than me, and appears much younger than his profile picture, but he's ordered a pitcher of something called Love Potion No. 9, and I am at that point, alcohol-wise, where my whistle has been whetted and I'm no longer thinking about how I'm going to feel when I wake up tomorrow.

For some reason the E on our lane's computer doesn't work, so on the screen I'm named as Charli. I think it makes me seem cooler and more relevant than I actually am.

Cathal has a Samsung which makes me incredibly suspicious considering his job with Apple. I mention the need for an upgrade a couple of times but this seems to go unnoticed. I bowl terribly – at one point nearly decapitating a group of twelve-year-old girls three lanes over.

"I thought you were a professional?!" he asks me, incredulously.

"Ex-professional."

I don't know what's in the Love Potion but it's 100% spirit and 0% dignity because after a few bowling balls I'm standing in from of him, making intense eye contact and pretending to polish the ball like a porn star washing daddy's car on the front yard for cash. It's working on Cathal though because he keeps touching the small of my back which screams Please Let's Have Sex. The conversation is still a bit dry. It's mainly about phones and bowling ability, but we do spend at least five minutes talking about a rare bird he saw this afternoon and I'm not being sarcastic but it was quite thrilling. At least he's making more of an effort than Jack did. Or at least the alcohol in my blood stream is making it feel like that.

We're on our third pitcher and nearing the end of our second game of bowling and my fingers feel huge and I can't get them into the holes in the ball anymore so I call time out. Cathal says I'm funny, but doesn't elaborate any further than that which obviously sends my brain into overdrive. I know I should cut it off and leave now because I've got absolutely no intention of seeing him again, but I'm suddenly finding him incredibly attractive. I don't know what it is, but it's as though his score of 110 – which included two consecutive spares – has bequeathed him with the looks of a young David Beckham. He lives in a flat only ten minutes' walk from here, and my appointment to meet Monty isn't for another two hours so I take him up on his kind offer of one more drink.

He only has a bit of scotch at home and I hate scotch but I gulp it down like a fish. His place is filthy – like Kim and Aggie from *How Clean is Your House?* wouldn't even bother – and I wonder if I might end up leaving with some form of scabies. Suddenly, that thing happens when you're at a level of inebriated where you have total clarity. It's a very fine moment where you tip from the fun part of drinking into the bit where you're looking at yourself in the mirror and telling yourself to snap out of it. I look at Cathal and he doesn't look like a young David Beckham but instead now resembles a sort of middle-aged Nosferatu, and I try to look up an Uber on my phone but I'm on two percent battery – which I need to save in order to locate Monty – and I don't want to ask for a charger in case he works out that I'm trying to leave, and the only way he can stop me is by turning into a bat and sucking my blood until I go limp. The scotch is making me sleepy and he kisses me, and I kiss him back. I don't know why. I feel as though I should do, seeing as he's gone to all this effort. It's all tongue and gum from him. He's making this weird noise, whilst he pokes his tongue against the back of my molars in a thrusting motion. Back and forth, back and forth, as though he's trying to penetrate my wisdom teeth. Luckily I had them removed a few years ago. I absolutely know I want to stop, and I'm aware that I've never been so un-horny in my life, but he paid for the bowling and now I'm at his house and because of this I'm letting him push my head down and unbuckle his belt and soon something else is penetrating the back of my mouth. My eyes gently water.

He tells me to slow down because he's going to finish, but I'd rather this just hurried along and ended, so I keep going until he judders into my mouth, clutching at my shoulders with his long vampiric fingers. He begs me to swallow but it's bitter and salty. I retch. As he lays back onto the sofa, I spit into some tissue in the bathroom. I spend a good few moments browsing his toiletries. It's amazing what you can tell about somebody from the products they use – it's invading their privacy, yes, but it's a tiny window into what life with them would be like. Do they floss and mouthwash and moisturise? Apparently Cathal doesn't do any of these, but there are quite a lot of painkillers in here. There's also streaks of brown down the toilet bowl and no air freshener. I drink some water from the tap with my palm. I'll shower twice when I eventually get home.

"Do you want to sleep here and we can fuck in the morning?"

I say that I've suddenly remembered how religious I am and I need to go to church early tomorrow. The vicar would have a field day with all that I've got to confess. He begrudgingly lets me out of his Fort Knox-style front door, and then I'm wandering around Stratford trying to find my way to the tube

217

because there's no way I can afford the luxury of a car-ride in order to get to date number three, which I am now deeply regretting organising. I can still taste Cathal, so I forcibly remove his scent from my mouth by riding the Central Line accompanied by five chicken selects, four mozzarella dippers and a large vanilla milkshake, which ironically is the only part of the evening that feels akin to scoring a strike.

* * *

"And the thing about being in a relationship with somebody for an intense period of time like that, is that when they leave you it's a kind of bereavement, I mean, you must have felt the same with George?"

I am somewhere underneath Soho in a place that's so dark I can barely see the cocktail glass in front of me. Monty sits opposite me. He looks exactly like his picture, but the plummy, well-spoken voice is a surprise. I try to lean my head on my hands to stop myself from falling asleep, because I've now mixed so much alcohol I can barely string a sentence together, but I miss and nearly head-butt the table. It's OK, because Monty has been out for drinks before this and assures me that he's just as drunk as I am.

"When Frazer left me I was genuinely in mourning for I'd say a good three days, but at the time actually I was doing this play where I had this incredibly emotional scene around drink-driving, hang on ... to give you some context, basically my girlfriend – in the play obviously – was ten times over the limit and she went through the windscreen, and actually the director we had was insanely talented with these beautifully creative ideas and we used this light blue taffeta and a song by Enya to depict her spiralling out of control leading up to the accident – it was honestly just stunning – so, yeah, so I had this monologue where it was just me in a spotlight at her funeral and this was what ... maybe ... a week after Frazer

218

left me, so I mean, my God. My God! Luckily my agent was in because fuck me I absolutely nailed it. Tears, snot, the lot. Had the audience in the palm of my hands, and afterwards in the pub everyone was congratulating me and saying it was the standout performance of the Wandsworth Fringe and then I thought about Frazer and I called him and I said Thank You, and I Forgive You. Wow, I'm choking up just thinking about how raw and stripped back that phone call was, because thanks to him I was able to give that raw moment on stage some real clout and clarity, which I truly believe I would not have found were it not for him dumping me and trying to take Belle. Oh, did I show you a picture of her? We bought her as a puppy a week after we met, so we're currently going through everything with the solicitors but she's handling the split really well I think, although she wouldn't eat any of her food or play with any toys for the first couple of hours once Frazer had left the flat. Frazer said she wouldn't be affected but psychologically I really feel it's taken its toll. I'm taking her to doggy therapy once a week. Oh look, here she is, my ray of sunshine in the darkness."

Monty holds his phone directly in front of my face. I can't do this anymore, I'm practically drooling onto the table I'm so smashed. I'm Dated-Out. I slap both hands against my thighs – the British sign language for I Should Get Going.

"Yeah, look, so I'm going to be honest but I just don't give a fuck about other people's dogs, and I've been out already today on two different dates – don't take it personally they were both shit anyway – but do you think we could just wrap this up now?"

"Oh. Right."

Monty places his phone back into his pocket, then looks up at me, puppy-eyed.

"Do you want to come back to mine for a shag, I only live around the corner from you don't I?"

I inhale and let out one of those sighs that makes your lips trill like a horse.

"Yeah, alright then."

★ ★ ★

This pattern repeats for the next few weeks. I cycle my way through various first dates with a number of people, all of whom I find no romantic spark with, but still willingly pull my pants down for. There is Lewis and Kyle and Sean and Joshua and Jared and Rikki and Ryan and Luke and Darren and Aaron and Riyadh and Mitch and Chris and another Joshua and Ali and Kem and even someone called Charlie. I've never had a calendar so full, yet felt so entirely empty.

★ ★ ★

Niamh has gone on holiday to Jamaica to see her Grandma's side of the family, and I'm trying to not ache with longing for Dylan, so I gladly take up Zachary's offer of cocktails despite having approximately thirty pounds in my account until I get paid on Friday, which coincidentally is when my rent comes out, so it's only a fleeting visit from my wages.

I made the mistake of forwarding Zachary the email I got from George and they want to discuss it – in detail – but really I just want to talk about books and funny PR stories and celebrity gossip and literally anything else in the entire world except boys.

"And you haven't responded to George?"

"No."

"But you want to?"

"I don't really know what to say to him."

"You can just thank him for the birthday message."

"And ignore the subtext that he's not having a nice time out there?"

"I mean absolutely, you must find out what the tea is there. I take it he hasn't said anything to Niamh or Dylan then?"

George and Niamh never really confided in each other – they were very much housemates who only had me in common. Dylan and George were much more pally on the surface, but they were the first two to get into a disagreement about house stuff like bills and the washing up, and who put the bins out last. Now I think about it, it felt a little as though without me being a linking factor, they never would have kept in touch much after uni. My phone vibrates. Another message from a potential suitor; I click the screen to darkness.

"As far as I'm aware they haven't heard from him."

"He'll be feeling pretty terrible about all of this, as he quite rightly should, so I imagine he'd steer clear of everyone you two were associated with, because he knows his name will be mud."

I sigh wearily and scoop some jelly from the passionfruit bobbing at the top of my glass. The sharpness makes my eyes water.

I've had this conversation with myself over and over again, mainly at night, in the quiet prison of my own bedroom. George's relative radio silence. No real heartfelt acknowledgement of what he did – just a "so so sorry". No real effort to at least try and explain himself. And then there's the matter of Axel's comment about the open relationship, a topic which Zachary is an expert on.

"There is something I wanted to ask you actually, Zachy."

"I'm on tenterhooks, go on darling."

"Well, I know that you and Steven are in an open relationship and it works really well for you both and I'm really proud of you, because that can't be the easiest thing to keep communicating about, but . . ."

"Oh no, you're not going to ask me if you can join us for a night or something are you, because one of our rules is no friends."

"Christ no! You're gorgeous, but no, bloody hell no, I wasn't going to ask that."

"Because George mentioned it once."

I stop breathing for just a second.

"What do you mean?"

"Well, I can't remember where we were now, but you were there too, just not part of the conversation, and it's when Steven and I had only been open for a couple of months and understandably you were all very inquisitive, which I didn't mind, you know, Steven and I were working it all out too, and George said would we ever want to do something with you and him. I mean, we were all very drunk, and he never mentioned it again, so I just forgot about it. I didn't know the arrangement you had and I didn't want to pry. I knew you'd talk to us if you wanted to know anything, but what I did know is that Steven and I wouldn't have done anything with the two of you."

I can feel my heart rate quickening, like it always does when I seem to discover something else about George that other people knew and I didn't.

"I didn't know about that conversation, Zach, and I'm mortified that he even asked you that."

"No, don't be. He was drunk. Open relationships weren't what they are now, they were an anomaly, he was probably just curious and didn't even mean it."

"Axel said that George told him that we were in an open relationship."

"Ah . . . But you weren't?"

I shake my head. Just when I think I'm doing really well, and feeling better about . . . him, something stirs it all back up again, picks me up and plops me right back down at square one again.

"Why would he lie to me, Zach? Why would he keep things from me? I thought I knew him, but it turns out I really didn't . . . at all."

"Maybe that's what you need to say to him – when you reply."

"I just don't know if I've got the words to convey how all this is making me feel. I feel sick all the time, Zach. It's making me act crazy, I'm thinking stupid things about everything, about Dylan and . . ."

"What about Dylan? He said he hasn't seen you for a few weeks, has something happened? When we were in the cottage I thought something was up, but I put it down to the weed."

"It doesn't matter, I just feel like I'm losing my mind. How can this one person be there every day and then suddenly be gone, and then I'm finding things out that makes me question whether he even loved me in the first place."

"You'll tie yourself up in knots darling, doing all the what-ifs. You need to talk to him, properly. You need closure. You need to reply to his email and say you need some answers. You won't move on until you have."

I start to cry. Big, gloopy tears that dribble down my cheeks and straight onto the bar table. Zachary rubs my back.

"Oh darling, it's not the first time I've seen someone cry in The Ivy Club, and it won't be the last."

My phone flashes up with another message from another unidentified male I've been having meaningless online inter-actions with. I turn the screen over to face the table – like it's a naughty child being sent to the corner of the room.

I know that the time to speak to George is coming, I know it is, but the more time I leave it, the more I have to say and the harder it gets to know where to begin.

★ ★ ★

I have chlamydia.

I'd had a coffee with Dylan last week, our first in a long while, and he was talking about how he'd had a patient who'd

223

been admitted to A&E after a minor accident and when examining him they found a nasty bout of gonorrhoea that had gone untreated for goodness knows how long, and his genitals were so red and sore that he could barely sit down and when Dylan touched his shaft, a stream of thick yellow discharge had escaped, and Dylan had thrown up in one of those little cardboard hats. He asked me when I'd last had a sexual health check up, and when I said I'd never had one, he helped me book an appointment there and then on the spot. I didn't have any symptoms so it was a real shock when the doctor phoned me and asked me to come in to begin treatment.

"Do you have a lot of unprotected sex?"

"No, no, I don't really have sex I just, well, I just put them in my mouth really."

"So unprotected oral sex?"

"If that's what we want to officially call it then yes. I am currently having quite a bit of unprotected oral sex."

"And do you ever pay or get paid for anal or oral sex?"

"Oh god, wouldn't that be nice!"

The doctor exchanges a withered glance with the nurse. Tough crowd.

"No, I don't get paid."

"And do you ever inject drugs?"

"No."

"Or take anything orally?"

"Only the penises."

The doctor prescribes me with antibiotics and advises me not to have any sexual contact for a week, which really throws my upcoming schedule into chaos.

The nurse is telling me I should get in contact with the last person I had sexual contact with to let them know that they might have it too and I laugh. I actually burst out laughing, almost verging on hysterical. I wouldn't even know where to begin. Who knew you could get an STI from oral. I've been purposely avoiding having any kind of anal sex to make sure I stayed disease-free and all along I've been dicing with danger the entire time.

As I'm leaving, the nurse hands me a leaflet for counselling, pats my hand and smiles gently at me.

CHAPTER EIGHTEEN

N iamh is back from Jamaica, so over some poached eggs
on sourdough, we're catching up.

"So, you won't believe it but the woman who made the
complaint in the first place – the one who Dylan ended up
being paired with, well she's not been in contact with the
school for weeks, and she's not been letting her son come in
either. So they've had to get the authorities involved and now
she's facing a huge fine."

"Well that serves her right, doesn't it?"

"I'm not concerned about her, it's her son I'm worried
about. He's gone home, feeling all emboldened from the assembly having met you and Kato and Sammy and Coco, and
he's told her that he might be gay and now he's had to suffer
from being taken out of school, and she's in trouble with the
education folk. Well, just imagine what she's saying to him,
or blaming him for."

"I see your point but, Niamh, that's hypothetical, we don't
know that's happening, she might not have told him anything
about it."

Niamh mops some yolk with a piece of bread.

"But she's stopped him coming to school, Charlie, a few

days after he's gone home and said he's maybe gay. What kind of message do you think that's sending to him?"

"What are you gonna do?"

"There's nothing we can do. It's sending a strong message to the parents that the school is standing behind me, but it's ruffled enough feathers, and the kids, I mean ... we think that at their age they don't know their arse from their elbow, but they do, they really do. We did! We know that at the age of eleven you're so switched on to things, but the older we get the more we forget and so we act as if they're these little thoughtless, opinionless blobs with no autonomy, and that's not true. They're starting to really form who they are, and something like this can have a huge knock-on effect, the likes of which they won't realise for years."

"At least my mum is only fucking me up now, rather than when I was growing up."

"I don't know, Charlie, from what you've told me, I don't think she did the best by you."

We finish our food and head out for a stroll along the Southbank of the Thames, past Tower Bridge and The Oxo Tower and towards Waterloo and the London Eye. Sunday dog walkers and joggers and families litter the small pathway as we weave around them all. Niamh holds my hand.

"Do you think I shouldn't have done it, Charlie?"

"The assembly?"

Niamh nods, her face crumpled with worry.

"Oh my God, Niamh, you absolutely should have done. I'm so proud that you did. There's some kids in there who will have really heard what you said. Whether that's to think twice before they say something homophobic, or whether a seed has been planted to allow them to be who they authentically are. Don't let this fallout make you feel bad. There will always be people ready to shout us down. We just have to shout louder."

"Thanks mate. And thank you for suggesting we do that

parent session. It was the right thing to do. I'm very proud of you too."

We stop at a little clearing and sit on a bench that looks out towards St Paul's Cathedral.

"Oh, Niamh. Look at us, huh? Who'd have thought we'd still be together after so long?"

"Me. I did. On that first day I met you at uni, I knew, I just knew we'd be friends for life. I don't know what I'd do without you."

"Do you know what I've realised since George? That it really is friendship that stands the test of time. It's remarkable how unbreakable it is."

"You've handled it all very well. Much better than I would have done."

"Really?! I think I've gone really quite mad over these past five months."

"Well, you're still breathing aren't you? You found a job and somewhere to live."

"Yeah, but . . ."

"No, no buts. You have to say you're proud of yourself too sometimes. You can't always wait for somebody else to say it."

"OK. I'm proud of myself."

"See!" Niamh shrieks.

"I mean that felt horrible."

"I tell my class all the time to say, 'I love myself' and they do, those little cherubic five-year-olds say it, they shout it, and they mean it. It's just a shame that we stop saying it eventually."

"Will you still be proud of me if I told you I've got chlamydia?"

Niamh turns to look at me and bursts out laughing.

"Do you know what, I actually am proud because it means you're getting some! Who gave it to you?"

"Will you still be proud when I tell you, I don't know?"

Niamh shoves me so hard I nearly fall off the bench.

"You are disgusting Charles Dowdeswell. But I bloody love you."

"It's put me off dating for a while, that's for sure."

"Come on, I'm freezing, you can walk me back to the station."

We head in the direction of Waterloo, stopping for mini donuts at a caravan to keep us filled with sugary warmth on our journey, arm-in-arm, towards the train home.

★ ★ ★

The next day it's my interview for the position of maternity cover at Waterstones. It's with a lady from Head Office called Manda who is very friendly and responds well to everything I say. I don't know where this new-found confidence is coming from but I'm enjoying this version of myself – he's charming, and surprisingly he knows what he's talking about. I could absolutely do this job. I talk to her about wanting to write my own books, and she seems quite impressed with that. She's also impressed with the impact I've made in the short time I've been there. Even Farrah has told her how she's learnt so much from me. She tells me I'll find out in the next couple of weeks. There's potential that they could bring somebody else in from The Outside, but I'm hoping my knowledge of the store, mixed in with a good word from Noma and Lana, should go in my favour.

I've barely taken any holiday since I started working – apart from the couple of days in Wales – so I'm landed with three days off with nothing to do. Everyone is at work, and after talking to Niamh so much about the assembly, and parents, for the first time in a long time I have an overwhelming desire to visit *home* home.

★ ★ ★

229

Essex is a wonderful and weird place. It's so close to London but couldn't feel further away. I automatically dress more conservatively; I keep my head down, try to be invisible. I wonder what the kids at Niamh's school would think of me standing proudly on their stage but dumbing myself down on one of my rare trips back to The Motherland.

Mum and I haven't done one of our usual coffee shop meets for a while because she's Been Too Busy, which is code for Can't Be Arsed.

Whenever I step off the train and onto the platform – the sound of seagulls screeching overhead and the smell of salt in the air – I feel immediately frantic. It's a strange emotion to not feel at home in the town that you did all of your growing up in.

My village near the seaside would be described as Picturesque and Idyllic on any of those TV relocation shows. There are ice cream parlours and cobbles and inns and ponds and boats and a relatively small amount of graffiti. It's a mix of old and young – people don't come here just to die – although there is a defibrillator attached to the wall outside The Co-op, which means the nightlife is still going strong. Not that I'd ever go Out Out around here. Rural clubbing is a very different beast. The biggest nightclub here has a café where you can purchase microwaved sausage rolls and pasties throughout the evening. To be fair, that did prevent many a hangover during my youth, and nothing beats dancing to Nelly Furtado with a Ginsters Pie hanging out the side of your mouth.

★ ★ ★

I have never kissed a boy in Essex. Until the age of thirteen I hadn't knowingly met anyone queer. Apart from the incident when those boys at school called me a 'lezzie' I genuinely didn't know one thing about the potential to be different.

The first time I remember feeling Turned On was at the

age of nine, when I was watching the television at home and Johnny Bravo came onto the screen. He had these huge arm muscles and a tiny waist and cool sunglasses and the most incredible unmovable blonde quiff and I instantly felt something for him. I didn't know what that was, but I knew that I couldn't take my eyes off him. Mum used to chide me for sitting too close to the screen; this was the time when everyone thought you might actually get Square Eyes if you watched too many cartoons. My little infatuation with Mr Bravo was the start of a cataclysmic change that wouldn't really come into full effect for many years.

I was round at Gran and Grandad's one day using a net tablecloth as a makeshift skirt and my gran hit me so hard around the back of the legs that I cried for at least an hour. Grandad was telling her to leave me be, but it was her best tablecloth and she didn't want me using it to be a Silly Bugger. No doubt this is why I hated the idea of drag until I'd moved to London and seen enough performances in pubs. It scared me at first. I know I'd only worn a tablecloth, but I'd been trying on a lot more in secret – Mum's dresses, scarves and tights. Twirling in that mix of netting and fabric was my way of testing the waters to see if it was OK to bring a bit of that into the public of my living room. The slap to the legs told me it definitely wasn't. This was to be my first burn from The Shame Dragon.

Fancying an animated all-American jock on TV and wearing a couple of silky garments from C&A didn't scream You Are a Gay to me because at the age of nine you don't know what *That* is, because back then nobody told you what *That* was. I continued to experiment privately whenever I could. Mum would pop to the shops and there would be lipstick rouged on my cheeks; she'd be kept back late at work and I would dance to S Club Seven in the mirror but exclusively singing only Rachel's lines; she'd be at the pub until it closed so I would write stories about being a princess and then hide them inside my socks. I knew it wasn't Normal Behaviour but I wanted to do it so I did it.

At the age of thirteen I was picked out at school to be in an amateur production of *Gypsy* at a local society. This fabulous man came into our hall at lunch time and taught us a little routine – something about being a paperboy – and somehow I was picked out to go and be in the show. The company were only looking for children aged eleven or twelve, but my form tutor saw me looking sad when they announced the auditions in the key stage three assembly, so she pushed for me to be allowed to try out. She'll never know how much that meant to me.

They rehearsed every Tuesday and Thursday evening, but as Mum was always out every night she never noticed I wasn't at home. This nice lady who worked at the school on reception was also a member of the society, and because the rehearsals were a long bus ride and a walk away, she offered to give me a lift. This lady – Joan – always had Murray Mints in her car and she continuously played musical theatre soundtracks on the journey and told me stories about all the other productions she'd been involved with. Those were happy drives with Joan. The best part about belonging to a group was suddenly being around older people who weren't Mum or Gran or Grandad. These people greeted each other every week with shrieks of excitement and hugs and told anecdotes and laughed. I desperately wanted to be them. The most astonishing part is that so many of the male members of the society were in relationships – with each other. Men. Holding hands with other men, and nobody was saying anything nasty to them. In fact, they were friends with them. All I'd ever heard was how being anything other than Completely and Absolutely Heterosexual was weird and odd and you should keep it to yourself because everyone will hate you, and here I was in a world surrounded by gay men who were the life and soul of the party. I had no idea how important those years in the theatre would be for me. I learnt more about myself in that one show than I'd learnt in over a decade of living.

Coming home makes me sad because it forces me to realise that lots of people don't get to experience that. The warmth of another queer person. The sense of belonging. The brief respite of understanding.

Mum found out that I was going to this theatre group and I think she was relieved because she knew, she absolutely knew I wasn't Normal, and this way she didn't have to have any kind of discussion with me. I came home from rehearsals for the next show – *Singin' In The Rain* – twirling and time-stepping around my bedroom, practicing my dancing, and she said possibly the only sentimental thing that's ever escaped her lips: It's Good to See You Passionate About Something. And she was right, I was passionate – I was passionate about myself.

Despite being able to credit this very town for introducing me to its own merry band of flaming homosexuals, it's still not as progressive as The Big Smoke.

I can't escape that niggling bit of guilt. You're Not Like the Rest of Us it whispers as I walk past my old school, and the bit of green where kids still hang out on Fridays, and the under 16s disco that I never went to because I didn't know how to just Be Me. The Shame Dragon torched so much of the land here, it'll never fully grow back.

* * *

Mum is at work and apparently Leanne is still knocking around the market pretending that she's employed, so I let myself in and take the car keys. Gran only lives three roads away, but I pick her up and drive us the five minutes to the sea-side. It's early October and it's still warm down here, warmer than London, but Gran is wearing two jumpers, a coat and a

233

bobble hat. We sit with a bag of chips – like every romantic movie set in a town like this – and watch the tide draw back, revealing slick mud and shiny grey seaweed.

"Your Grandad liked it here."

"I know."

"We used to come here sometimes when the water had gone out to see how far we could walk. One time we nearly got as far as Kent."

It's incredible how memories work. That would have been some years ago with Grandad, yet when I arrived at her house earlier she was surprised to see me, even though I'd telephoned this morning to remind her I was coming.

"That's a long way isn't it? I didn't realise you could get as far as that!"

"I'm not lying, don't accuse me of lying, I know what I did, you weren't there," she huffs, and a couple of chips fall onto her lap. A few pigeons hover underneath her legs.

"I believe you."

"I've got a picture somewhere to prove it. You can ask your Grandad."

She picks up the chips from her lap and thumbs them into her mouth.

"Eurgh, these are cold."

The bag is thrust into my hands and I finish them greedily – they're still boiling. The vinegar almost burns my fingers.

"Gran, have I done something wrong?"

"What?"

"It's just, I feel as though nobody really likes me in this family."

"Don't be soft."

"It's true. Mum and Leanne make it very obvious, and you, well you never really seem pleased to see me."

"Oh Charlie, of course I like seeing you, but I'm old, and I forget things, I know I do. I see that look in your eyes sometimes and I think, oh Christ, I'm bloody repeating myself again, but you never say anything, you just listen patiently. When you've been around as long as I have people get on your nerves for no reason. Sometimes I'm tired or confused or a little bit afraid and it just makes me a bit snappy, I suppose."

This rare moment of lucidness from Gran completely floors me, but she picks away at a scab on her wrist as if this is a generic conversation filled only with pleasantries and not the answer to all of my worries over the past three decades.

"This whole thing about being friends with your family is a load of old toot. That's what you have other people for. Your mum isn't supposed to be your best friend, she's your mum. Even your sister – you don't have to like her – you're related yes, but nobody is forcing you to put the effort in. If you two don't get along it's a shame, but I wouldn't punish yourself for it. I never made too many friends. Your grandad was enough for me, but since he's gone I realise that was a mistake now."

Gran's voice wobbles slightly.

"You've always had lots of friends, you have. That's why your sister is rude, because she's envious. Her and your mum stick together like two peas in a pod, because neither of them can make friends, and there you are having a lovely time in London and they both don't like it because they wish they were doing the same. I give your sister a bit of love and a tenner every now and then just to keep her happy. You don't need me to do that for you."

"Sometimes I do."

"It's all about bloody money isn't it?"

She starts to fumble around in her purse.

"No, no I don't mean the money."

Gran sighs – but it's not a loaded one – it's a soft, almost pitying sigh.

"Your grandad idolised you. You were his most favourite thing in the world. I suppose I was a little bit envious."

"Why?"

"I don't know really. We behave in odd ways sometimes. You never quite know your own mind, no matter how much you tell yourself you do – there's always something new to surprise yourself with. We're monsters really, all of us, selfish bloody monsters, but we all know – on a deeper level – that we're all just as bad as each other. If you think that I know the answer to it all at my age then I can tell you now, I don't. And when you reach this part of living then you won't either. Just enjoy yourself and stop worrying."

An aeroplane leaves a perfect line of white past the sun and I look at it for a little bit too long so that my eyes blur. Gran hands me a fiver. I drive her back home, to the sounds of her whistling along to an Abba song on the radio, and that's the last time I ever see her. The memory of her tapping her hand on the dashboard to 'Dancing Queen' is the final thing she leaves me with. That, and the fiver.

★ ★ ★

Nobody really knows what it was that sent Gran back to Grandad, but I'm convinced that she knew because of that End of the Play final act speech she gave me when we were sitting on the beach. Imparting wisdom feels like a common side effect of dying. Mum tried to tell me that maybe me taking Gran out that day was the final nail in the coffin, but even Leanne told her to Fuck Off with that one.

I tell Noma that I'll be staying at home a few days longer and she's fine with it. She whispers down the phone that Things Are Looking Good with the promotion and I smile.

Dylan, Niamh and Zachary all call. They all make me feel loved and cared for. I might be away from them, but they remind me how they are easily just a phone call away. Dylan's coming down to stay this evening. I know that I've been pushing him away because I was scared that I'd say something to him that I'd regret, but he offered and it would be really lovely to see him. He must be confused as to why I was spending every day with him for a period of time and then suddenly vanished but I'll explain it to him somehow.

I feel as though I'm going to have to. I owe it to him. I owe it to myself.

* * *

We're in this afternoon tea place – that apparently Gran used to like coming to – but I've never heard her mention it. Mum checks us in on Facebook with a picture of a delicious looking plate of finger sandwiches that she's got off Google, the caption underneath reading, 'Remembering Mum and Gran'. I have mixed emotions. It's the first time that the three of us have sat down together in a long, long time. The bread in our real-life sandwiches isn't as good as the stock image Mum used – the crusts are stale on the edges but there was no food in her house this morning so I wolf them down anyway. Mum dabs at the corner of her mouth with her napkin.

"I only saw Mum yesterday morning and she was fine."

She tries to squeeze a tear but nothing comes. Leanne appears to be sulking. Or maybe she's grieving, it's difficult to tell since her hand is always glued to her phone. Nobody has moved on to the scones tier yet but I'm not waiting about.

"Slow down, you'll get indigestion."

"I'm fine, Mum."

"Leanne can you eat something please before your brother scoffs it all?"

"I'm not hungry."

I slather a small amount of clotted cream onto my scone, leaving plenty for the other two. Usually I'd use most of the pot, just to make a point, but I'm tired of the petty fighting.

Mum pushes Leanne's phone down onto the table.

"I said eat something."

"And I said, I'm not fucking hungry."

Leanne storms off into the bathroom at the back of the shop. Two cute old ladies shake their heads and go back to their hushed conversation over their clacking needles. They are exactly the sort of people that Niamh and I will become. Going to stitch'n'bitch every Wednesday morning and eavesdropping.

Mum fixes me with a look.

"Mum, don't. It's not my fault that she's just shouted at you."

"Isn't it?"

"No. It's not. It's you. You're always in this constant mood, it's exhausting."

"My mother has just died, Charlie."

"I don't just mean now, I mean all the time. Why do you think I don't come down and see you? Why I don't pick up the phone very often? Because you constantly, constantly make me feel completely horrendous about myself. You've spent most of my life telling me I'm useless and that I'll never amount to anything. Why? For God's sake, why? You should be proud of me! Parents are supposed to be proud of their children. When I was with George you just fawned all over him and told me that he was brilliant and wonderful and basically the fucking Patron Saint of Your Happiness and I appreciated that you liked him, I mean, Jesus, it's much better than you hating him as well as me, but do you have any idea how unworthy that made me feel? You turned up on my doorstep on the day we were meant to be moving to New York and you wanted to thank *him* for giving me something to do. That's what you said. My own mum was thanking somebody for getting me out of her hair when I've done absolutely nothing wrong. Why don't you like me? What have I done that makes you behave so cruelly towards me? Why do you make me feel like I'm not a good son?"

There's jam spittle from my mouth all over the tablecloth,

which is adorned with illustrated cups and saucers, and I'm looking at Mum and she's dumbfounded. Her eyes are glassy and her mouth has fallen open a tiny bit. I realise I am crying.

Leanne comes out of the toilet and slumps down in her chair, so totally unaware that the atmosphere has changed. Mum falters.

"I didn't know you felt like that."

"Mum, come on, when I told you George had slept with someone else, you said I should have tried harder to keep him interested. What kind of person says that?"

Leanne looks up from her screen for the first time.

"George shagged someone else? Who?" She stares at me waiting for an answer.

"That doesn't matter Leanne."

"Yes it does, I wanna know. Charlie, who was it?"

"Who it was is irrelevant."

"It's not because you tell me who and I'll stick some fireworks through his letterbox. George is lucky he's not in this country because he wouldn't know what was gonna hit him, nobody does that to my brother."

I guess maybe I should be flattered that she cares about it this much, but it's months too late, and I don't want to be a part of some suburban seaside mafia who go around popping kneecaps with buckets and spades for revenge.

"Leanne it's fine, just leave it. I've dealt with it."

"Pushover."

She goes back to her phone. Mum is still gawking at me. I wipe my face with a tissue. I wish Dylan would hurry up and get here, so I can have some space from them.

"I don't really know how to be your mum."

Leanne and I both look at her now.

"Both of your dads didn't want to know me once I got pregnant. My mum couldn't really be bothered with me ... actually I think she hated me, and I've never liked my job,

239

or the way I looked or really had any friends, and I just don't know how to be a mum. Particularly to you, Charlie. You don't live here and you've never needed me, so I thought it would be better for you to just do it on your own and not take on any of this crap that I feel. I've never been a fifty-eight-year-old woman with a thirty-one-year-old son living in London and a ninteen-year-old daughter living at home – this is all new to me."

I hand her a napkin. She blows her nose.

"But you do pass on that stuff to me, Mum, you know you do, and I'd rather you didn't, because I'm your son – not a punching bag for you to direct all your anger towards, because you know I'll sit there and take it and not say anything back because you're my biological mother and I'm supposed to be grateful that you brought me into this world, so therefore I'm meant to just take everything you say and do and swallow it down, but I don't want to do that anymore. We're not going to be friends and that's fine, but I just want you to be nice and ask me how I am and support me – not financially, before you start – but for fuck's sake just be kind. Be a mum! Don't do what Gran did with you because you know how crap that is. When I came out you just got on with it, which was weird because I thought you'd hate me, but you just carried on. You never said anything bad about me being gay, but you've never said anything good about it either. It's almost like, if you just sort of ignored me then it would all go away. Is that what it was? The best way to accept me was to just ignore me?"

"I don't know, Charlie. I don't know why I'm like this."

And now it's Mum's turn to cry, and she cries and cries and cries so much that the waitress comes over and asks us if everything's OK, and we tell her that our gran just died and she gets Mum some camomile tea, and says that everything is On The House. The cute old ladies pass on their condolences and talk about how they felt when they lost their husbands and soon everyone is crying, and this tearoom has accidentally become some weird sort of safe space for bereaved misfits, and for a second, just for a second, I feel as if Mum, Leanne and I are on the same page of our fucked-up book. Just for a second though.

* * *

I tell Dylan not to come down tonight. A change of personality would certainly blow away some of the cobwebs, but the house feels full with the three of us in it. It's been a rough day. Besides, having him here would feel a little too much like couple behaviour, and I don't want my already jumbled, over-emotional, grieving mind to jump to any conclusions.

My bedroom remains trapped in 2007, when I last lived here. There's a faded poster of McFly on the wall and stacks of *Desperate Housewives* boxsets and *Now That's What I Call Music* CDs. Weirdly, my school uniform still hangs in the otherwise empty wardrobe – ironed and waiting to never be worn again. My prefect pin clutching onto the blazer lapel by a few loose threads. I haven't slept in this room since the night before I left for university. This room that saw my tears and my growth and my first wank and my anger and frustration and exhaustion and confusion and highs and lows and utter contempt for being alive, until I suddenly dropped it and ran away to find my people and never looked back. Yet here I am, sitting in it for the second night in a row, reacquainting myself with its musty scent and showing it that things did genuinely get better. They got a lot worse on some occasions and will continue to do so, but they really did get better.

* * *

I help with the funeral arrangements and Mum seems grateful. She doesn't know how to act around me after our conversation in the tearoom. I don't know what she could say, or what I

241

even want her to say, but when I go back again nine days later, I stand at the front of the church with her and pass her a tissue as she weeps tears of regret and anger and sadness onto the stone floor and in that moment, united by our grief, I am glad she is there next to me. She squeezes my hand as the curtain envelops the casket, and in that moment I know she's glad I'm there next to her too.

CHAPTER NINETEEN

"I think I just don't have any direction in life. At all."

Sour cream dribbles down my chin and drips onto the table. I hastily place my half-eaten burrito in its red plastic basket and paw at my face with a napkin. Dylan hands me a clean one.

"I hear what you're saying, Charlie, I do, but I don't believe that for a second."

"Well what is my direction then?"

"You're about to become supervisor of a shop you've always wanted to work in since you were little! If that's not direction then you tell me what is."

"I don't even know if I've got the job yet. It's all gone quiet. And even if I have got it, then it's only cover."

"So? It'll look fantastic on your CV, and when your boss does come back from maternity then you can either decide to stay and go back to your old position—"

"Which is shit."

"No it isn't! If you like what you do, then why do you need to progress? We're always looking for the next bloody step-up all the time when maybe we should just be enjoying what we're doing now. Not saying you won't make a great

243

leader, but after this you can do whatever you like. There's no rule book."

There's a tiny piece of guacamole on Dylan's cheek. I pick it off and show him the evidence. He licks it off my fingertip.

"What did you do that for?!"

"I paid an extra three quid for that. I'm not wasting it."

To any onlookers we might as well be completely and utterly in love – the familiarity between us is almost nauseating. I try to remember what my new online therapist said: To Ignore the Narrative That My Mind is Constantly Writing: Dylan licked my finger therefore he finds me attractive, therefore he's in love with me, therefore we should be boyfriends forever. The real storyline is far more basic: he feels comfortable around me and is a disgustingly stingy bastard – so much so that he'll eat avocado off my finger to get his money's worth. There's nothing more to it than that. Our four-book epic romance should remain unwritten.

Dylan takes another bite out of his wrap.

"I keep meaning to ask you, did you want to come to Mighty Hoopla next year in June? I can get you a ticket if you like. They've just put some more early bird ones on sale."

"I don't know, Dyl. Is it a bit full on?"

"What do you mean?"

"Like people in leather everywhere, and everyone's looking for who they're going to take home?"

"No, Charlie, not every queer thing is predatory."

"I know, but I'm still getting to used to all this stuff."

"I know, but it'll be fun. We're all going. And Zachary might use it as the basis of their Hag do."

"Hag?"

"Yeah, they don't want to call it a Stag or a Hen, so they've mixed it together and are calling it a Hag do. I love it."

"Then of course I'll come."

We chew in an easy silence. That's the best thing about

Dylan and me. We never feel the need to fill a quiet void. It's reassuring. Niamh on the other hand can talk for days. Zachary will check their phone after a while, but Dylan and I will sit. Exchanging the same air. Gently. Until we feel the need to converse again. I wonder if we'll still be like this when he eventually meets somebody who is worth his time. Whether the silences between us will be filled with inane chatter to appease his lover.

"Did I leave you out whilst I was with George?"

Dylan slurps his lemonade.

"What do you mean?"

"I don't know what I mean really."

"Well you do know because you asked me."

"I mean . . . did you ever feel excluded or left out, or not a part of my life anymore?"

"I missed you sometimes, yeah, but also he was your boyfriend so of course he's more important than me."

"Did I ever make you feel not as important?"

"Erm, a little bit, maybe . . . no not really."

"Well I'm sorry if I did. You're very important to me, you know that."

"I know."

"Even if we bicker, and I call you names sometimes behind your back."

"You don't need to apologise, Charlie. I do the same."

"Do you?!"

"Yeah. It's what friends do."

"Oh right."

"I keep picking up the phone to eat Mexican food with you at 11 pm on a Thursday night though, don't I?"

"Yeah you do."

"Well there you go then."

★ ★ ★

I've told everybody that I'm having therapy and to my amazement none of them are even remotely phased. Niamh sees someone that her school provides, Dylan has regular contact with a counsellor at the hospital and Zachary tells me that a few years ago they went to a rehabilitation centre to sort out their drug addiction – a piece of information that rocks me.

"I always made jokes about you always disappearing off to the toilet."

"Had my face deep in cocaine, darling. I was a mess."

"And now?"

"Each day is different. But I haven't touched a drop of the stuff for three years and two months now."

"But you still vanish quite a lot."

"Mindfulness. Whenever the mood overtakes me and I can feel that burning rage for a sniff, I take myself to the nearest bathroom and breathe."

"I had no idea."

"Nobody did. I didn't want you to know."

It's as though I've been cruising through life with blinkers on. Were all these signs right in front of me? That my friends were suffering with everyday life and I just could't see them – or did I not want to see them? I was blissfully happy with George. Selfishly happy, even. It's comforting to come to the realisation that everyone I know is constantly battling with something. We're all just making it up as we go.

★ ★ ★

Dylan and Niamh's Halloween party is on the horizon – they've done one every year since uni, and this is the first time I'm not living with them so I don't have to contribute in any way or clear up after – which is thrilling. They call the evening Shalloween – encouraging people to dress as slutty and shallow as possible, which for our group of friends is somewhat challenging. Three years ago Zachary came as Debt which just involved them wearing a designer suit with actual five-pound notes safety pinned to it. Apparently they arrived wearing eighty pounds' worth but got home to find only sixty-five remaining. Everybody categorically denied involvement despite the threat of legal action from Steven – which I truly believe he meant – and although Dylan did wear a very nice new jacket out to dinner three days later, I said nothing. This year however, Axel is co-hosting with them, and his track record of fancy dress leads me to expect the Shallow to be very much spliced back into Shalloween.

I have a long-standing issue with two words that are put together to make one: Bromance, Chillax, Chocoholic, Gaydar and don't get me started on Glamping. It all started when I was forced to attend something called Crunch at the age of eight – Crunch being a portmanteau of Church and Brunch. Of course the main selling point of this weekly jaunt on a Sunday morning was the Brunch part, but when it became apparent that this constituted merely a plain croissant (*no jam*) and that really you were there to attend a regular Church service, I complained furiously to Mum and anybody else who would listen – I even prayed that I wouldn't have to go anymore. Apparently I'd signed up for a full twelve-week course of Crunch – and Sunday morning was the time when Mum would Go For A Drive with Pete who worked in the petrol station – so the vicar and the croissants essentially became glorified babysitters and the best part was Mum didn't have to pay a penny. The deception of it all stayed with me for years – dangling the prospect of a delicious breakfast in exchange for an endless morning of Hymns and Hail Marys. And Shalloween was the same. I'm never going to look sexy at Halloween. I will always look terrifying in a costume, because that's the only way it should be. It's Halloween for goodness' sake.

I contemplate wearing my hotdog outfit from the American-themed leaving party, just with some blood splashed about on my face and a bit of talc on my hair but I fear that I'll look a bit Not Over My Ex-Boyfriend so I shall be cutting a hole in a sheet from Primark and going as a ghost. The Ghost of Fancy Dress Parties Gone By.

CHAPTER TWENTY

I'm standing at the door of my old house in the Dodgy End of Wandsworth, shifting nervously from one leg to the other. I've painted my eyes with black rings but my ghost-sheet remained in a bag for the entire bus ride here. The woman sitting opposite gave me a sympathetic smile before I got off, which read as You Work Too Hard and Look Very Tired whilst the man next to her had an expression of Stop Doing Drugs You Massive Junkie.

The last time I was here with this many people it didn't end well, but I'm determined that this party will feel different.

There's a loud cheer from inside the house and I'm aware that my teeth are chattering together. I ring the bell and after a few seconds a werewolf opens the door. I can tell from the naked torso and Very Small Pants that it's Axel. He lifts up his mask and flashes those bright gnashers at me.

"Charlie! My man! Come in!"

He kisses me. Square on the lips. As usual. Stepping into a place that feels so familiar when you have become a stranger to it is the most dizzying of moments. Everything is the same yet so totally unrecognisable. I smile around the room – a witch waves – I've absolutely no idea who it is. Niamh is in the kitchen pouring Basic Vodka into a large orange bowl adorned with cartoon bats. Something is burning in the oven.

"Are you joking? You're doing Trump again?" I ask.

"It was a great fucking costume. Plus if he can get a second term then I can get a second use out of this wig."

"Well I hope you at least washed it since you last had it on."

"You can't wash a wig."

"I'm absolutely certain that you can but whatever."

"And what the hell have you come as?" Niamh pouts.

"Tired. I've come as somebody who is tired of life."

"Well that's all of us, but tiredness isn't sexy."

"Neither is Trump."

"I disagree," says a voice from behind the fridge door.

As it shuts I see a beautiful bumblebee in a skintight yellow-and-black bodycon slink towards us. It takes me a moment to recognise Kayo, the incredibly eloquent transwoman from the assembly, and by the time I do she's already planting a kiss firmly on Niamh's lips. Kayo touches me on the arm and says It's Good to See You and hands me some sort of vodka jelly thing before leaving the kitchen.

"When did that start happening?!" I ask Niamh as I suck at the green stuff, which makes a satisfying sound as it peels away from the edges of the shot glass.

Niamh smiles this wicked toothy grin and carries on pouring more unidentifiable spirits into the bowl.

"Oh, I've had a thing for Kayo for a while, and it just sort of happened between us not long after she came into assembly. And then, she just kept coming!"

I laugh and feel the fuzzy bloom of familiarity in my chest – the gentle ribbing of a friend, a tiny perfect fragment of time. This exact scene could be taking place in the first year of university. In ten years absolutely nothing has changed. Niamh and I are still in a messy kitchen making mistakes and changing our minds about who we like and what we like and in this moment I am so glad we're here. We are exactly where we're supposed to be.

"I'm pleased for you Niamhy baby. You deserve something good."

"And so do you my darling."

"Well actually, I found out yesterday that I got the maternity cover job!"

"Yes! Of course you did! You superstar. Now there's extra cause for celebration! Go on, get yourself a big glass of something!"

I take a bottle of something on the countertop – a bottle that I didn't bring because everybody knows you don't put anything in the kitchen at a party that isn't for sharing. I fill a pint glass with bubbles. Niamh now has her head under the tap because she's just tried some of her concoction and she's spluttering something about it tasting like Paint Stripper and now I'm laughing so hard that a bit of wee absolutely dribbles out and I don't even care.

Back amongst the ghouls of the lounge I say hello to Steven who is dressed as Frankenstein's Monster – which mainly involves him wearing two bolts in his neck fixed to a hairband. I congratulate him for making as much effort as I have. He tells me to keep Saturday the 4th of September free next year. The sound of wedding bells swells in my ears.

Zachary is dressed in black denim hot pants and very little else. They have tyre tracks across their chests and red contact lenses in. To be fair they do look scary, but also extremely Instagrammable.

There's a group of people I don't know – they must be Axel's friends. There's a ladybird and a French maid and a couple of nuns and one man in a particularly fetching – and tight – Spiderman patterned-Lycra. No sign of Dylan though. The door goes and more monsters pile in and the music is upbeat and pumping through my body and I've drained the pint glass and filled it up with the punch, because I know it's going to eventually send me into a catatonic state, which I'll then wake up from on the sofa in time to spend my Sunday with the others laughing about all the stupid things we did at the party, and we'll order dumplings and watch trashy television and make the absolute most of being inside on what will inevitably be a gloriously sunny day.

★ ★ ★

Thirty minutes later I'm lying on the bathroom floor desperately trying to cool my forehead down on the tiles. There's frantic knocking at the door and somebody says to Fucking Hurry Up because they're going to piss themselves but I have become a slug and the effort of rolling my body over to the door and unlocking it is too much to contemplate. I manage to shout that there's another toilet in Dylan's room and the knocking subsides. I lay my head on the toilet bowl. I didn't eat anything for dinner or even lunch as I didn't want to feel bloated tonight so there's nothing to come up. I lay there for an unquantifiable amount of time and potentially take three short naps and then this glorious momentum of second wind sweeps my body and after a splash of cold water directly to my face I'm back in the room. In the mirror my black kohl eyes have trickled down my cheeks. I roll the sleeves of my t-shirt up. I find some nail scissors in the bathroom cabinet and spend ten painstaking minutes snipping my jeans into short shorts. I eyeball myself again. I'd never usually get into the spirit of things like this, but if this past year has taught me anything, it's that trying something new is the best way to get over heartache. A new job, a new house, hundreds of app-based dates, my first ever STI and an ill-advised but enjoyable foray into bondage. That's quite a lot of things in a short space of time isn't it? And it's nice to know that there's parts of myself I'm yet to discover, even if for a long time I've been hiding them away.

I run what is probably Axel's wax through my hair. Now I look like Shalloween.

★ ★ ★

It's 11.30 pm. Some people have left, others are talking, limbs intertwined, heads bobbing to the music. Nobody is dancing. I look at The Wall. And there's Dylan sitting with his back against it, sipping from a pumpkin-decorated cup. His face lights up.

"Where have you been!"

"I had a moment with myself in the bathroom. Niamh's punch is fucking lethal."

"You know never to go near that stuff."

"I've been here for ages though – I haven't seen you all night."

"I only got home about an hour ago, work was mad, as usual."

He picks a piece of glitter out of his eyelash. I sit down next to him on the floor.

"You work too hard."

Dylan rests his head on my shoulder. A shower of green and black sparkles from his face land on my lap. I don't know what he's dressed as and I don't care to find out either.

"You not on the pull then, Dyl?"

"Not tonight. Can't be arsed."

"But Axel has got a lot of hot friends here."

"You trying to get rid of me, Charles?"

"No! I'm just saying . . ."

"What, that it's not like me to let the talent go untouched?"

"It's Shalloween. That's why you throw this party."

"Fair. I like your costume. It's a bit edgy for you – everything OK?"

"Everything's fine!"

Neither of us move for a bit. Niamh and Kayo are

253

kissing on the sofa. Axel has discarded his werewolf mask. The playlist has unintentionally become more mellow. It's comforting.

"I'm doing that airplane jump next week – finally."

"Jesus, how long has that been in the pipeline now?!"

"Well it wasn't my fault – they called it off once because of the weather, and obviously the second time I cancelled because of Gran's funeral, but I've got a good feeling about this one. Third time lucky. I'm gonna use it to raise a bit of money for the hospital Gran was in, too – I got some sponsorships from people at work, so that's nice."

"Can I still come and watch? Y'know – just in case you go splat."

"You'd want to be there when I become soup?"

"Well somebody would have to bring you home in a Tupperware."

"You know full well that none of the lunchboxes in this house have a lid that matches."

"We might have invested in some new ones since you've been gone."

"And have you?"

He smirks. His tongue pressing between his teeth.

"No . . ."

"If you want to come, Dyl, I'm not going to stop you."

"Good, then I'll come."

"Fine."

"You're fucking mad you are, Charles, jumping out of a plane! You're crazy."

He puts his arms around my waist. I'm aware that the thump of my heart is making his head move up and down. I adore being this close to him. He makes me feel so safe.

"Oh, Charlie, I keep meaning to say, you know it's nearly the end of the contract here."

"Is it?"

"Yeah, it'll be a year in a few months since you moved out, so the landlord asked us if we all wanted to renew."

"Right."

My tummy is getting damp from the warmth of Dylan's hand, which is still rested upon it, but I don't want to stir him.

"I don't think I'm going to stay here."

"Oh. Why?"

"Need a change of scene I think."

"What about Niamh?"

"She's happy here. Coco, the barmaid from the pub, is looking for somewhere with her girlfriend so she might have my room. If I decide to go, that is."

"OK."

"And Axel might be going back to America or something, I don't know."

"He told me his family don't talk to him."

"Oh," Dylan drinks, "Well he said he was going somewhere else in America, not to his family."

"So everyone's moving on?"

"Not moving on, but just trying something else, so I was gonna ask you – are you happy with the house you're in?"

"I'm OK, but it's not exactly the place you want to be living when you're thirty-something. We don't have an oven for fuck's sake. And I still don't actually know the names of the two girls upstairs."

"But you've been there for ages."

"I know but it's been too long for me to ask now. It's just awkward."

"You dick ... wait, when does your contract run out?"

"I'm not on one, I'm on a rolling thing."

"Let's find a place together!"

I gulp. I'm at that level of pissed where I can fully form coherent sentences but I'm also not sure what's going to come out of my mouth before I'm saying it.

"Really?"

"What do you mean really? We used to live together, we haven't for a bit, and now we can live together again."

"Well I mean, OK."

"Yeah?!"

"Yeah, OK."

"Fuck yes! It'll be just like old times."

Dylan squeezes my hand and then I sway a little bit and go in for a hug, peeling my back away from The Wall, but for some reason our lips meet. We hold the moment for a few seconds and then I move my head back. Neither of us says anything. I look at him and see him in the student union and at the first newspaper meeting and in the nightclub and in the smoking area and in my bed in the cottage in Wales.

"I love you Dylan."

"I know you do, mate."

"Exactly, and that's the reason why we can't live together."

"What do you mean?"

"Dyl, I love you so much, and you're such a good friend to me and sometimes when I think about you my heart feels like it's going to burst out of my chest, and I'm so glad we found each other, but my love for you is so astronomically strong that I don't understand it a lot of the time, and so as much as living together would be nostalgic, it wouldn't be like old times, because we want different things from each other, and I don't even really know what it is I want from you, but I do know that I want you in my life as much as I can have you, but since George left I've been wandering around a bit lost and I don't want to spoil our friendship by living together because I don't know how I'll behave around you. I think I'm clinging onto the idea of something with you that wouldn't really work, and I'm confusing your loyalty and dependability for something else."

"You're not making much sense, I'm gonna be honest."

"I'm not really sure what I'm saying either, but I think I need to be on my own for a bit and do less sleeping around, and less dating, and less making up scenarios for my life in my head and just actually work out who I am and what I want?"

"You've had a rough bloody year, Charlie. I don't know many people who'd be able to cope with the amount of shit you've had thrown at you. I couldn't do it, but you have done it. And that's incredible."

"I don't feel incredible."

Dylan puts his drink down and grabs my head with both of his hands and brings me towards him, very close, our noses almost touching. His breath is hot on my face.

"You are one of the most important people in my life. Please don't ever forget how special you are."

It's incredible how the power of friendship can hold you so strongly that you feel as though you might choke.

"Dylan, let's not move in together again yet but let's be best friends until we're old and grey and incontinent and then let's live in an old people's home where we can shit ourselves in the same room on a daily basis and eventually forget who we are but always remember the familiarity of each others faces."

"Charlie, that's the nicest thing you've ever said to me."

I don't know what came over me, but I know Dylan isn't the answer for right now, or maybe even ever. A song comes on and I can't remember any of the words but my feet are moving and I'm in the middle of the living room dancing, and I'm pretty sure that somebody else is with me, but Dylan is still by The Wall laughing at me, and Niamh gives me a loud cheer so I keep dancing – and I'm trying to incorporate some of the moves we used to do to S Club but my limbs are all over the place – and then the song finishes and I get a little smattering of applause from some people even though I didn't notice that I've been dancing on my own. I go to sit back with Dylan but the next song that plays immediately after is an Absolute Banger and I have my audience so I'm going to carry on dancing. I do that until it's 2 am and everyone has gone and I'm exhausted. Exhausted but happy.

★ ★ ★

It's June and the sun is beating down on Brockwell Park. Strands of multi-coloured tinsel hang on string between trees, splaying out in the gentle breeze – the homosexual version of the Northern Lights. The hill is full of queer people of every shape, colour and size. The only sounds are laughter and chatter and the steady thrum of pop music. Carly Rae Jepson alongside Bananarama and Destiny's Child mixed with Bewitched. The air fizzes with excitement.

I was dreading this day. Poring over a number of different outfits for months on end – nothing representing how I felt on the inside. But standing in the middle of my friends, adorned in rainbow socks, a slick of purple glitter on each cheek, and a can of Red Stripe in my fist, I am overwhelmed with how good it feels – watching festival-goers who are unapologetically living their absolute best life. I allow the safe atmosphere of acceptance to seep through me, calming any anxiety I had about attending. I hold hands and I kiss and I dance and I roll my shorts up to make them even shorter and I fall over and I scream in ecstasy and wave my arms to old favourites and clutch onto my friend's faces and tell them how much they mean to me as I enjoy being content in this community of the brave and wonderful. I remember Sarah-Beth asking me at university if I was frustrated that I was Different. Looking at Zachary on Steven's shoulders, and Niamh and Kayo dancing, hands intertwined, moving their limbs to the euphoric music I scream Never. This is my team, and no matter what people want to throw at us, or how loudly they try to hate us, I wouldn't have it any other way. Those people only fuel my determination to live my life, the way I want to, whether I'm single or not. I am good enough. Dylan slides another can into my hand and pecks me on the cheek.

"I bloody love you, Charlie D."

I'm good enough. And for the people that matter, I always will be.

I still don't know where I'm going. But for now my head is definitely above the water and I can see land and that's all you can ever really ask for isn't it?

★ ★ ★

I'm sitting in a little coffee shop just around the corner from work on my lunch break and I'm staring at a white page and a flashing cursor. Niamh managed to smuggle me a laptop from school over the holidays so I've only got six weeks to finally write the book I've been wanting to pen for so long, but I've always loved a challenge during the summer. I've no idea what's going to emerge from my fingers but I'm going to give it my best shot.

Before I write my masterpiece though, there's something else I need to write first, and it starts with two very simple words. Two simple words that might lead me to the closure that I need.

"Dear George."

I begin to type.
And away we go.

259

Acknowledgements

Firstly, I have dreamed of writing an acknowledgements section in my head for so long and it feels very surreal now having to do it. What a THRILL.

Thank you to my editor Matthew Bates, and Sarah and Kate Beal at Muswell Press for believing in my writing, and for all your support and encouragement during the process – especially when having to answer all my silly questions. I am indebted to you for taking a chance on me.

Mum! I wrote a book! Before I thank her, I will point out that my mum is nothing like Charlie's mum – we'd never split an almond Bakewell, we'd have one each. She is so kind, thoughtful and supportive and I love her eternally. Thank you for letting me do the Reading Challenge at the library every year, and for letting me find my own voice, and for allowing me to do all the madcap things I do without any judgement. I am so very lucky. P.S. Sorry about all the swearing and the sex but it's Charlie, not me.

Dad, thank you for your unending support and always believing in me too, and never failing to be delighted and surprised when I call you to tell you what I'm up to now.

And Grandad, who I sadly said goodbye to in March, you wouldn't have read this because it's too rude but I know you'd be proud as punch and Nan would have been too, and I love you and miss you both.

This book actually started off as a TV pilot many moons ago – so to all those actors I hassled to do table reads of it – I apologise, but also thank you, because hearing it out loud made me realise I knew fuck all about TV and so should make it into a book instead.

To all my wonderful beautiful and brilliant friends who were early readers of the first drafts of NOT GOOD ENOUGH in 2019 – Alex P, Wes D, Greg A, Debbie C, Molly H, Clare T, Joe B, Ben T, Emily D, Kirsty A, George K and Grace H – your encouragement and kind words made me keep going. And to my other close friends whom I never sent it to so now you'll have to buy it (sorry) – Luke H, Chris J, Lottie C, Flora D, Katie C, Molly R, Cheryl F, Jimmy P, Lucie-Mae S, Pip G, Claire D, Zoe B, Eleanor W, Geri A, Ross T, Jane G, Conor HH, Will HH, Drew M and Mark S – I am so lucky to have you all in my life. Thank you for lifting me up on a daily basis, calming down my anxieties and shaking me every time I said I wasn't good enough. I love you all. Ian W – thank you for lining the dominos up to make this happen. I can't thank you enough.

And finally, thank YOU dear reader. I hope you liked it, and I hope it made you laugh, and I hope it makes you love yourself a little bit more and reminds you that you have autonomy and independence even when you're feeling at your lowest, but I also hope it helps you remember: if your partner gets a job in New York and wants to take you with them, don't have a leaving party.

James xoxo

ABOUT THE AUTHOR

James Robert Moore is a theatre director, actor and writer from Essex. He's worked on productions including *The Hunger Games, Shirley Valentine, 2:22 A Ghost Story, Greatest Days, The Full Monty* and the *Calendar Girls* musical. *Not Good Enough* was shortlisted for the Penguin Random House WriteNow competition and won the Literary Consultancy Free Reads Scheme. It is his debut novel.

@jamesrobertmooreauthor on Instagram.